Hotel Europejski

The Judge's Chambers

The Judge's Chambers and Other Stories

The Lawyer's Chambers and Other Stories

The Last Jewish Shortstop in America

The Night Swimmer—A Man in London and Other Stories

Conversations with a Golden Ballerina

The Humpback of Lodz

The Legal Fiction of Lowell B.Komie

The Silhouette Maker of Copenhagen

Hotel Europejski

A Novel

Lowell B. Komie

Swordfish/Chicago
Publishers

 For information, address Swordfish/Chicago, Publishers, 431 Elm Street, Deerfield, IL 60015

Book Design: Miles Zimmerman
Book Production: The Chestnut House Group, Inc.

Library of Congress Catalog Card Number: Applied For

Komie, Lowell B.

Hotel Europejski

1. Fiction I. Title

ISBN: 978-0-9641957-7-6

A portion of this novel was published as a novella in 2006 under the title "The Silhouette Maker of Copenhagen" (Swordfish/Chicago). "The Silhouette Maker of Copenhagen" was listed by Oxford University (England) in its journal, *Holocaust Genocide Studies*, Winter 2006. *Holocaust Genocide Studies* is a joint publication of Oxford University and the United States Holocaust Memorial Museum.

For
Mary Lou Schwall-Komie
and
William B. Laurie

Preface

After I finished this book, I remembered that there was a Jewish cemetery that I visited in Faborg on the island of Fyn in Denmark when I was there several years ago. I rented a bicycle and inquired at the town hall whether there had been a synagogue in Faborg at one time. A very gracious woman clerk told me that there had been a synagogue and showed me the building on a small map. I think it had been converted to a town hall. There was now no Jewish presence in Faborg. She also asked me if I would like to visit the Jewish cemetery and showed me how to ride along the sea to the gate. Then she handed me the key.

I set out thinking of the wonderful Danish people and as I rode along the sea wall into the tiny road that led to the cemetery I began to think how someday I would like to write a book honoring their valor and courage in saving from the Germans almost their entire Jewish population. This was on my mind when I opened the gate of the cemetery. I walked in and saw that the

Danes had preserved the Jewish cemetery with great care. The grass was cut. There were no broken stones. All was in order. Obviously, even though there may have been no Jews living in Faborg, the Danish people had taken the task upon themselves to preserve the cemetery and the synagogue.

I walked through the paths looking at the names on the stones. I noticed that one small gravestone was set apart from the others. The name on it was, in my memory, Jonny Levin. It was very weathered and stood alone overlooking the sea. I think this is true although I might have dreamt this because I named the major character in my novel Jonny Levin. I hope this book does him honor and all the Danish people honor.

I had also intended to visit Lithuania on this trip but I cancelled that portion of the trip. My family came from Mariampole, Lithuania, to the United States in the 1870's. I knew that almost all the Jews of Mariampole had been murdered by the Germans and their Lithuanian accomplices during the Holocaust. I have annexed to the book a report by an SS colonel, the Jäger Report, which details the killing of the Jews of Lithuania by the murder squads of the Germans and Lithuanians. The Jäger Report details the killing of the Jews by these murderers from July 1941 through November 1941. In that period 137,346 people were killed. To this date no Lithuanian has ever served a day in prison for these killings even though many of the men who did the killing are still alive.

On September 1,1941, the Jäger Report lists the killings in Mariampole as "1763 Jews, 1812 Jewesses, 1404 Jewish children, 109 mentally sick, 1 German subject (f.) married to a Jew, 1 Russian (f.) - 5090."

I am certain that members of my family were murdered on that day. We have never heard from any of them again although my grandmother used to correspond with them. In their memory and in memory of all the people killed by the Germans and their Lithuanian accomplices I dedicate this book. If the victims could speak, they would testify as to the crimes, but since they are silent, I will try to testify for them.

Fiction can often reveal the truth.

Hotel Europejski

L · B · K

1

HIS NAME IS JONNY LEVIN. He has come to Copenhagen in Denmark on his sabbatical, perhaps to write a history. What kind of history? He doesn't really know. He's always wanted to write a history of the Levin family, but has never attempted it. He's an English professor at one of the universities in Chicago. Let's leave it nameless. All we can say is that it has a football team. Last term he taught a new course on Jewish Literature. It was a first for the university and he established it. It was the last course he taught before leaving for his sabbatical year. He's 62 and twice divorced with two daughters from his fractious first marriage. He lives alone in a large two-bedroom flat in Evanston in an old 1920s courtyard brown brick building with two regal lions on colonnades with cannonballs in their paws guarding its entrance.

He and his second wife, Ramona, had lived there for ten years until their divorce. They had no children. The second divorce was friendly. They just split and went their separate ways – she to California and he to his sabbatical year. He'd always wanted to visit Denmark. He felt drawn to this small, courageous country because of its rescue of its Jewish citizens during the war. He knew he would feel comfortable among the Danes. Just being among them would be a comfort to him and he wouldn't feel so alone. Also, instead of a history of the Levin family, he really wanted to attempt to write a novel. He had a quiet flame insisting that if only he would try, he would be successful. He would perhaps be likened to an undiscovered Bellow. He could be an undiscovered and even more misunderstood Roth. Or perhaps Irwin Shaw, no, no longer Irwin Shaw, Shaw's dead. Perhaps Bernard Malamud, no, also dead, Alfred Kazin, dead. Lionel Trilling, dead. But Jonny Levin, a talented unknown Jewish novelist with a bizarre and whimsical sense of humor, still alive with this tiny secret flame burning of a novelist *manqué*. But since the divorce, blocked. He hasn't been able to write a word.

Actually, the name is Professor John Levin, not Jonny Levin. Perhaps this is the beginning of whimsy? Jonny Levin is only a pseudonym he's been using the four days he's been in Denmark. It makes him feel slightly Danish and allows him to blend and not be just an aging, dried out American professor on sabbatical, but seemingly a youthful energetic Jewish Dane. A Dane still with some liveliness in his heart and vigor and longing. So, a Dane simply named, the name foreshortened, John to Jon and given the diminutive Jonny. Is this the beginning of a farce? No, it's just the changing of a name.

He's staying at the Hotel Angleterre, a small hotel right on the edge of Copenhagen's red light district. The hotel has a dignified paneled lobby with leather, brass-studded chairs and two gracious, even beautiful, blonde Danish women in their mid-twenties behind the front desk, dressed in black waist-coats and bow ties, politely greeting him each evening and handing him his key on a large, oblong wooden block. He doesn't know the Danish word for key, but he does know the word for thank you, *Tak*, and he says thank you to them. *Tak*. They smile at an American who tries to speak Danish and answer him with the same word, *Tak*. So he converts it to "*Tak, Tak* Jonny Levin" as the answer that spins through his mind, the two lovely blondes still whirring in his head as the elevator doors close and it begins its ascent. "*Tak*, *Tak*, Jonny Levin." Each of the four nights he's been here he's hesitated at the front door of his hotel before going up to his room to look down the street Colbjornsengade to see if there were any prostitutes on the street, but so far he's seen no one. He feels like a rather foolish man gazing down the street each night for prostitutes, but he's far from foolish. He simply wants to learn the rhythm of the city, and more importantly the rhythm of himself in this city.

So far each night he's had dinner outdoors in a restaurant in Tivoli, the beautiful gardens and amusement park. It's early in April and the restaurants are chilly but open. He's only spoken to two people at Tivoli. One is the young woman in charge of a shooting booth where you can target shoot at clay targets with a compressed air pellet rifle. She's perhaps 18. The other woman is a woman almost his age, in her late fifties. She's a tall, heavy woman with a seamed face in charge of a roulette wheel in the section of Tivoli devoted to slot machines and roulette. She says "Skål" perfunctorily to him when he wins. She's like a peasant lady croupier. It's not really a roulette wheel. It's more like an old-fashioned wooden carnival wheel and you bet ten kroner pieces on symbols, caricatures, farm animal figures, numbers and flags. He's picked the American flag as his symbol and each night has come back to the hotel with a small plastic sack half full of kroner pieces. His winnings. They're only worth a dime, which, at best, isn't worth anything in Denmark. It's just half of a small plastic sack full of dimes. Perhaps a total of five or six dollars.

After dinner tonight, the fourth night, he again headed toward the shooting booth down the flower-edged gravel paths of Tivoli. He'd had a good meal, again outdoors, different types of small boiled potatoes, and four different types of herring. Herring and sour cream, herring and mustard sauce, herring with onions, and matjes herring, all this over thick slabs of dark Danish bread and washed down with glasses of Carlsberg beer and a tiny glass of Aquavit on the side.

The bored young woman at the shooting booth looked up and smiled at him tonight when she saw him coming down the path and handed him the same rifle he'd used last night. The prizes are foolish little things. A caricature of a Tivoli toy soldier guard standing in his striped conical guard's hut in his red waist coat and bearskin hat. A China cup with a photo of Queen Margrethe, some balloons on sticks, a red paddle with a white ball on a rubber band, the usual teddy bears and stuffed animals. Some multi-colored joss sticks, some of which have been lit, are set in a gold rimmed dish wafting incense across the front of the shooting booth. The combination of the incense and the Aquavit blurs his vision, and he holds the heavy stock of the rifle to his cheek. Last night, of ten shots, he'd put eight on the target, even two in the tiny circle of the bulls eye. The young attendant had said nothing. Neither approbation nor disapproval, but without expression she tore off his target sheet and handed it to him as he left. He'd come close. Three shots in the bulls eye circle would have won a prize. He kept the paper target and had it propped up on the dresser in his room if the maid hadn't thrown it away. Tonight the gun swayed as he aimed not at a bulls eye sheet, but at a rack of clay pipes. If he could shatter four pipes in the rack he'd win his choice of a Danish flag lapel pin or a figure of the Little Mermaid. He aimed at the pipes and blinked several times to clear the blurring and then held his breath and squeezed off the first shot. He shattered the first pipe, hitting it exactly on the bowl. He moved the rifle to the left, just a minute adjustment, held his breath for a long moment, blinked again to clear his vision and squeezed the trigger. He shattered the bowl of the second pipe. Again, an infinitely miniscule adjustment, he held his breath, and squeezed and he hit the third pipe. Now only one more for a prize. He rested for a moment and looked over at the attendant. She was a typical red-faced Danish teenager, with a cherub face, a tiny snub nose, blonde hair held in back with a large plastic clip, and fair blue eyes. She was listening to a yellow iPod with ear phones and dropping pellets in a tube. But tonight she was also watching him. He knew she was watching him. He aimed again, but this time he wet the front sight of the rifle with saliva on his finger. He'd seen Gary Cooper do that in a movie, "Sergeant York". He aimed and immediately smashed the fourth clay bowl.

The young woman got down off her perch and said to him, "You're a good shot," in an almost-perfect English accent. "Americans love to shoot. You're early though. We don't get them in spring, only in the summer. Do you have shooting booths like this in America? What do you want, the Little Mermaid?"

"No, the pin."

She handed him his trophy, a Danish flag lapel pin. She dropped it into his hand.

"We have shooting booths on the main boulevards in most of our cities," he told her.

"So you practiced before you came over here."

"Yes I practiced."

He thanked her and put the Danish lapel pin on, pinning it on the lapel of his navy blue sports coat and with his blue jacket and his red and white lapel pin, he thought he looked like a Danish yachtsman. All he needed was a white yachtsman's cap. While he'd been shooting, a group of Spanish tourists had quietly gathered around him, standing silently watching him. "Good evening," he said to them in English as he left, and several people smiled but didn't answer him. He could hear a few words of Spanish, "Buenos Noches," he said to them and pointed to the rifles, "Buena Suerte." Was that the right phrase for good luck? One of the men, short with glasses and a white dress shirt smiled up at him as he hugged his wife to protect her from the chill.

He walked down the flowered gravel paths of Tivoli wearing his Danish flag pin, a white cross on a red background, and went out the old wooden archway gate and crossed Hans Christian Andersen Boulevard. He'd seen the hulking bronze statue of the seated figure of Andersen across the boulevard. It was a nice touch, placing a statue of the old poet directly across from the amusement park. He crossed the street and he was alone with the huge statue of Andersen who was shown seated wearing a top hat and a cravat and a long waistcoat, holding a cane in one hand and a book in the other, his head turned up in the direction of Tivoli. What about giving a little hello to Andersen? A little shry in the moonlight with the bulb-lit towers of the Tivoli pagodas in the background. A shry for all the pain the old bachelor writer had to endure to grind out those magical tales. A Reichean shry. He'd read James Atlas's biography of Bellow. According to Atlas, Bellow practiced Reichean primal scream therapy sitting on the benches of Hyde Park in Chicago. He put his hand on Hans Christian Andersen's hand, over his thick fingers holding the book. They were worn smooth from so many tourists' hands touching them. He opened his mouth. Not a word. Not even a sound. Andersen's smooth bronze fingers were as cold as the barrel of the gun. The only sounds were the shrieks of the riders dropping from the parachute towers at Tivoli. Finally a sound came out of his own mouth and it sounded like – eech – a weak little glottal puff. Not even a shry. Not a cry. Bellow would have really sounded off in the moonlight in Copenhagen. When he was Jonny Levin's age, he would have given Andersen a real primal shry in honor of Andersen's work. Bellow fathered a daughter at 83 and wrote a novel, *Ravelstein.* And he, Jonny Levin, he Jonny Levin could only manage – "eech". But maybe, by touching Andersen's hand, he'd unblock and he'd be able to go back to the room and write something marvelous.

2

INSTEAD OF THE TWO LOVELY BLONDES on duty at the hotel desk, he was met by a sour-faced old man doing a crossword puzzle in the evening paper who said nothing to him when he handed him his key. Also no prostitutes were hanging around the hotel on the street, just some kids beered up and singing. Many of them wearing those silly little white yachting caps. He was told that those white caps signified graduation from high school so he really didn't need one to go with his blue blazer and the Danish flag pin.

Up in the room, he sat on the edge of the bed and turned on Danish TV. Some kind of quiz show with two dour tweed-jacketed men and a big breasted cheerful hostess. He watched for a moment but couldn't understand a word, and muted it. He took his writing tablet out of the night stand drawer and found a pen and wrote two lines.

KAENE MICKEY BERNSTEIN (MARRIED TO ROSE LEVIN)

Perhaps this would be the beginning of his Levin Family history which hopefully he could turn into a novel if he could just keep the faces of his old loves from suddenly appearing. For years he'd been carrying a set of images of his old loves, college girls, high school girls, women from his bachelor days and lately they would appear flashing through his mind almost every day, particularly in the morning in the shower, or in the evenings just before he went to bed. In the evenings, the faces would always appear about this time so if he was to do any serious work he would have to stop them. *Kaene* is the Danish word for "Dear". He'd cut through a small church cemetery during his exploration today and he'd seen the word "Kaene" chiseled into the gravemarkers before the name on many headstones. The stones were small compared to American headstones. He would read "Kaene Peter Christiansen," date of birth, date of death. Or "Kaene Margaret Mortensen", date of birth, date of death. Or "Kaene Peter Jensen". The stones were also often bordered by one or two tiny songbirds modeled on the top edge of the gravemarkers, perhaps a set of lovebirds or doves or pigeons. Often "Kaene Peter Christiansen, etc." would be finished off with a separate line ... *Tak*. On some stones, a separate line, *Tak Tak Tak*. Again, *Tak*, the word for thank you. So apparently you have "Dear Peter Christiansen" thanking those who have come to visit his grave. He was told by an older man dressed in formal black with a white wing bow-tie, some aide in the church, that *Kaene* is the word for "dear" and instead of the deceased thanking his mourners, *Tak Tak Tak* represented his friends and family thanking the deceased for his life.

If ever he was to write something it would be much easier, it seemed, if he could construct something within the pages, something useful, but also something mystical. Perhaps he would try to construct a cemetery, a beautiful little Danish cemetery with trellises of doves and love birds crawling on top of the headstones and each of the dead memorialized with the lovely Danish prefix – *Kaene*. "Dear." The cemetery would be an attempt to build something that would be a special gift to the reader. Something that would last, beyond the life of his book, a magical construct.

So again—KAENE MICKEY BERNSTEIN

Fat. Pig-eyed. Shrewd Mickey Bernstein. A cigar always stuck in the side of his mouth. A drunk. Never got out of eighth grade. My uncle. Married to Rose, my father's sister, childless, a barren marriage. Mickey made millions in the *smatteh* business. Dress factories. King of the oversized woman's trade. Blew it all. Not quite. Left Rose enough to have a black Cadillac, a maid and a chauffeur, and a fancy rented apartment at an apartment hotel on the edge of Lincoln Park in Chicago. The chauffeur stole what was left of Rose's money, her diamond pendant disappeared into the projects, Cabrini Green. Her sapphire ring. The black Cadillac went too, her bank accounts, her stock, they ripped at her like piranhas and when nothing was left but a little, old, frightened Jewish lady, mute and alone in her room, they gave her back to her family, her brothers, who supported her until she died.

Mickey Bernstein never lived to see how Rose died. He lived his last days dressed in diapers with Rose as his nurse. Mickey profanely mumbling for a drink through a haze of small strokes. A tough kid out of the west side of Chicago. He used to wear a pink carnation in his lapel, big camel's hair coats and a white broad-brimmed fedora. No kids. Never any kids. A yacht in Florida he named after Rose. In a way I became their child. I remember they gave me a model toy car when I was eight or nine for Chanukah, a Pierce Arrow. A beautiful model of a Pierce Arrow with headlights sculpted in its fenders, whitewalls and red wheels, and a working rumble seat. It was made of heavy metal and I filled in the windows with a light blue-colored wax that I got by melting my mother's candles. The windows were like waxy glass – a gray blue-colored glass that I smoothed with my fingers.

KAENE ROSE LEVIN BERNSTEIN

Mickey's wife, my Aunt Rose. Not like Allen Ginsberg's "Aunt Rose". She didn't have hair on her chin. She was a cosmopolitan woman. She had a lovely singing voice like an opera star. She was a big woman. They were big people, Mickey and Rose. She always wore a black silk dress and posed in photographs in profile so she would look thinner. She also had a big heart. When I had graduated college she gave me a car, a two-door two-toned brown and beige Chevrolet. A brown bottom with a beige top and red wheels. She bought it on her own. Rose never had her own money. Mickey controlled the money doling out a weekly allowance to her. He bought her jewelry in restaurants. It was always "hot" being fenced in whispers by the restaurant's owner. I was with them in "The Singapore" on Rush Street when Mickey bought Rose the star sapphire. She was a consummate nagger and he bought her gifts to keep her quiet. She bought the car on time even though Mickey had at least two million in the bank. She paid for my car secretly each month from her household allowance. I thanked her and used the car to seduce college girls. At least I would try. I hardly ever succeeded. No, I don't think I ever succeeded. No one would go to bed with you even if you had a brand new car given to you by your aunt.

Hotel Europejski

Kaene Elaine Marks

I knew it would happen. The faces of the young women would begin intruding. I can't keep writing without seeing the faces that keep floating into my mind. I really shouldn't put Elaine Marks into my cemetery here in Copenhagen. But I haven't seen her in over forty years and she'll never know. She was a real Jewish beauty. She had dark eyes and dark, long, shining hair that hung straight down from her shoulders and she was very slender. I lied when I said I never succeeded with the car. I think I can say I succeeded often if you can view the car as an accessory to the seduction. Even then, if a place could be found, a room, an apartment, your parents' home, it was much more preferable than the backseat of a car. By putting Elaine Marks in the cemetery I am in a sense handing her the gift of death to protect her identity. She's probably very much alive. I hope she is and I hope she doesn't read this because she was always kind to me, a lovely, kind, intelligent young woman and she doesn't deserve my kind of memorial.

I remember making love to her or at least trying to make love to her. My parents were gone. I lived at home and we had the evening together. No one would bother us. She came home with me in my new car and we got into my bed, naked. No, she wore one of my summer robes, but she was naked underneath the robe. I found an ancient rubber in my top drawer. I was inside of her quickly and she held me back for a moment and said to me, "If we were married, we could do this all the time." Elaine Marks. Perhaps the most beautiful Jewish girl I had ever known. I was twenty-three, she was maybe twenty. I pushed. I was caught in a tight little chamber. I was inside her maybe three or four inches. I didn't realize that I was attempting to make love to a virgin. That she was a virgin. That's how dumb I was, how unskilled at love-

> making. I pushed again and again, but I couldn't break through her maidenhead. I didn't want to hurt her. She was a true virgin, maybe a doctor could do the job. I couldn't. Still, she is pinned by that moment into my memory, the fragrance of the evening, my triumph and yet failure at love.

He closed the notebook and put his pen down. He had no justification for writing about Elaine Marks. Why should he invade her privacy? She was probably a grandmother. He'd heard she was living in Boston. He could just rip up the pages about her. Mickey and Rose, they were beyond caring. Each a pile of bones rotting in a cemetery in Chicago. They weren't even buried together. Mickey was buried with his family, Rose with her family. He should have written about Mickey's trick with his double-jointed toes simulating trench foot, the trick that got him out of the trenches in France in 1917, and his imitation of Jimmy Durante with his teeth. He could add that tomorrow. Tomorrow he'd describe how Mickey would take his teeth out and hold them in his open palm and imitate Durante singing in Durante's mumbling accent, "a one tooth, a whole tooth, a one tooth, a two tooth." He made a few notes in the notebook where he'd stopped, "Mickey – France, imitate Durante, trench foot – double-jointed, 'a one tooth, a whole tooth.' 'Sing Rosie – Sing.'" He would also do a riff on Rose's opera voice. How the brothers would always encourage her to sing. He put the notebook down and went into the bathroom and looked at himself in the mirror. Wisps of gray hair growing over his ears, a mole removed from below his throat leaving a round nickel-sized scar. Thank God it wasn't melanoma. He'd had a friend die of a melanoma on his scalp. He'd discovered it one day in the mirror and six weeks later he was dead. Kaene/Malcolm Cohen, his dear friend, Mel Cohen. A professor of classic Greek. His own forehead was spotted with tiny lesions and age marks. Which one would darken into Kaene

Jonny/Levin? Did Nikos Kazantzakis worry about melanoma? No. He worried about getting laid and loving life. "Report to Greco." Learn to love, Jonny Levin. He looked at himself in the mirror, learn all over again to love.

3

IT'S THE NEXT MORNING. It had been very hard to sleep, so warm in the room because he had to close the windows. Sounds of kids singing in the street and shouting all night after he stopped constructing the little gravestones. At least he'd left Elaine Marks in peace. He hopes he left her in peace. He doesn't know if he can really continue with the history but it seems he's constructed a beginning. A fragile beginning.

So if he's to be Jonny Levin and see more of Copenhagen, he thinks about renting a bicycle this morning. What about it, Jonny Levin? Stop building the cemetery, and get up and out of the room and rent a bicycle.

But first breakfast, and he just makes the 9:30 deadline. The hostess is at the door and is about to close it. A young black woman in a uniform with a white collar and dancing eyes. She seats him with a man and two women. The man looks up at him with a smile and immediately speaks to him in English. The women pay no attention.

"So where are you from fella?" the man asks. "I know you're from the States."

"How do you know?"

"The shoes. I always look at the shoes. You've got American shoes. Hush Puppies."

"Am I wearing American shoes?"

He leans over toward Jonny Levin and picks a piece of thread off of his shirt.

"*Smutz*, you've got a piece of *smutz* there. I got rid of it for you." He flicked at a piece of thread.

The man was about his age in his early sixties. He had a fluid, expressive Jewish face, a long bulbous nose, his cheeks were flushed and a full head of hair brownish and yellowing in a pompadour. He wore an initialed English purple dress shirt with a white round open collar. The shirt was initialed on the breast pocket with his initials "ML" in a circle of laurel leaves and on the white cuffs "ML" in straight cleft letters. His fingernails were immaculately manicured and his thick fingers glistened.

The two ladies, one round faced, the other slim and rather attractive, in their late fifties or early sixties, pretended to be inspecting their menus, but they were watching and listening.

"I didn't get your name."

"Mooney Levine, and yours?"

"Jonny Levin."

"You're Jonny Levine? You're kidding me. Johnny Levine is my nephew. Maybe we're *mishpocheh*? Except Johnny Levine's from Philly and I'm from Manhattan, 86th and Central Park West."

"You really have a nephew named Johnny Levin? How do you spell Levin?"

"L.e.v.i.n.e. Sure. Johnny Levine. He's a dentist in Philly. An oral surgeon"

"We're not related. I spell my name L-e-v-i-n. And I'm from Chicago. Also my first name is J.o.n, not J.o.h.n. What are you doing in Denmark?"

"I sell carnie equipment."

"Carnie equipment?"

"For carnivals. The horses and the chariots in the carousel in Tivoli. They're all mine. Thirty six Jumpers, fourteen Standers, it's the same size as the carousel on Coney Island. Those Coney Island horses are mine too. All my horses are hand-carved in Brooklyn. I sell the most beautiful Jumpers and Standers in the world." Mooney Levine set his coffee aside and pulled a binder of photos up from the floor, put his glasses on and spread the binder on the table. There were glossy color photos of wild-eyed thick-maned carved wooden horses with red-cheeked wooden cavaliers and dirndled wooden maidens with blonde tresses standing as attendants.

"My Jumpers, all pure Lipizzan stallions."

The two women each were giving their orders. They both ordered curried eggs over toast and cold salmon. They were still listening but pretended to be talking about friends they were expecting.

"What's your line of business in Chicago, Jonny?"

"I teach at a university."

"What do you teach?"

"English. English Literature. I'm a professor."

"So you're a professor. Good. How's business?" he asked.

"I'm making a living."

"I'll tell you a little joke, Professor," he held Jonny Levin's arm down on the table. "There's this little Jewish guy in Brooklyn who throws himself in front of a cab and lies there moaning on the street under the wheels. A crowd gathers. One of his friends sees him lying under the cab and rushes over and bends down to help him. 'Irving, Irving, are you all right? What are you doing?'

"*Ich machen a leben,*" the little guy says. "You know Yiddish, Jonny?"

"I know a little."

"'*Ich machen a leben'* means 'I'm making a living.'" Mooney Levine laughs and laughs and then flipped to some more photos.

"I also sell jewelry. Rings. Men's and women's costume jewelry. Special rings. Here, watch, I want my check. Now watch the hostess." He was wearing a big clear glass stone on his ring and he caught a slant of sunlight falling across the table with the ring and shined it in the hostess's eye. "Check, Miss," he signalled with a little wave.

"You could hurt that young woman's eye," one of the women said to him. "You really shouldn't do that."

"No, it don't hurt, it just gets their attention."

The hostess brought the check over.

"Did I startle you miss?"

"No, I just suddenly saw this huge flash of light. Do you have some kind of flashlight?"

"No, just this." He flashed the ring around the room, flashing sunlight on the tiered, jellied sardine mold and the plaster cupids along the tops of the heavy drawn maroon velvet drapes.

He signed his bill with a flourish and handed the hostess back her pen as if it were a gift.

"Nice talking to you Professor, ladies. Come over to Tivoli and see my horses. I'll get you on the carousel with a pass. They've got a brass ring machine there. Grab a brass ring and you take home a set of Royal Copenhagen china free."

"I'm renting a bike today."

"So come over tonight, Professor. It's only a few blocks. I've also got my other merchandise in a booth with some Danish ladies. I do a little magic on the side." He flipped to another photo of an emerald green ring flecked with gold. "That's a séance ring. We've got a séance going on over there tonight at eight. What about it ladies? Want to come to a séance? Here's my card. Bring the Professor. I'll take you all for a carousel ride in the moonlight. Ever ride a giraffe? I've got them too." He flipped his album to a glossy photo of an astonished looking wooden giraffe.

"See you later," he said. Then he was gone, snapping his fingers for the elevators. "*Hiss*," he called, the Danish word for elevator. "Hold that *hiss*."

"That man is really bizarre, very strange," one of the women said after Mooney Levine left the table. "Look at his card."Her friend looked at the card, pushed her glasses back on her head and continued, "Let's go, Martha. One free question."

"No, first you pay the entrance fee, Elyse."

"No, I don't think so. I think you get a free question and then if you want to stay you pay the entrance fee."

Martha handed the card to Jonny Levin.

> Mooney F. Levine, New York City, U.S.A. and International Productions, Inc. presents a séance tonight at eight. Booth 33 at Tivoli. Josefina, the internationally acclaimed Seeress, will cure your heartache, love, and money problems. Josefina accepts Visa, MasterCard, and American Express. No tape recorders or video cameras. Proven results and testimonials. Modest entrance fee. One free question. Performance in English. Danish translation.,

She let her glasses fall back on the chain. She was a heavy woman with an intelligent face and a cultured accent. "You're from Chicago?" she said to him pleasantly. "Where in Chicago?"

"Evanston."

"Oh, Evanston, I have friends there. The Koenigsbergs. Where in Evanston?"

"Near the university."

"Do you know Fred and Enid Koenigsberg?"

The second woman was elegantly slim, in a black slack suit. She had a smooth face with obviously a few cosmetic changes. She wore horn-rimmed glasses on a chain and dressed in a black jacket and a crème-colored cashmere turtleneck sweater. "Do you know Harold and Sally Hechman?" she asked him. Harold practically owns one of the banks in Evanston. I think he's the president of the biggest bank there. I also think he's a trustee of Northwestern. I heard you say you teach at a university. I'm Elyse Friedberg." She extended her hand and he shook it. She was rather sexy. It was perhaps the first time he'd touched a woman since he'd been in Copenhagen.

He wasn't about to tell her where he taught. He didn't want to make American friends in Denmark. These were obviously two wealthy Jewish women from Chicago. He didn't want to play status games with them at breakfast.

"I'm Jonny Levin," he said quietly to Elyse Friedberg. He thought of dropping the "Jonny" with these two American ladies, but he didn't.

"Hello Jonny Levin. A fellow Chicagoan," The heavier woman extended her hand and he shook it. "I'm Martha Selig. Did you say you taught at Northwestern?"

"No I didn't say that."

"Where do you teach?"

"Martha, leave him alone. The man doesn't want to tell where he teaches. He has a reason. So leave it alone."

"I just think it's so strange."

Already he was annoyed by her. "Do you have an occupation you want to tell me about?" he asked her.

"Occupation? Hell no. We're just running around Europe. I can't stand Copenhagen. What a provincial town. There's nothing here. Just a square, a few towers and statues, a shopping street, Strøget. Is that what it's called? We're on our way to Stockholm then Helsinki and St. Petersburg. What did we buy here Elyse? I don't even remember."

"You bought some silver at Georg Jensen."

He ordered French toast and some tea.

"Have you been to Tivoli?" he asked them.

"No, but I'd really like to go see that man's production," Elyse Friedberg answered him. "I'd like to go to a séance. I've never been to a séance. I think I'd love it."

"I hate all those yiddishisms he used, Elyse. *Smutz*. What's *smutz*?"

"Dirt," he told her. "*Smutz* is a speck of dirt."

"Can't he just say 'dirt'? What about *mishpocheh*? I know what that means. Family. *Meshugana*? That's what he is. A real New York *meshugana*. He says he sells carnival horses. He runs séances. He's a real New York *meshugana*. I'm not going anywhere near that man, Elyse."

"He said he'd give us each one free question, Martha, and a pass to the carousel."

"That's just what I need. A pass to the carousel. I'm too old to go twirling."

"Martha, where are we going tonight? We let the driver go. We don't have a car. The ballet is closed, the opera is closed. Why not a séance? We can walk over there. It's only a few blocks." She suddenly put her slender hand on top of Jonny Levin's hand with a half-smile. "If you don't have plans, join us."

Both women stood up and took their bills. She touched his hand again. "I'll save you a place at the séance table."

She was a direct woman. And she'd given him an invitation. He watched them head into the lobby toward the elevator. She had a graceful walk. Her friend was a busybody, a gossip, but the woman who touched his hand had a certain elegance about her, a kind of graceful elegance in her walk and even in her directness. He turned to his French toast. An interesting woman, but did he really want to hook up in Copenhagen with a woman from Chicago? If she wouldn't intrude on him when they returned it might be nice. He could go into the city occasionally and meet her for theater or perhaps even the opera. It would be better than falling asleep in his chair watching television. He'd been doing a lot of that lately. But not since he'd arrived in Denmark. Not one night asleep in the chair. And he'd finally begun writing again. He looked up and saw Mooney Levine coming out of the elevator and watched him at the front desk where he began talking to the two, young blonde receptionists. They were both laughing with him and he leaned towards them and one of them seemed to sniff his cheek and then she took a white carnation from the vase of flowers on the marble countertop and carefully pinned the flower to his lapel. She did it laughing and tossing her hair. They both then pretended to admire him. He turned and headed towards the dining room. He was dressed in an Italian-cut brown jacket with padded shoulders and a yellow silk ascot. He came directly to Jonny Levin's table.

"How do you do it Mooney?"

"Easy. I just put a little of my cologne on. Just a spritz. It's my own brand. I have it made for me in Paris."

"Cologne?"

"Here's a small sample bottle. On the house. Wear it. The women will never leave you alone. It's got a special chemical in it."

"I couldn't do that."

"So be a *putz*. An older man needs a lift. It's the Viagra of the aftershaves. It's got a pheromone in it, like an aphrodisiac."

He set the tiny bottle beside Jonny Levin's plate.

"It's a gift. I'll see you tonight, professor. Wear a few drops of this stuff. The Danish women love it. And here's one more joke." He looked around the dining room to see if anyone was listening and lowered his voice. "A man goes to a doctor for some Viagra, 'Doc, I can't get it up. What should I do?' The doc says, 'Take this Viagra and then call me.' The guy takes it that night and just before he tries to make love to his wife he falls over dead on the couch. She calls the paramedics and they work on him for an hour, but he's dead, and she gets out his best suit and a nice tie and calls the funeral parlor and they come over. They take him back to the funeral home and get him all dressed up and put him in the coffin, but they can't get the coffin closed. Why? It was the Viagra. It killed him but it worked."

"You get it, Professor? He had such a big hard-on that they couldn't get the lid down on him." He slapped Jonny Levin on the back and pointed to the bottle.

"Put a few drops of my stuff on, burchik. Just try it. Only a few drops. You won't be sorry. Here, I'll give you just a little spritz." He removed an inlaid pearl spritzer from inside his jacket and spritzed a touch on his index finger and chucked Jonny Levin under the chin. "Just a drop, Professor. It don't take much. If you put on too much it becomes like a repellant. The women start running away. So just a touch, under the chin, behind the ears, on the wrists. You work it out."

He set the inlaid spritzer on the table and gave it to Jonny Levin. "Mother of pearl made for me in Indonesia. It's yours. I get them by the gross. Keep it. There's a war on there, but they still make good spritzers. They make them out of abalone shells."

He chucked Jonny Levin under the chin again, punched him lightly on the shoulder and turned and walked out of the dining room.

4

HE RENTED A BICYCLE. He found a small shop near Radhus Pladsen, the main square of Copenhagen. Radhus was the old red brick tower City Hall. The main square surrounding it was filled with people, lines of tourists, families, water fountains with people sitting on the edges their faces to the sunlight. There were small crowds in circles around the street performers. Also Kierkegaard's gray stone house, very large and formal. Kierkegaard must have come from a wealthy family. As he tried to become more in control of his bicycle, he thought of a line of Kierkegaard that he always gave to his students, "Life can only be understood backwards, but it must be lived forwards." No time for philosophy in the middle of this square. He almost ran over a woman looking at her guidebook, just wobbled around her. He'd rented an old comfortable black bicycle, a woman's bike with three gears, a large straw basket, a bell, handbrakes and a low soft seat and thick tires. He felt quite comfortable on it. It had cost thirty kroner, about three dollars, for the afternoon.

As he rode carefully toward the edge of the square, he thought about the bicycles he'd owned in his life. The first, when he was a boy about ten, was a "Shelby Flyer". It had shiny aluminum fenders, thick balloon tires and a streamlined light built into its front fender. He grew up in Glencoe on Chicago's North Shore. His father owned a small stamping plant that sold parts to the automotive industry. His father was a successful businessman who bought everything for his family wholesale, and the "Shelby

Flyer" was a proud gift to his ten year old son. The son wanted a lightweight, thin-tired bike, like his friends' bikes, not a fat-tired heavy aluminum-fendered bike with an aero-flow light built into the fender. In eighth grade and in high school and in his teens, there was a black Schwinn, finally a thin-tired fast bike with a three-speed gearshift. It was also bought wholesale and picked up by father and son at a Chicago freight yard on Roosevelt Road in a packing crate. It took two weeks to assemble and he'd used it for five years, to ride to school, to play baseball, basketball, hockey, and most importantly, to visit girlfriends at night. He was a man about town on a bicycle, like Saroyan's Messenger. He couldn't remember the name of Saroyan's book with the bicycle messenger engraved into the cover. No it wasn't on the cover, it was drawn as one of the chapter headings and the name of the book was "The Bicycle Rider of Beverly Hills". Saroyan's Messenger was drawn as a boy on a bike wearing a Western Union uniform. After reading Saroyan's book, he'd foolishly tried his hand at being a Western Union boy and delivered telegrams during the Korean war. But when the death messages began to come he quit, and put his bicycle away for the rest of high school. Then when he went to college in Champaign after the war, there was the old red bike, a used bike that he rented from a campus bike shop. It was sort of a maroon color. He tried to remember it, but he could only dimly see it lying on its side at a bike rack. No more bicycles until he was a young married man. He bought a suburban Schwinn with a child's seat, and used to ride the children after dinner. The dog, a black Lab, running ahead of them. She would disappear and he could never see her, but he could hear her padded swift footsteps in the suburban darkness and the light tinkling sound of her collar.

He parked the bike at a small sidewalk café and sat down and ordered coffee. He felt good, proud to have bicycled confidently across the square, and now sitting in the Danish sunlight, closed his eyes for a moment and put on his sunglasses. Poor Saroyan. Whatever happened to him? He used to teach Saroyan in his short story course. "The Bicycle Rider of Beverly Hills," "My Name is Aram," "The Daring Young Man on the Flying Trapeze". He hadn't read any Saroyan in years. Could he name another Armenian writer? There was Michael Arlen, a fine essayist. He used to write for the New Yorker. He hadn't seen anything by Michael Arlen for several years. Michael Arlen's father was Harold Arlen who wrote, "The Green Hat," one of the most popular novels of the '20s. He'd never read "The Green Hat". He would never read "The Green Hat". Was it true that Stalin's wife had been reading it a few weeks before she committed suicide? According to their daughter, Svetlana, that was true. Didn't Stalin partially blame his wife's suicide on Arlen? And then who gave her the pistol? A member of the Inner Circle? Who was it? He had Svetlana Stalin's book, "Thirty Letters to a Friend", in his library at home. If he was home, he could easily look it up. He'd actually seen Svetlana once. She lived in Wisconsin south of Madison where Frank Lloyd Wright had built Taliesen East. He and the children and Magdalena, his first wife, had spent a weekend there. They went to see Chekov's "The Cherry Orchard" in an outdoor arena and just before the lights dimmed, two young ushers seated a heavy set older woman with a round Russian face in her sixties. She was seated across the stage, and when he saw her as the lights went on he realized at once that it was Svetlana. He recognized her from her photo on the cover of her book. He knew that she had married the architect in charge of Taliesen East and she was living there. So he'd come full circle. Armenian writers, Harold Arlen, "The Green Hat" and finally Stalin's daughter Svetlana Alliluyeva. He could have given a lecture on Armenian writers. He'd left out Elia Kazan's "America, America". He smiled at his list making and his didactism.

Now his coffee came and he drank it and began to watch the crowds of people. There was a soccer game between Denmark and the Netherlands. People were walking through the square on their way to the soccer game dressed in their country's colors. The Danes in red and white soccer shirts, some in red tams with white tassels or red oversized stovepipe hats that they would bow to the Dutch in mock greetings. The Dutch wore red, white and blue, the colors of the Dutch tri-color, many also in the tall, silly hats or carrying paper streamers they would toss. Some wore rubber masks of their favorite players. As they passed each other there would be occasional bursts of song and cheering.

There were some street performers moving along the edges of the tables and they stopped almost in front of him. There were two women, one was dancing, a pretty young woman dressed in a black cutaway with a cane and a black silk top hat and a formal white shirt and bow tie. She tipped her hat to him and began to dance in front of him. She apparently recognized he was an American. She began singing in English, "I'm a Very Stylish Woman". She bowed and tapped his table with her cane. Suddenly she put her cheek against his and whispered in his ear, "I'm a Very Stylish Woman". Then she quickly moved away and danced around several of the other tables. Her companion was a tall, blonde woman in her late twenties dressed in a full Indian headdress, a war bonnet. She was quite beautiful, full breasted, wearing a flesh colored bikini top as she played the accordion.

She also swayed toward him and put her cheek up against his and whispered to him, "Hello, mister".

What was it? One minute he was sitting in the sunlight brooding about Armenian writers and Stalin's daughter. Now two Danish beauties were dancing and swaying in front of him. The one with the accordion almost sat down on his lap. "Do you have a request sir?" she asked him smiling and laughing with her friend.

"What kind of request?"

"A song of course. A favorite song."

"Do you know 'Lady of Spain'?"

"Oh, come on sir, that's not our kind of song. You're a sophisticated gentleman and you smell delicious."

"Do I really?"

"Inge, did you notice the gentleman's aftershaving lotion? Do you think he's a movie star from America? Are you in the cinema sir?"

Inge twirled over to him and put her cheek against his again and sniffed.

"Oh he does. He smells delicious."

She held her cane horizontally and did a little swaying shuffle. "He looks like an American movie star or perhaps a director or producer. You will want both of us in your film, won't you?"

She put her top hat down in front of her by having it roll down her arm and they both bowed to the audience. The open hat on the ground was a gesture to him and the others that they would like some money dropped in it.

The people at adjoining tables put some coins in it and began to applaud.

He reached for his billfold and put a twenty kroner note in her hat.

"Oh thank you sir, 'I'm a Very Stylish Woman'," the dancer sang in her husky voice and tapped his shoulder with her cane. She danced over to the adjoining café. The blonde with the accordion followed her and waved goodbye to him and blew him a kiss and gave him a shake of her hips and began playing "Ta Ra Ra Boom Dee-ay". They both began dancing in unison doing bumps and grinds like in the old lithographs of the dancing cabaret girls in the cabarets of Tivoli.

Another woman approached him, a woman in her forties

with long brown hair and a very sad ivory oval face. She was holding up a scissors and she wore a placard board around her neck with several black paper silhouettes pasted on the board. She was a silhouette artist and she stood before him and held her scissors up and began cutting a silhouette of his face. She said nothing to him and as she worked she leaned toward him so that her hair brushed his cheek as she moved to one side of his face, and then the other, cutting solemnly and without expression. Then she handed him a finished silhouette of himself in profile.

"Thank you," he said. He held it up to the sunlight. "Thank you very much."

She took the figure back and turned toward him frowning, her hair brushing his face again, and then she snipped off a fragment, a tiny sliver of paper and gave the silhouette back to him.

She said something to him in Danish in a soft voice.

"I'm sorry, I don't speak Danish. I'm an American. Do you speak English?"

"Yes sir, I speak English. Not too well though. Would you care to buy my silhouette? One hundred kroner, sir." She seemed to be slightly smiling at him and then she lapsed back into her somber expression. She had lovely planes to her face and dark eyelashes and pale blue, almost green eyes.

"It's very nice."

"If you like it then you should buy it."

"What will I do with a silhouette?"

"You could frame it. I carry frames in my shop." She quickly handed him a card. "Beautiful frames. You should visit my shop, it's quite near here."

He reached in his pocket and found a hundred kroner note and handed it to her. The silhouette was about ten dollars. "You're very talented."

"Thank you sir," she said. She looked at him again for a moment and then began moving alongside the adjoining tables holding her scissors up to the customers.

He glanced at her card.Suddenly she returned to him and in

Marguerite Berenstyne

24 Helgoland, Brunsdrata 24
Silhouette Artiste
Berenstyne Frame Shoppe & Antiquaries
Telephone 721-1390

a moment cut out a swan and handed it to him, leaning in again toward him and then turning her back and snipping something and turning away again. She then handed him a white rabbit and turned abruptly and walked toward the next tables. She said nothing to him as she handed him the new cuttings. In five seconds she had produced a beautiful swan with a tail spread in a fan and a rabbit with long ears cut precisely and evenly. She was a master artist and also a dancer as she cut her silhouettes and whirled at first toward him, handing him her gifts, and then turning away and moving down along the other tables.

He looked at the figure of the white swan. It made him remember the small inn he'd stayed in, "The White Swan", in northwestern Holland with Magdalena, who was born in Belgium and had led him on a bicycle trip to Holland. He remembered "The White Swan" in Raalte, with its old feather beds and dormer windows overlooking the square with plane trees and a horse fountain. When they went down for breakfast in the dining room, they faced a scene right out of Rembrandt. Old men in black caps, jackets and trousers, wearing wooden shoes and smoking clay pipes. He hadn't thought of that tiny inn in Holland in years, but suddenly the silhouette of the swan she handed him brought him back to Magdalena and their trip to Holland just before their marriage. He usually tried not to think of her because it would bring back only bad memories. But this was a good memory, almost a tableau of Rembrandt. They had hot chocolate and carried the tray of hot chocolate back upstairs to the feather beds and drank it and made love.

He carefully folded the swan and the rabbit and put them in his wallet. He paid his bill and then rode his bicycle back to the bike rental shop and turned the bike in and walked back to the hotel.

5

BACK AT THE HOTEL HE STOPPED AT THE COUNTER and asked if he had any mail or messages. The two young lovely blondes were on duty. Very crisp and efficient in their black bow ties and black waistcoats with gold crossed keys pinned in the lapels. They wore white plastic name tags, Dagne and Karen. Both greeted him. There was a bowl of apples on the desk and he thought of taking an apple, but he was afraid he'd break his lower bridge if he tried to bite down. Then he remembered he had a tiny knife in his shaving kit, so he took a green apple. He searched the numbered cubicles behind the counter for a message. He couldn't see well enough to make out his room number and he bent toward Dagne who suddenly leaned in toward him with a pink carnation in her hand and held the flower up to him. "Thank you," he said. *Tak.*

She replied, *Tak,* and brushed her hair back with one hand and turned and searched his cubicle and said in perfect English, "No messages, Mr. Levin, but now instead you have our flower."

"Yes, a pink one. I saw that you gave the other Mr. Levin a white one this morning."

"Oh yes, the other gentleman from America. Also a Mr. Levin but he has added an 'e' to his name, Mr. Levine." She sniffed and leaned in toward him again. "Yours is pink, though, for the afternoon our flowers are always pink. Isn't that true Karen?"

"What?"

"Pink flowers for our guests in the post-noon."

"Yes, that is true."

"So, Mr. Levin without an 'e', your key. Here it is and please have a pleasant evening." She handed him his key and touched his hand, like Elyse Friedberg. Now two women in Copenhagen had touched his hand. He was keeping score.

Again, the elevator ascending and behind the barred cage he held the green stem of the single pink carnation and twisted it under his nose. "*Tak. Tak.* Jonny Levin," he said to himself as the ancient cage climbed up to his floor.

In the room he put his carnation in an empty Coke bottle that he filled with water.

There were some remnants of petunias on the small balcony. He opened the sliding door to let fresh air into the room. The glass panel of the door was filthy. Absolutely scabrous and filthy. He hadn't noticed it behind the brocade curtain, but the glass was dulled with grime and he filled a cup of water and took the Kleenex box from the bathroom and began to clean the door panel. He wasn't doing a very good job though, he barely made a dent in the city grime and only succeeded in making whirlpools on the window. He thought of calling the front desk. What would Dagne and Karen think of Mr. Levin without an 'e' if he immediately called to complain about Copenhagen's grime after receiving a pink carnation? No, he wouldn't call. He stepped out on the balcony. He could see the towers of the old city in the distance. Some of the Dutch soccer fans were on the street alongside the hotel that led to Tivoli. They were shouting and pumping their fists. Several of the women wore the tri-color red, white and blue Dutch flag as capes. The Dutch must have beaten the Danes.

He took a shower and used several of the small plastic bottles of skin gel and conditioner the hotel had provided. After showering and using the bath gel, he realized he had washed away Mooney Levine's pheromone. It was probably just nonsense, this Viagra of aftershave lotions, but just as one final touch after he changed, he took Mooney's abalone shell sprayer and gave himself a little spritz. He felt refreshed after the shower and put on his navy sports coat with brass buttons, almost the uniform of the middle-aged American tourist in Europe. He wore a bright red patterned tie. With the red tie, he looked like a member of Bush's cabinet. They all wore red ties. None of them, though, would spritz themselves with a pheromone after shave or be on their way to a séance. None of them would have been invited to a séance, and with their red power ties, none of them would ever be invited to a séance. Was there one Jew in Bush's Cabinet? He couldn't think of one. The former Press Secretary was a Jew, Ari Fleisher, but he'd resigned, probably to write a book. Just as a precaution, he dropped a Viagra pill into his pillbox. There was something about the woman from Chicago, the thin woman, her invitation to him, her hand on his hand, even the sound of her voice that told him that he would not only need Mooney's cologne, but also the reassurance of the hidden blue pill. He dropped it in his pillbox hidden in his pocket. It was like a *pushkeh.* A Yiddish word for a little hidden purse. He also folded three Danish one hundred kroner notes into a small wad and hid them in the secret compartment of his billfold. Now he had his own *pushkeh.*Except if he really wanted a *pushkeh*, he should take along not only the Viagra pill but a condom. He'd bought a new six-pack of condoms on impulse in the O'Hare washroom. A horny middle-aged Jewish professor on sabbatical doesn't enter Denmark without a six-pack of condoms. A six-pack of thin, rubber French condoms with a cover on the package of a beautiful young couple embracing beneath a cascading waterfall.

He hadn't attempted making love to anyone in six months. There'd been a drunken failure six months ago with a teaching assistant in her mid-forties in his department who was as drunk as he was and when he didn't have a condom, she refused to have sex with him unless he went out and bought one and a pack of cigarettes. But he couldn't really get it up anyway, so when he came back to her fortieth-floor apartment, all he'd bought was a pack of cigarettes instead of condoms. She took the cigarettes and pushed him out the door. Now every time he saw her in the corridors or at a staff meeting she avoided him. Since his divorce from Ramona a year ago, that sad, drunken night was his only attempt at sex. When at three in the morning he'd gone for the condoms to an all night drug store on Rush Street, he'd had a premonition that she might attempt to jump out of her apartment window. She was very depressed. She'd been talking about suicide. As he left the apartment he could barely see her outlined in the darkness of the room, her head tilted back on the window pane, the ember glowing from her cigarette, "This is my last cigarette, John. I need some cigarettes, please get me a pack of Winstons." So he'd come back with the cigarettes, but not the condoms and she'd pushed him out the door. After that night he went to a urologist and got a prescription for Viagra. So he'd not only come to Denmark with a box of French condoms, he had a bottle of Viagra pills to go with his new identity.

Before he left on his trip, he received a note from her. It was in a small, white gift envelope, with a white card stuck into his office mail slot. "Bon voyage, John, from your friend – Patricia Bregemann." She'd put the envelope under a rubber band that held a scroll, Lewis Carroll's "Jabberwocky" in Danish also translated into English in alternate paragraphs. A strange going away gift. He'd brought the scroll along to Denmark. Now as he added a French condom to the secret billfold compartment he went to his suitcase and found the tightly-rolled scroll of "Jabberwocky". He read some lines aloud.

> "Min so°n, pas godt på Jabberwock!
> Han river, og hans tand er hvas."
> "Beware the Jabberwock, my son!
> The jaws that bite, the claws that catch!"

Maybe he should take it along to read to Elyse Friedberg. Or at least he could try to memorize the two lines and say them to the desk clerks as he left. But he left the scroll in the room.

When he went downstairs he was quite pleased with himself. He skipped the elevator cage and instead took the stairway down to the lobby. He'd have to learn to count in Danish so he could count the stairs. One of the men in his department had a pedometer that he always wore and did three miles a day. It was a tiny blue belt pedometer and when you pushed a button it announced the number of steps you'd taken. He didn't really need a pedometer. His walking was good. He could bicycle. His aim was steady at the shooting booth. He was beginning to relax. He wasn't certain about the cemetery construction. Maybe he'd give that up, but at least he'd begun writing again. He didn't stop at the desk in the lobby to go through the charade with the two young women. Anyway, they were registering some new arrivals. As he entered the street, the Danish night seemed fragrant and a soft wind blew on his cheek. And then he spotted her, a young Danish prostitute approaching him as he passed the tavern next to the hotel.

"Sir, are you looking for a companion," she called to him in English.

She was about twenty, maybe twenty-two, dressed in a black tank top with a head of black curls. She wobbled toward him on heavy black platform shoes. She was thin and ungainly, very pale, younger than his youngest daughter, and she had a jewel in her navel, a black faceted jewel. She also had a ring clipped to her left ear with a tiny companion black jewel, lavender toenails, a tiny black shoulder purse, and a red string of ribbon underneath her hair. She was quite exotic, even beautiful, like a young hawk descending on him from the night and landing at his feet. She was smoking and she flipped the cigarette away and asked him again, "Do you, sir, want a companion for the evening?" She spoke English with an unusual accent. "I am a licensed guide. I can show you Copenhagen."

"Where are you from?" he said to her.

"What difference does it make where I am from? You're an American, no? Or maybe an Englishman, a London man? I can tell from your clothes and you're speaking English. I am from Lithuania, if that should make a difference. Now, does it make a difference? Have you heard of Lithuania?"

"I am not looking for a companion."

"Oh, that is a pity. Do you think I am a streetwalker? Is that what you think? I am a guide and a commission agent. I will take you shopping. You seem like a gentleman. Are you really from America? Most Americans come in the summer, not in spring."

"Yes, I'm an American."

"And you're here in Denmark as a visitor?"

"Yes."

"So I can show you Copenhagen. It's a beautiful city. I have excellent connections. I will be your guide. Have you been to the casino at the Radisson? We can take a taxi and have dinner there."

She held his wrist and looked down the street for a taxi. She was the third woman who'd touched him in Denmark. Elyse Friedberg, Karen at the hotel desk, and now this young Lithuanian woman. He was still keeping score. He should have a pedometer that counted the touches, a pedometer with a button you could push that would announce the number of women who had touched your wrist.

"Where are you from in America?"

"I'm from Chicago."

"I shall visit there someday." She was quite tall, about three or four inches taller than him. Even without her platform shoes she would be taller. She wore tiny square-shaped snap-on sunglasses that reflected green. She also wore wire-rimmed glasses underneath the sunglasses.

She pointed to the stairs that led down to a tavern.

"Let's go downstairs and have a drink and discuss our situation."

"No, I'm not interested in having a drink and we don't have a situation."

"Where are you going?"

"I'm going to Tivoli."

"Well, then I'll be your guide to Tivoli. I am a licensed, commission agent for Royal Copenhagen. We will visit their showroom and then we will visit the ballet. It's an outdoor ballet. We can stand in the garden and watch Pierrot together. I am also an official guide for the ballet. I will show you my pass. Then to the swan boats. And then we will take a swan boat to a restaurant for dinner. I am connected to several excellent restaurants."

She pulled on his wrist and began to lead him down the street. Her thumb and index finger each had a glass ring and she wore a heavy silver flanged cross around her neck. Also she leaned her head against his shoulder as they walked.

"You're wearing a lovely cologne, sir. Are you a married gentleman?"

"No I'm not married, I'm a divorced gentleman." If he really wanted to open himself up to a new experience, this could be one. She was forty years younger and probably a prostitute and not a guide for Royal Copenhagen or the ballet. Yet the prospect of eating boiled potatoes and herring again by himself wasn't so compelling that he could tell this young woman to get lost.

"What do you charge for your guided tour?" he asked her.

"Well I charge nothing for Royal Copenhagen. If you buy something I receive a commission from the store. The ballet is also without charge. We will just stand at the rear. The swan boat is also free. The dinner is at your expense and I will also eat, but there is no charge for my meal, the restaurant will pay for me."

"So the entire time with you is free?"

She laughed. "Yes, absolutely free. Can you believe it as a capitalist? Americans are always worried about money. That is why you have so much. You are such a rich and powerful country. I do not worry about money. I am a free spirit. That is why I have so little, but I am a free spirit. My spirit is free. Is your spirit free sir?"

"No, I don't think my spirit is free."

They were within a block of Tivoli. He could see the strings of white bulbs outlining the wooden towers and the parachute rides looming up down the street. There were silk-screened banners on the lamp posts advertising a Chinese opera from Peking. She guided him across the street through the roundabout of traffic, ignoring the cars, pointing at one to stop, and then crossing to the curb.

"You will have no need for a ticket to Tivoli, sir. You are with me." She smiled at the two young attendants at the ticket booth, both dressed in dark navy braided jackets with gold buttons, like the King's Guards.

"See, you're perfectly welcome here as my guest and there is Royal Copenhagen." She pointed to the entrance of the showroom and opened the door.

She was immediately met by the manager, a fat-faced, red-cheeked blonde balding man. He wore a dark blue suit and vest and a red and blue striped tie with tiny Danish crowns.

"I have brought you a customer, a gentleman from America."

"How nice to see you sir. You are most welcome to our showroom." The manager looked at her rather skeptically.

"I will show the gentleman around. I am quite familiar with the store."

"You are very welcome sir." The man bowed his head and smiled and walked to another section of the store without saying anything further.

"They also have beautiful glassware here as well as china." She pointed to the department in the other room. "Crystal and glass lined with silver, also lead goblets. May I ask your name sir?"

"Jonny."

"You also have a last name?"

"Jonny Levin."

"My name is Leda, like Leda and the Swan. My last name is too complicated." She laughed and bowed and spread her arms in an exaggerated imitation of a swan. As she bowed her purse swung out and hit a china sugar bowl and pitcher set and knocked them off their pedestal. They both shattered as they hit the tile floor.

"Oh, sweet Jesus, what have I done now?"

"You are a rather clumsy swan, Leda."

"Oh, dear Jesus. I'm so sorry. I am always foolish. This will cost me a fortune. I cannot pay for these." She pushed her sunglasses up on her head and began to pick up the pieces. "Oh, these poor angels. They'll never fly again."

The shattered pieces were blue ceramic angels painted on Italian ceramic earthenware. "I've broken their wings. I've shattered their wings. Did you see their eyes? You can see how angry they are at me."

"They didn't look angry to me. They looked happy. How would you like to spend your whole life painted on a bowl. Now they can just fly away."

"They can't fly away with broken wings. Let's just leave. I'll take the pieces with me. I have a friend who will fix them."

She turned quickly and took his wrist again and led him toward the door and then outside to the gravel paths edged by flower beds.

"Are we just sneaking out without paying for them. I don't think that's very honest Leda."

"Honesty is a relative thing, Mr. American, depending on the size of your purse. We'll walk to the ballet now. I will have these pieces repaired by my friend. She's a master with ceramics. I will return the angels with their wings put back together."

"You speak excellent English, Leda. Where did you learn to speak English?"

"I studied for several years. When I started school at the Lycee, as children in Lithuania we were taught Russian. It was compulsory. But when we broke away from Russia and won our freedom, English was taught in the Gymnasium and I became an advanced student of English."

"Where are you from in Lithuania?"

"I'm from Kaunas. Do you know Kaunas? It is the second largest city in Lithuania next to Vilnius, the capital city."

"Yes, I know both Kaunas and Vilnius."

"Over there is the ballet." She pointed at a crowd standing in front of a small stage in a grove of trees strung with colored lights. There was an orchestra playing and a performer dressed as a Harlequin in a yellow and blue costume and a lace collar dancing with a black mask over his eyes and wearing a black tri-corner hat. He looked exactly like a Picasso Harlequin.

She took his hand and led him to the rear. "That's Pierrot," she said her eyes flashing up at him as she leaned back against him. Her body felt hard and thin and he sensed the fragrance of her hair brushing against his face as she leaned back against him and they watched Pierrot dancing to Swan Lake. He almost put his hands around her waist as she nestled her body against him and he felt the warmth of her bare shoulders on his chest. The performance was quite lovely, very simple. The solo performer was Pierrot as a Harlequin dancing gracefully to Tchaikovsky. He would have to watch himself with this young woman. He was surprised that in just a few moments of touching up against her he was already filled with longing and so attracted by her fragrance, the touch of her skin and her laughter. He didn't move away from her.

"Now to the swan boats," she said turning. "The swan boats are over there." She pointed to a lagoon filled with children and parents. Danish couples with their children were riding in motorized boats with carved swans as prows moving through a lagoon of castles and waterwheels, Chinese pagodas and miniature waterfalls. The children were mostly high-crowned little blonde boys and girls who wore enormous silken hair ribbons and knit sweaters, steering proudly beside their fathers and mothers.

Suddenly he realized that he'd become enveloped in an intoxicating mixture of swans – first the memory of The White Swan, the inn in Raalte in the Netherlands with Magdelena. Then Leda the swan girl from Lithuania with the shattered angels in her purse. The Harlequin Pierrot dancing to Swan Lake and now the astonished laughter of children guiding the swan boats through the ancient lagoon.

"Do you always commandeer a swan boat when you want to escape Royal Copenhagen, Leda?"

"Always."

She already had the hawser in her hand and held the boat steady against the pier. She knew the young man in charge of the boats who stood watching her. He was barefooted and wore a straw Venetian gondolier's hat.

"Get in, Jonny Levin, and I will hold the boat for you."

She steered them carefully through the boats of children and their parents, occasionally bumping one of them and saying, "*Unskold*", "Excuse me", and smiling at the parents. She steered them away from the pack of boats to a clear channel in the lagoon. She was a skilled swan boat operator. When they reached the channel she turned and put his hand on the tiller and moved behind him.

"Just steer a straight course to the restaurant. You can see it down there. The one with the blue awning and all the flags."

So here he was, steering a swan boat under the stars and with a secret *pushkeh* in his back pocket filled with mysterious oddments all unknown to this young Leda. He took the tiller.

"You know Leda," he said pointing to a constellation, "there are Leda's two twin sons, Pollex and Castor. The two brightest stars."

She looked up as he pointed and then she reached over his shoulder and held the tiller with her hand over his hand and her lips on the back of his neck.

"You really have this marvelous cologne, Jonny Levin. I seem to want to put my arms around you."

They were passing several swan boats with parents and children coming in the opposite direction. She squeezed a rubber bulb at the nape of the swan's neck and blew a horn at them which approximated the claxon bray of a swan and the children screeched and were delighted. All this with her lips still pressed against his neck and their boat rocking in the channel in the wake of the passing boats.

Now he could feel the touch of her mouth against his ear as she steered over him with her hand on top of his hand.

"You also had a daughter named 'Helen', 'Helen of Troy'. The Trojan War was fought over her. She was stolen by the Trojan king."

"I know," she said into his ear. "They brought that big wooden horse to rescue her. Steer carefully Jonny Levin. You sound like a school teacher. Are you a teacher?" She put her lips on his ear again.

"Turn right Jonny Levin. Right into that little passageway there beside that pier with the Danish flags."

She suddenly crawled onto the bow of the boat and crouched and took the coil of rope.

"The lever on your left, move it down."

He did as he was told and they began to glide into the dock and she jumped off the bow onto the pier and tied them to a cleat.

"Now there'll be a big bump and my American teacher friend will be careful."

He stepped out of the boat carefully and adjusted his blue jacket and his tie and wiped the spray off his shoulders. "Leda, what do you know about Helen of Troy?"

"I know I am not Helen of Troy. Leda is the mother of Helen. Helen of Troy is my daughter."

"Yes, you're right."

"I know that legend. I am most of the time right."

"I've noticed that."

"Also I am totally attracted to your alluring cologne."

"I've also noticed that. But, I think off the swan boat I won't be so alluring."

"I don't understand."

"I mean, are you really attracted to older men on land, Leda, not just at sea? I can understand the attraction on a sea voyage, but now back on land I doubt if it will last."

"You will buy me dinner and we will see. You are not an ordinary older man. Also you are not so old. There is something very mysterious about you, some secret. I will find it."

The hostess smiled at them as they approached her and said something in Danish to Leda which he presumed was "Good Evening." She led them to a small table that faced open French doors and the lagoon. She lit a candle and held the chair for him. He thanked her, but instead took his jacket off and put it over Leda's shoulders and held her chair. The hostess watched without expression and still held his chair. She was a slim woman in a white nylon blouse, black jacket, and long black skirt, a high cheekboned Danish blonde in her forties. She picked up and held the large menus against her breasts and her eyes seemed to engage his with both amusement and Danish formality.

She asked him in English if they would like something to drink.

He saw the two men at the table across from them drinking Carlsberg beer and chasers of Aquavit.

"Leda, would you like what they're drinking? Do you like beer?"

"I love the Danish beer, Carlsberg. It's not too strong. Very pleasant."

"Then bring us just the same combination that the two men are having, a bottle of Carlsberg beer for each of us and a bottle of Aquavit and two shot glasses." He felt that he sounded like Victor Borge. A paternalistic Victor Borge ordering drinks for his daughter. Borge was a Danish Jew so there would be some validity assuming Borge's manner.

When the hostess left the table, she touched his hand. He'd add that gratuitous gesture to his hand touching count.

A young waitress brought them a tray with two bottles of Carlsberg and a blue bottle of Aquavit. He poured a glass of beer for each of them. He looked at the bottle of Carlsberg "by appointment of the Danish royal court". He turned the green bottle and pointed to the crown on the label.

"Is that crest the Danish royal crown?"

"I don't know, but Carlsberg is very popular beer here. The most popular. The most favorite." She raised her glass of beer to him and licking the foam off her lips as she drank she said, *Skål* to him.

"*Skål*? Is that the Danish drinking toast?"

"Yes it is. The same as 'Cheers'."

"They also say *Skål* when you win at roulette."

"Oh, I didn't know that. *Skål* at roulette?"

"Only when you win. They say nothing when you lose."

"You are a winner at roulette?"

"I only win ten kroner pieces. I have a bag full of ten kroner coins."

"Are you a wealthy man in America? If you're a school teacher you must not be too wealthy. The teachers in Lithuania are very poor."

"I am a school teacher and I'm not a wealthy man."

"I need to borrow some money from you Jonny, even if you are not a wealthy man. I need four thousand kroner. I have to have it tonight."

"I don't lend money."

"I need desperately to borrow money."

"Have you some collateral?"

"Collateral, of course. What is that?" She filled each of their shot glasses with a shot of Aquavit from the blue bottle and held her beer glass up to him. "Skål." She held one finger up and motioned him to drink the shot down in one swallow.

"Collateral is security for a debt, like a mortgage on a house. Do you know what a mortgage is?"

He took a sip of the Aquavit while she stared at him. It was very strong and tasted like ouzo or slivovitz.

"This is very good. Good and strong."

"Just swallow it down in one swallow like I did. You don't just touch it with the tongue, you take it down like this." She poured herself another shot and held it up to him. *Skål.* She gestured at him again to drink and held up two fingers.

He drank his shot down and felt it searing his throat and then burning in his stomach.

"No I can't loan you four thousand kroner. You're trying to get me drunk. Why do you need four thousand kroner?"

"To pay my room rent. Otherwise my landlady will put my things on the street tonight. She told me that when I left. Not to come back without four thousand kroner."

"And you expect me to pay your rent? You probably say that to every man you meet."

"That's cruel. It's not true. I only ask you because I can see that you're a gentleman. A gentleman will always help a lady if the lady truly needs his help. I truly need your help."

She bent her head down and shook her hair out and took off the heavy silver cross she wore on a leather thong around her neck and handed it across to him. "This cross will be my security, or what you call collateral."

"I don't want your cross."

"I insist. It is my most precious possession. It was given to me by an elderly priest in Vilnius before I left Lithuania. Father Brecevius. He blessed it and told me it would always protect me. I will give it to you and put it around your neck as a symbol of my honesty." She poured them each another shot of Aquavit and filled his beer glass.

"Drink up – *Skål.* She clicked their glasses." It was her third shot and his second. She held up three fingers and held her nose and tossed her shot down.

"Just hold your nose and close your eyes like I do and drink it down, Jonny Levin."

He tried her technique and again he could feel the shot burning its way down into his stomach and he put his hand over his glass. Why was he drinking like this?

"No more Leda. We've got to order something. Some bread, some herring, some appetizers, some potatoes." He looked around for the waitress.

Suddenly Leda stood up and moved in back of him and put her arms around him. "You have such a fragrance my dear American man. I can't keep my arms off you." She dropped the necklace with the heavy cross over his neck.

"Now you have what you call my collateral and you will be like my priest and protect me." .

The two men opposite them stopped their drinking and began watching them.

"I won't give you the money, Leda. Sit down. Also I don't want your cross." He reached back and took it off and dropped it on her plate.

She gave his ear a wet kiss and nipped his earlobe and staggered back to the table and sat down. "I'm already drunk. You're such a mean man. Why do you let me get this way? You have made me drunk and dizzy."

She dropped the cross around her neck again and stood up. "I can't understand you. A wealthy American. You are so selfish. Wealthy and selfish. I will have to go back on the street and find someone else."

She stood for a moment looking at him and put one of the rolls in her purse and turned and walked away through the tables without looking back at him. Suddenly she turned and came back and took his jacket off and put it over his shoulders.

"I can't take your coat even if you're selfish. I am not a thief. Here it is. Thank you for letting me wear it."

She stumbled against the table.

"Sit down," he said to her. "Sit down Leda."

"I won't sit."

He put his hand out to her and pulled her down.

"Sit down and listen to me."

"I don't have to listen to you."

"How can you expect me to pay your rent? We've known each other for one hour."

"And we have learned a lot about each other." She tossed her hair. "Haven't we, Mr. American?"

"Don't call me Mr. American."

"I have learned that you will not help me. I cannot rely on you. What do you think I am, a prostitute? A street walker? I am not a prostitute. I am a licensed tour guide and physical therapist. If you give me the money I will come to your room and massage you or make an appointment for you and you can come to my studio. If I still have a studio. The landlady has probably put my things on the street."

"I don't want a massage."

She tried to pour herself another shot of Aquavit but he held the bottle away from her.

"All right. I won't massage you. I will just manipulate you. I can see you have very poor posture."

"I have a back problem."

"I will very gently manipulate your back. Where is the problem, upper or lower?"

The young waitress came now with a tray of appetizers, different types of herring and sliced bread and tiny boiled red potatoes.

"I have a lovely studio with all the equipment, candles and oils and fragrances, but I am about to lose all my possessions. I am a desperate woman. Can't you see that?" Tears were glistening on her cheeks.

"All right, I'll help you Leda. But I won't give you four thousand kroner, that's four hundred dollars. I will give you only what I have and I'll buy you a dinner."

"What do you have?"

He took out his *pushkeh* and removed the tightly wadded bills.

"I have three hundred kroner. Give it to your landlady as a down payment. It will be a gift from me, not a loan." He handed her the money and she quickly stuffed the bills in her bra with no expression. She wiped the tears off her cheek with the edge of the napkin.

"Thank you. I will give you a massage by appointment. I will walk on your back and straighten you. That will cost only three hundred kroner. I will not accept a gift. I will not be indebted to you. I will excuse my debt by walking on your back."

She stood up and began to leave again.

"Leda, sit."

"I won't sit. Thank you for the money."

"You will wait. How will I get back without you steering the swan boat?"

"You will steer it yourself."

"Hold on. Sit down. Have some bread and potatoes."

"Danish potatoes. Kartofler. I don't eat this kartofler. I'm not hungry. Danes love kartofler. I do not eat them. They put weight on my hips. Here is my card. Jonny Levin, you are a decent man after all. I have to go back to the street now to search for the rest of the money. Ciao. You will call me or I will call you."

She dropped her card on his plate.

Leda Renauskas Vicivious
Masseuse and Physical Therapist
Shopping Service
Discounts at all stores
Private Studio
Model, Your Guide
Adventures

Tel. — 920758 - 4
20 Konigsgaard Krulesfjord

"I'm going to the ladies' toilet to warm my hands on the hand dryer. It is freezing here. Ask my friend Petrius at the dock. He will help you with the swan boat. I will go on foot. Do not try to go on foot. You will never find your way. Petrius will help you with a good boat."

She bent over him and kissed him on the lips.

"Goodbye, Jonny Levin."

He watched her turn and walk through the crowd in the opposite direction and in a moment she was gone.

He shook his head and made a small sandwich of matjes herring, thin slices of potato with vinaigrette and onions on a square of rye bread. He took a sip of Aquavit and looked at her card.

He called for the check and left the waitress what he thought was a decent tip. Then he got up and walked through the crowd. The Aquavit had affected his legs and they felt slightly numb. He'd weakened and given in to her. She was quite an actress, but three hundred kroner, what was that—thirty dollars? It wouldn't be much help to her if she really was about to be evicted. What would Victor Borge have done if he'd been alive and faced with Leda? Would he have handed her his secret *pushkeh*? No, Borge was too shrewd. He'd become an American millionaire. A chicken farmer somewhere on the East Coast. A purveyor of packaged chicken. Borge would have been too smart to have become involved with her. He should have given her more than thirty dollars. He could have asked her to meet him later at the hotel and cashed a traveler's check for her and really helped her. Still he knew she wasn't telling him the truth. He had her card, though. He could call on her, look her studio over and see if she really was a masseuse. He could make an assessment of her situation. He'd be like an appraiser. He felt a real attraction for this young woman. Her hair had a lovely fragrance. It was still in his nostrils as he wandered down to the dock and looked for her friend Petrius.

Petrius was barefoot in a blue striped T-shirt and a white Danish flat sailor's cap with a black ribbon embossed in gold with the name of a Danish ship. He seemed to be in his early twenties. Petrius held the swan boat steady for him while he got in and sat down. Then he showed him the steering wheel, the throttle lever, the klaxon and turned on the motor and running lights. He pointed in the direction of the main Tivoli pier and shoved the boat with his foot out into the channel and gestured to accelerate by pulling down the lever. The swan boat quickly began to move away from the pier and in a moment he was alone navigating toward the lights of the Tivoli dock.

He looked up at the stars and there were his old friends Castor and Pollux. He would just hold the nape of the swan's graceful carved prow between the two constellations.

Maybe Victor Borge would have given her the entire four thousand kroner. But Borge was a cautious gentleman, an elegant man who could charm an audience in a hundred ways. Borge wouldn't have let himself become enchanted by Leda. He had too much self-control. But Borge was dead and he felt very much alive steering by the polarity of Castor and Pollux, adrift in the swan boat channel, moving through the colored lights reflected on the channel.

He tried to imitate a few of Borge's famous tongue clicks. Borge would have just pushed his piano bench back and given her a few clicks of his tongue and shaken his head in commiseration and given her nothing. No *rachmones* from Borge. Although tongue clicks were probably the earliest form of communicating sorrow.

Still she was really a beautiful young woman. He could still feel her lips pressed against his neck and the touch of her breasts on his back. She made him think of Robert Herrick's poem about "Julia" although Herrick wasn't steering a swan boat when he wrote it.

He looked up again at Castor and Pollux and kept his hand on the tiller, cleared his throat, and began reciting Herrick's poem quietly to himself.

UPON JULIA'S CLOTHES -

Wheneas in silks my Julia goes,
Then, then, methinks, how sweetly flows
The liquefaction of her clothes!

Next, when I cast mine eyes and see
That brave vibration each way free,
— O how that glittering taketh me!

He pulled into the swan boat pier rather easily, touching with just a little bump. He handed the hawser to another young man barefoot in white trousers and a straw Venetian gondolier's hat. The Danes were good with hats. He'd have to learn to interchange hats. He could be a different person with each hat. He could be a sea captain, a lover, a gambler, or a money lender. If he'd given her four thousand kroner he could be a Danish shylock and wear a little red Venetian yarmulke, "Hath not a Jew blood? Doth not a Jew bleed?" Something like that from "The Merchant of Venice". He should have given her the money and taken her cross as collateral.

6

THERE WAS THE CONSTANT SOUND of the screaming of the riders on a huge lighted Twirl-A-Wheel. Round and round they were flung, screaming. Beyond the trees ahead he heard the piping of the carousel and walked over a little hill and there was Mooney Levine standing alone and slowly twirling on the edge of the carousel.

"Hi there Professor, I'm just giving this a test. I want to see if it's working right."

He watched Mooney slowly whirl by on the platform while the calliope played a Strauss Waltz, what was it, 'The Merry Widow'? That wasn't Strauss that was Lehar.

The platform slowed and Mooney stepped off and the carousel came to a stop. He was in his shirtsleeves and was wearing the same initialed blue shirt with the white round tab collar and the ML crest on the pocket and one cuff.

"How do you like my stallions? I have to do a little cosmetic job on a few."

"Hold this Professor." He handed Jonny a leather case that had tiny bottles of paint and brushes.

"Now, look at this lion's mouth. I'll take the red paint and just barely outline the lips. They're not right. They should snarl. If you do the lips with just another touch of red they'll look ferocious. Scare the crap out of the kids."

He held the brush between his teeth and carefully traced a thin red line around the lion's mouth that he curled into a snarl. Just as quickly he took a tiny pointed brush from the case and edged the red line with a thin black line. "There, now they look like they could bite your *toches* off."

"See that rose on that chariot over there? Its petals are broken. Some kid probably kicked them off. I've got a tube of plastic wood." He took it out of the case and reformed a perfect set of rose petals, rounding them with his index finger.

"Now the eyes of some of the stallions. Take a walk with me around the platform and look at the eyes. Look for the eyes that don't gleam. It's got to be like magic for the kids. The horses gotta invite you to climb up on them. There's one. Look at its eyes. They've gone dead."

He took another brush and tube and quickly touched the pupils of the horse's eyes..

"I got another joke for you Professor," he said while he worked on the eyes.

"Big black Cadillac pulls up to the entrance of one of the Miami hotels. Like the Americana, the Eden Roc, the Saxony. A little old Jewish lady is helped out by her chauffeur. Her girlfriend who lives at the hotel is standing there to meet her.

"'Where's your grandson, Rose? I thought you were bringing him,' the girlfriend says.

"'Wait a minute.' The old lady points at her chauffeur and

he wraps the grandson, an eleven year old boy, in a blanket and carries him into the hotel.

"The girlfriend says, 'you didn't tell me he can't walk.'

"'He can walk – but thank God he doesn't have to.'

"You've got to laugh at that one, Jonny – 'He can walk – but thank God he don't have to' – so there, how do you like those eyes? Don't they look like evil eyes? You've gotta scare the crap out of the ladies, too, not just the kids."

"Okay, Professor, I've got another one for you – little old Jewish lady goes to her travel agent and insists on buying a ticket to Tibet.

"'Tibet, Mrs. Goldstein? At your age? Why Tibet?' the travel agent asks her.

"'I want to go, that's all. It's none of your business why. Just book the ticket.'

"'Okay, so I won't ask. Such a big journey. I won't ask any more questions.' She books a round trip ticket to Katmandu.

"A week later Mrs. Goldstein arrives in Tibet and is met by a guide. 'Where do you want to go madam?' he asks her.

"I want to see the Dalai Lama.'

"'I don't think so. That isn't possible.'

"'I want to see the Dalai Lama.'

"'I don't think that can be arranged madam.'

"'You just tell him that Mrs. Goldstein is here from Newark to see him.'

"She goes back to the hotel and goes to sleep. In the morning, to the amazement of the guide, an official car is sent for her and she's taken to the top of the mountain to the palace where she's ushered in, but stopped by the palace guard.

"'I want to see the Dalai Lama,' she tells him.

"'And who shall I tell His Eminence are you?'

"'Tell him Mrs. Goldstein from Newark.'

"Much to his surprise, the guard is told by the Dalai Lama's aide to bring her in immediately.

"So she's shown down the long red carpet leading to a dais. There, sitting on a platform covered with flowers, is a short bald man with glasses peering at her over his bifocals. You can see by his expression that there's a hint of recognition.

The aide steps forward, a gold bell is rung.

"'Madam, you may address the Dalai Lama.'

"Mrs. Goldstein stands before him, clears her throat, purses her lips and waggles her finger.

"'Elliott,' she says, 'All right already, your father wants you to come home.'"

Mooney Levine shakes with laughter. "'All right already, Elliott, your father wants you to come home."

"Do you get it Jonny? Her son Elliott is the Dalai Lama."

"How's that, is that a good one? First—'He can walk, but thank God he don't have to.' Now—'Elliott, come home already.' Now it's your turn Jonny. You got any good ones? I need some good jokes. I collect them at home and I send them out by email to my friends and my customers."

"No, I don't think I know a joke. Not one."

"Not one?"

"I can't think of one."

"Not one Jewish joke?"

"I can't think of one."

"Some Professor you are. You can't tell me a Jewish joke. If you tell me one I'll tell you the one place in Copenhagen you can buy a piece of halvah."

"I don't eat halvah."

"There's only one Jewish deli in Copenhagen. It's right near our hotel. Everyone eats halvah. Even Arafat loved halvah. What do you think the first thing he asked for when they took him to the hospital in Paris from his headquarters in Ramallah? He asked for some halvah."

"Okay, I got one for you Mooney. I just remembered it. Myron Cohen's favorite joke."

"I love Myron Cohen. What is it, the one about the lady on the plane and her diamond ring that she shows to the Texan sitting next to her?"

"No this is Myron Cohen's most famous joke – 'Lady is home in bed with her lover. They're both middle aged and having this affair once a week on Thursday afternoons. But this Thursday, the husband unexpectedly comes home. They hear the front door open. They're up in the master bedroom. The man who's the lover, he's a little guy, jumps out of bed, grabs his clothes and shoes and hides in her closet. The wife pretends she's asleep.

"The husband comes upstairs into the bedroom and he senses something going on. He says to the wife, 'What's happening here?' – 'Nothing', she says. He sees the rumpled sheets and the bedspread thrown back.

"Who's here? There's someone here.'

"There's no one here.'

"Oh yeah?' He starts looking around, poking the bedcovers and looking around the bedroom. Suddenly he opens the closet door and there's the little man.

"The man looks up at the husband, shrugs and says, 'Everyone's gotta be somewhere.'"

Mooney laughs, "That's a great joke, Jonny. 'Everyone's gotta be somewhere.' That's a famous joke. I heard it already, but it's a great joke."

"Okay, one more for you Jonny and then I got to set up the brass ring machine and the calliope. Those two ladies from the hotel are coming here at eight and then we're all going to the séance as my guests. You're coming too. I've got three seats reserved in the front row."

"Here's my last joke Jonny. The famous diamond joke. A little Jewish lady on a plane to London seated next to a big Texan in a ten gallon hat. She's got a huge ring and the Texan taps her on the shoulder and says to her, 'Pardon me ma'am, but is that the Hope Diamond?' 'No,' she says to him, 'that's the Klopman diamond.' 'Well,' he says, 'it's just beautiful. Tell me ma'am, does that diamond have a curse on it like the Hope Diamond?' 'Yes it does,' she says. 'Tell me, what is the curse ma'am?' 'The curse? The curse is Mr. Klopman.'"

He slaps Jonny on the back. "You get it Jonny – 'The curse is Mr. Klopman.'"

"That's an old joke Mooney."

"You've heard it?"

"The Klopman diamond joke, I've heard it."

"Okay, I've got to set up the brass ring machine. You climb up on the neck of that giraffe and hold your hand out. I'll turn on the machine. There are only three or four brass ring machines left in the world. I've got one here and one on Coney Island. All the rings are silver except one is brass. When they come flying by you see if you can grab the brass ring. Silver don't count. You get nothing for silver, *bupkes.* Grab the brass ring, you get a free table setting for four of Royal Copenhagen. Each time I turn it on though, if you play, it costs you fifty kroner. You got the best chance leaning from the neck of the giraffe. You'll be closer than you are sitting on a stallion."

"I'm not going to get up on a giraffe." When he said the word "giraffe" a line of poetry from an author whose name he couldn't remember began to throb in his head... "Maculate Giraffe".

"Why not?"

"I'm leaving. You finish your work. I'll be back at eight to watch the ladies grab for the brass rings."

"Suit yourself, Jonny. But don't forget, I've got all of you booked for the séance. She's a great fortune teller, Josefina. There's no one like her. You'll be glad you came. If you've got any problems, she'll solve them for you."

"I don't have any problems."

"Everyone's got problems. Here, I'll give you another little spritz." Mooney took out his abalone shell spritzer and gave Jonny a spritz of pheromone. "I call it "Danish Delight." The Danish girls go nuts for it. It worked for me, has it worked for you?"

"Mooney, no more spritzing. I don't want more."

"Just another tiny little spritz. It only lasts for maybe an hour or two burchik. Men our age need some extra allure." He sprayed Jonny's lapels. "I just put it lightly on your lapels. It seems to work best when it's absorbed on your clothes. I gave you just a touch. A scent like a woman's musk perfume. Do you remember the ads for Tabu? Are you old enough Jonny to remember Tabu? The girls in my high school in the Bronx all wore Tabu. They used to drive me crazy. Beautiful young Jewish girls soaked in Tabu with pearls and cashmere sweaters no one could afford."

"I remember Tabu. The ad with the violinist with the lady in his arms. He's holding his violin and kissing her over the piano."

"That's how my stuff works. It even works on American ladies. Those two from the hotel. The thin one goes for you Jonny. I can tell. The fat one's not my type. But the thin one, she's got a nice body. A couple of rich broads from Chicago. I like the young blonde Danish ladies, like the two desk clerks. They're my type."

"They seem to go for you Mooney. They give you special flowers."

"I told both of them to meet me later tonight at the Radisson SAS at the casino. I said I'd back them at roulette. Why don't you come along? I can't handle two of them. They said they might show."

"No, I'll come to the séance, but not to the casino."

"Okay, Jonny, suit yourself." He stuck his hand out and touched his knuckles to Jonny's. "Eight o'clock. Listen to what Josefina has to say. Your luck will change."

He walked away from Mooney to a carnival booth where darts were thrown at yellow balloons tied to a wall. Three darts for ten kroner, a dollar. If you broke three balloons you got your pick of cheap prizes. He bought three darts and aimed and tossed one and broke a yellow balloon. He tossed a second dart and broke another yellow balloon. He aimed carefully on the third try and hit the balloon, but the dart bounced off obliquely. The man who ran the booth shrugged, but then smiled and handed him a fourth dart and pointed at the balloons. Another chance for free. He carefully aimed the dart, threw it and the balloon popped. "*Tak*," he said. The man pointed to the prizes and picked one out for him. It was a framed photo of Queen Margrethe as a young woman. Just his kind of prize. "*Tak*," he said again. Then he mumbled, "Thank you."

Now he had a framed photograph of Queen Margrethe as a beautiful young woman. It would go with his prize from the shooting booth, a Danish flag pin. He'd forgotten to wear the Danish flag pin tonight. Mooney Levine was very annoying. He didn't want to be spritzed with pheromones. The whole incident on the swan boat seemed almost unreal, phantasmagoric. A word right out of Poe. It never happened.

There never was a young woman named Leda who put her arms around him and stuck her tongue in his ear and bit his earlobe. It never happened. He had too much dignity to have allowed it to happen. Still, there was her lingering fragrance. That was real.

The next booth was a shooting booth of sorts, only the guns were water guns. You aimed a stream of water flowing from a mounted water machine gun at metal bullseye flanges. If you hit the bullseye flange in the center it caused a wooden rabbit to advance up a tube above the targets. A race of wooden rabbits and the first rabbit to climb to the finish line took home a prize. Better than a race of "Maculate Giraffes." Why maculate? Maybe because they eat the leaves off tree tops. He bought a ten kroner token and sat down at his machine gun with a seated group of Danes all waiting for a buzzer to sound. He toggled the gun so the sight was squarely on the bullseye. The buzzer rang. Little girls shrieked behind their fathers. The bullseye flange swayed as the water hit it, but he kept a steady stream of water on it. The buzzer rang again. His rabbit won the race. He chose a small teddy bear and walked away again a winner.

Two wins in a row. Maybe Mooney was right. His luck would change. What was the name of the tall slender woman from Chicago? Elyse Friedberg? Attractive and confident with slender long legs. He had a choice. He could walk back to the hotel, lock himself in his room and work on his novel. Maybe stop on the way and visit Andersen and give him a little shry. Something more than his last glottal eech. Maybe a real Bellowian shry. He could touch knuckles with Andersen in the moonlight then go back to the room, close the door and write. Or he could return to the carousel and see if Elyse Friedberg would show. He just didn't feel like sitting alone in his room with his teddy bear and framed photo of Queen Margrethe or further constructing the cemetery. The night was too beautiful to sit alone in the room.

He turned back toward the carousel. He'd read somewhere that Queen Margrethe was a chain smoker. She was still lovely though, in her fifties, in her newspaper photos. Now he had a plastic sack with her framed photograph and a teddy bear. He'd easily out shot the Danish fathers. As the young shooting booth attendant had told him, Americans are very good with guns. He'd stop by her booth again, perhaps after the séance, and see if he could win a Royal Guardsman, the tiny wooden statue of the blue, waistcoated royal guardsmen with the bearskin shako. Then he'd have a trio, the chain smoking beautiful queen, her shako-topped guardsman and the Danish flag pin. All because of his prowess as an American marksman.

He turned and walked back over the tiny rise to the carousel. It was exactly eight o'clock. *Klokken 8* as the Danes say. The two American women were standing there, both looking at their watches as he approached. They wore black slack suits and black cashmere sweaters with long bright colored silk floral scarves. Elyse Friedberg smiled brightly as she saw him.

"You came. I'm so pleased."

"Yes, I'm ready to be séanced."

"You remember Martha?"

"Hello Professor," Martha said to him. "We met at breakfast."

"Yes, I remember. Please call me John. J-O-H-N. John Levin." He'd be John with these American women.

"Where did you say you taught, John?"

"I didn't say."

"Martha, stop it. You promised me you weren't going to do that. Don't start."

"I don't see why he won't tell us where he teaches. If he lives in Evanston I already know where he teaches. What's the big secret?"

He answered her, "The secret is that there is no secret. It's sort of a Zen secret."

Mooney Levine hopped off the carousel and greeted them. He put his arm around Martha Selig.

"Hello sweetheart. Glad to see you ladies. Hi, professor. Okay, just get on any one of these animals. The lion, the giraffe, the stallions. I'll turn on the brass ring machine. There are only a few in the world. I have two. One here and one at Coney. Get up there before all those Danish mamas grab the best seats for their kids. I'll let you on free. You're all my guests. When the rings come flying by, see if you can grab the brass ring. There's only one. If you get it you win a place setting for four of Royal Copenhagen. Whoever sits on the giraffe has the best chance."

"That's me," Martha Selig said. "I want the giraffe."

"You got it Martha."

She stepped up on the platform. She was a big woman with a large behind and as Mooney helped her up on the giraffe he pinched her.

"My god, Elyse."

"What?"

"Be careful of that man, did you see him pinch me?"

"No."

"Get on, Elyse. Get on the lion behind me."

Elyse Friedberg swung herself easily on the lion. "Okay John, you get on. How about a lion next to me."

"I think I'll watch."

"No, no, that's not fair. Climb on the lion."

He got up on the lion and Mooney rang a bell and all the Danish children came running with their parents and climbed up on the animals. Some of the children were as young as two and were hoisted up. The fathers and mothers stood behind them. A few adults got on the stallions. Some rode in the chariots.

The calliope music began softly.

Mooney Levine was talking through a loudspeaker in English. His remarks were immediately translated into Danish after each sentence by a smiling young Danish teenage girl with a large yellow flower at her throat.

"Ladies and gentlemen, boys and girls, you are about to ride on one of the world's most famous carousels."

"The Tivoli carousel has 36 jumping horses – fourteen standing horses – they're all stallions. They're all hand-carved by the greatest wooden carousel carvers on earth from Brooklyn, New York. Notice the roses woven into their manes and the baby-faced angels on their flanks."

"We also have two wooden chariots, carved by the same carvers. Please don't let your children kick the wooden rose petals or the angels on the chariots and horses. We know kids get excited, but don't let them kick the rose petals and angels.

"All the animals and chariots are very safe. We don't go at high speeds. We twirl slowly and you'll all have a chance at the brass ring machine.

"We have a sixty-six key Gebruder organ. The Copenhagen organ is even larger than our Coney Island organ and plays only waltzes and love songs. It's like being at a concert at the Royal Opera House.

"We have one of the world's only brass ring machines. When the music starts, silver rings will come flying by you. One of them, though, isn't silver, it's made of brass. Grab at the rings and try to find it. Each ring you take will cost you fifty kroner. If you grab the brass ring you'll win a beautiful china table setting for four from Royal Copenhagen—no children can play though.

Only adults can reach for the rings. Remember, if you take one it will cost you fifty kroner and we'll collect when you get off.

"All right, is everyone ready? I'll start the Gebruder. See if you recognize the song. It's a very famous waltz. A Viennese waltz, a gift from Vienna to Copenhagen. Hold your children. Keep them firmly on their mounts. Have a good time. Adults only for the rings – okay – here we go – the "Merry Widow" waltz."

The organ began to play the waltz from the "Merry Widow" and the carousel began to slowly turn.

The children were frozen into silence when the carousel began to move. The younger ones sat very solemnly holding onto the brass poles with their parents alongside reassuring them. The older children quickly grew bored until the stallions began to move up and down and the children would post in the stirrups and point to each other and laugh. Then the rings began to descend, slowly at first then twirling and flashing tantalizingly as they whirled by just out of reach of the adults.

Mooney Levine's voice again came over the loudspeaker.

"Ladies and gentlemen, the rings have descended. As they fly by you, see if you can find the brass ring."

The young Danish woman with the yellow flower at her throat translated as Mooney paused and gazed at her with fatherly affection. She looked like a young, virginal, Danish Marilyn Monroe.

"Remember, there's only one brass ring, so look them over carefully before you pick one."

"They all look alike to me," Elyse said to Martha.

"No Elyse, I see it. That one there. It's coming around now." Martha pointed.

Some of the Danish men had reached up and plucked silver rings over the necks of their horses.

Suddenly Martha threw herself over the neck of the giraffe and lunged at what looked like a tiny comet whirring and flashing gold in the glistening circle of silver rings. "I got it," she screamed, and lunged over the neck of the giraffe falling to the floor of the carousel clutching the brass ring and twisting in agony.

"Oh my God Elyse, my rotor cuff. I tore it." She lay writhing on the floor as the carousel kept whirling and the Gebruder played on. She had the brass ring clutched in her hands.

"I tore my rotor cuff, Elyse. I can feel the tear. I've done it before. I can't move my right arm. Call an ambulance. Get me out of here."

Elyse bent over her.

"Martha are you okay?"

"No I'm not okay. I tore my rotor cuff. I could feel it rip. I'm in God-awful pain. I'm going to sue that man. Call an ambulance."

"Do you want to go to the hospital?"

"No hospital, just back to the hotel. This has happened to me before. A few days' rest and I'll be okay, but I'm going to sue. That giraffe's neck was so slippery and covered with some kind of grease to make it slippery, like a greased pig."

"A greased giraffe?"

"Go look at it and feel it yourself."

Mooney Levine and his young Danish assistant bent over Martha and helped her to her feet. Mooney took her long scarf and made a sling out of it and walked her over to one of the chariots and sat her down. He tried to soothe her.

"Martha, it was just an accident. People get excited and fall off the mounts as they reach for the rings. It happens all the time. There's no grease on the giraffe's neck. I'd have to be crazy to do something like that. We have a perfect safety record." He flashed the reflective light from his glass ring at two passing Tivoli guards and the guards came running over and stood next to him beside the chariot. They looked like large duplicates of the carved wooden guard figures on the carousel.

"Martha, these men will escort you to Royal Copenhagen. You can turn the brass ring over to them and they'll wait with you while you claim your prize and then they'll take you back to the hotel. Now just let me feel your shoulder for a minute." He pretended to adjust her sling, but instead with just a quick movement of his fingers manipulated her shoulder back into place.

"What are you doing to me?"

"Just relax Martha, you'll be okay."

"You're hurting me."

"Only for a second. Now try moving your arm." He untied her sling.

"You're going to be okay Martha."

"Elyse, look, I can move my arm."

"So go pick up your prize Martha." Mooney gave her a little pat on the behind. "And here's a flower from me." He plucked the yellow flower from his assistant's throat and fastened the wire stem around the zipper of Martha's sweater.

"I have to go with her John," Elyse began to follow Martha and the two guardsman. Then she turned back, "I can't go to the séance John, but call our room when you get back to the hotel." She said the hotel room number into his ear, "502". Her lips seemed to linger at his ear. "502," she said again. "Call me and I'll come down and we'll have a drink in the bar. Believe me, I'll need one."

They watched Martha being ushered away by the tall Tivoli guards.

"She'll be okay Jonny. I clicked her shoulder back into place. What a klutz."

"Did you really grease the giraffe's neck?"

"Just a little."

"What do you mean, 'just a little'?"

"I always put a thin film of neats foot oil on the giraffe's neck. If I didn't I'd have a winner every time. It's too easy to grab the brass ring from the giraffe's neck so I grease up the giraffe a little."

"What about at Coney Island?"

"No I never grease the giraffe up at Coney. I could get my throat cut at Coney if I got caught. But I don't give away such fancy prizes at Coney. No Royal Copenhagen. Sometimes I give away cheap china and silverware, but most often big plush dolls for the girlfriends."

Jonny thought about changing the phrase 'Maculate Giraffe' to 'Greased Giraffe' but he didn't feel any poetic sense from the change. The phrase would lose its symmetry. Maybe 'Maculate Giraffe' was a line of T.S. Eliot or perhaps a line of Auden's.

"Jonny, we'll walk over to the séance together, we're already late, but before we leave I've got one more joke for you. Just a short one." A young Danish man in an open guardsman's tunic and a Danish captain's hat gave Mooney a two-fingered salute and Mooney tossed his ring of keys for the carousel to him. "Okay, Jonny, listen to this one."

"Two Jewish men are walking past a Catholic church and as they pass they see a sign, 'Come in and convert. You'll be paid ten dollars'.

"'I think I'll go in for a minute,' one man says. 'Wait for me here.'

"The friend waits outside the church for maybe ten minutes and finally the man comes out.

"Well, did you convert?" he asked his friend.

"Yes I did."

"Did they pay you the ten dollars?"

"The friend looked at him. 'You people. All you think about is money.'"

"How do you like that one, Jonny? 'You people. All you think about is money.' Is that a keeper?"

He was still lost in exploring the parallelism of 'Maculate Giraffe' and 'Greased Giraffe' when suddenly a joke of his own popped into his head like an email popup. "Did you hear about Philip Roth's new book?" he could ask Mooney – "No," he'd answer. "What's it called?" – "The Grapes of Roth." Not bad he told himself, but Mooney wouldn't know who Philip Roth was so he didn't tell him, but that was fairly clever, "The Grapes of Roth". Maybe it could fit somewhere into his novel. He could put it on one of the little grave markers.

"Mine eyes have seen the glory of the coming of the Lord.

"He is trampling out the vintage where the Grapes of Roth are stored."

That would be good for a grave marker with a tiny grey dove perched on top and peeking over the side. Or maybe two grey doves. Kaene Philip Roth. He wrote his guts out trying to win the Nobel Prize and look what it did for him. He's made millions. But Bellow, that dessicated cocksman with the beautiful young wife, and Singer, that crafty old cocksman and son of a rabbi, who picked out his stories and novels in *mameloshen* on an old Yiddish typewriter, they each got the Nobel—and Roth, he got *bupkes, gornisht*—but he's still locking himself in his room all night writing, hoping for a Nobel. You call that a life?

7

The séance was held in a tent lit only by candlelight. There were about eight people seated in a circle around a large wooden table. Mooney led him to a card table, then Mooney disappeared behind a curtain. There were orange shadows of figures enlarged by the candlelight dancing on the walls of the tent. A scratchy record of a wailing Arab song of flutes and oboes began and an aroma of Middle Eastern fragrances wafted over the audience. A young woman dancer in veils, barefoot, her face hidden in the darkness, appeared and whirled and whirled around the room and clicked golden castanets as she turned and suddenly she also disappeared. Mooney's voice came from a microphone behind a curtain.

"Ladies and gentlemen, welcome. In a minute you will meet Madame Josefina who has just come to Copenhagen from her home in Jerusalem for this one time appearance for M. Levine International Productions. As you'll see, Madame Josefina is a talent of great magical powers. She can solve your problems in a New York minute. She can help you if you'll let her work her magic on you. Madame Josefina is an international sorceress, but even international sorceresses have to make a living. So remember, the first question to the Madame tonight is absolutely free. After that each question will be one-hundred kroner or ten dollars paid in advance to be collected by my assistant before the question is asked. Any questions will be put to the Madame in a private booth over there." Mooney flashed his ring and a beam of light, like a laser pointer, illuminated a ragged looking carnival booth that looked like a frayed cabana or an ancient canvas confessional.

"But before taking any private questions, Madame Josefina will conduct the séance you have all been waiting for." Suddenly the reedy music swelled into a crescendo – "Now here she is, direct from the ancient walls of Jerusalem. Welcome her to the beautiful towers of Tivoli Park Copenhagen—the International Seer and Sorceress, Madame Josefina. Give her a nice hand ladies and gentlemen. Give her a real Danish welcome."

A little old lady that looked as wrinkled and furtive as Mother Theresa dressed in the same kind of saffron robe limped out on the stage and sat down holding her cane and blinking at the audience.

"Vhy haf I come to Copenhagen?" she said in a heavy Polish/Yiddish accent. "God only knows. So cold here and the wrong kind of herring. No schmaltz herring. Vot kind of town with only von delicatessen and only chopped herring and matjes herring, but no schmaltz herring?"

She shook her head sadly. "But for Mister Levine I fly, but only for two nights I vill hold the séances. Already I feel pain in my heart. I need some special water with bubbles like greps vasser to take my nitro pill. So he's my friend and he gets me my special water which, by the way, they don't have on SAS. SAS, such a name. It was to me like SS only with an extra A. SS, the Gestapo, who killed my beloved Bruno Schulz in Drohobycz in Poland. Who vas Bruno Schulz? He vas my fiancé. A great Jewish-Polish writer and artist. We hoped to marry, but the Gestapo killed him and left me alone. Only do I haf memories. Only painful memories of one of the greatest writers and artists in the western world. He vas the Polish Kafka, Bruno Schulz.

"But I come here to honor another great writer and artist, a Dane not a *landsman*, but a maker of fairy tales. Who is dot man whose statue is standing in the moonlight right outside the walls of Tivoli vit his top hat, a book on his knee, and his cane? Dot man with the top hat and cane is the great Danish writer

Hans Christian Andersen. The spinner of fairy tales, which kind the world has not known since. 'The Ugly Duckling,' the von about a mermaid, 'The Little Mermaid,' the von about the match girl, 'The Little Match Girl,' not even a Yiddish writer could spin out such magic fairy tales like Hans Christian Andersen. No one – Anski, poof – he writes only about Hassids. No Hassids in Denmark. Zeitlin, poof – Julian Tuwim, that imposter, that fancy man who moved from Warsaw to New York, piff-poff. Not even my beloved Bruno could write about 'The Little Match Girl.' I vas Bruno's Little Match Girl, me Josefina. The little match girl of Bruno Schulz. He was engaged to another Josefina, a Catholisher Josefina Czelinska before me. But he dumped her and promised me the marriage. I am the real Josefina, Josefina Goldstyne, the Jewish Josefina, the love of Bruno Schulz's life.

"So for the Danes who saved their Jews from the Nazis, the only ones in all Europe brave enough to do so, I come to Copenhagen to honor their great writer, Hans Christian Andersen. With this séance, I will put him back in touch with Jenny Lind, his love. I will bring them back together. As I, Josefina Goldstyne, was loved by Bruno Schulz, Hans Christian Andersen was in love with the great soprano, the Swedish Nightingale,with a voice like an angel, Jenny Lind.

"Tonight I vill restore their love and bring them back together."

Suddenly a curtain was dropped and Madame Josefina was gone. More incense wafted into the tent. The reedy music began again, but then the record was pulled with a screech and the beautiful soprano voice of the Swedish soprano Jenny Lind began flowing into the tent and suddenly Jenny Lind, appeared in shadow behind the curtain.

The tones were dulcet, smooth, and ripe but the shadowy

figure of Jenny Lind looked vaguely familiar to him even in the sparse light of the candles. She turned and came out from behind the curtain and faced the audience. He recognized her. She was Mooney's assistant, the virginal, apple-cheeked Danish Marilyn Monroe. She was both the veiled dancer whirling with the golden castanets and the Swedish Nightingale, Jenny Lind. Madame Josefina came back on stage.

"Und now Jenny Lind will sing for us her famous aria, 'Svenska Flicka' vhich means a young Swedish girl in love. She vill sing this aria, not only for your ears, but also for the ears of Hans Christian Andersen who, by the vay if you've ever seen his picture, had big ears like an elephant and a big nose, a schnozz so big he had a very hard time getting women to fall in love with him. He vas, in fact, the original Ugly Duckling, that face, vot a *punnim*, but vot a magnificent heart. It was in his heart that he was such a great lover.

"Now vhile Jenny Lind sings her sweet aria, please all of you in the first row put your hands down flat on the table and vhen I tell you to knock on the table – you knock. If we hear someone knocking back, ve will know then that it's him, Mr. Andersen, the Ugly Duckling. So silence – absolute silence while Jenny sings her love song. The sad song of a young Swedish girl looking for her lover. Und by the vay, did the Little Mermaid ever find her lover? Who knows the answer? Did she ever find the prince – of course she did, but vhat price did she pay? Vot did she haf to give up to meet her love? Vot did the wicked witch of the underwater kingdom do to her before she fed the mermaid the magic potion to change her fins to legs and bring her up from the sea – she took her tongue. She cut out her tongue – so all you ladies who vant to be mermaids and rise from the sea – best to keep your mouths shut.

"Okay, in America they play this game—Knock, Knock.

"I say Knock, knock.

"You say who's there?"

There suddenly was a knocking on the table—knock, knock.

Jenny Lind kept singing, but now she began whirling and whirling as she sang.

"Who's dere? Who's dat knocking?"

"Isak," a tortured raspy voice answered.

"Isak who? Isak Bashevis Singer, the Yiddish writer who wrote 'Yentl'? You call that a fairy tale? A girl who dresses as a boy and tries to win the love of a yeshiva *bocher*. Dot Bashevis stole from 'Yidl Mitn Fidl,' the same story. A girl with her violin disguised as a boy wit Polish violinists on the road falls in love. Bashevis just stole Yidl and made her into Yentl but still no fairy tale like 'The Little Mermaid'. Nowhere near as good.

"Is that really you Bashevis? The boy who wit his brother Israel Joshua used to climb the trees in Swider by the seaside and sit up in the trees and try to write fairy tales?"

"It is not Bashevis," again the croaking voice.

"Well then who? Isak who?"

"Isak Dinesen."

"Isak Dinesen, the famous Danish woman writer, the Baroness Blixen? So vot message do you bring to us tonight, Baroness?"

" – All of you keep your hands on the table – vait for the knocking."

" – Knock, knock."

"Vot is the message?"

"The message is – 'I had a farm in Afrika'."

"Oy, ve all know that message. Tell me Isak Dinesen, haf you seen Hans Christian Andersen? Can you bring him to the table tonight? Knock three times if you can."

Again, the raspy, tortured voice.

"I have not seen him."

"Who? Who have you not seen?"

"Hans Christian Andersen."

"Vhere is Hans Christian Andersen. Do you know where he is, Baroness? All of you. Keep your hands down on the table."

"Denys Finch-Hatton. Where is he?"

"Vot about Denys Finch-Hatton?"

"He flew away from me."

"Ve all know about Finch-Hatton. He was your lover in 'Out of Africa' and he got in his plane and flew away like a bird and never came back. Only he crashed into a mountain. Den you buried him up on that hill where the lions came and laid down on his grave. I remember dot scene. But Finch-Hatton ve don't look for, ve vant only Hans Christian Andersen."

"I want Denys Finch-Hatton."

"Ve know all that already. But we vant 'The Ugly Duckling'. The man wit the big schnozz who wrote 'The Little Mermaid'. Haf you seen him?"

"I see him quite often. He comes to visit me at my grave in Helsingor. Always by moonlight. In his top hat and with his cane. We talk Danish together in the moonlight."

"Vot do you talk about?"

"I ask him if he has seen Denys."

"Vot does he say?"

"He says, 'no. never.' Then he tips his hat and walks away down the path. But always he turns and with his hat over his heart he asks me, if I have seen Jenny Lind."

"His great love. Jenny Lind, the 'Swedish Nightingale'?"

"Yes."

"And vot do you say to him?"

"No, I have never seen her. I don't know where she is."

"I know vhere she is Isak."

"Where?"

"If I tell you vhere is Jenny Lind, vill you bring Hans Christian back with you to meet her?"

"Oh yes."

"She is here with us tonight."

"In this tent?"

"Yes, we vill show you – now all of you lift your hands from the table."

As everyone raised their hands the music began again and Jenny Lind appeared singing in her beautiful, sweet voice, slowly whirling around the table, her veils swirling.

"Do you hear her Isak?"

"The voice. It is so beautiful."

"It is Jenny Lind. She is vaiting here for Hans Christian. Bring him to us tomorrow night. Bring him. If you bring him to us I promise ve vill look for Finch-Hatton. I think I know vhere he is."

"You do?"

"I might."

"I will give you anything, anything, if you find him."

"Good night Isak Dinesen. I am growing weary. My powers are leaving me. I cannot see you anymore. Please, please all of you keep your hands on the table. Say goodbye to Isak Dinesen. Ve vill see you tomorrow night at eight. Same place, same time, same table. Good night Isak Dinesen, the Baroness Blixen."

The music began again. The reedy, atonal music. Jenny Lind came whirling out on the stage, only this time she was dressed again as a harem girl and she held a very frightened white chicken in a bamboo cage.

"Okay, now if any of you vant a private session with me, I vill see you in one of the booths over there."

Madame Josefina limped off the stage as the audience applauded and the harem girl bowed and twirled once and followed her with the white chicken in the bamboo cage.

Jonny Levin was the first to follow her to the tent for a personal consultation. He was the first in line.

The tent panel opened after a few minutes and the young Danish harem dancer beckoned him inside.

Madame Josefina was seated behind a small table with one foot propped up on a tufted cushion. She was holding a bottle of water.

"Oy, I could *plotz*. Vot a job this is. Dat Isak Dinesen. Did you see her *punnim*? As ugly as Hans Christian Andersen. She looked like a dried prune. Uglier than Hans Christian. So, I'm supposed to find her true love vot flew away from her up into the sky in Africa? Dots vhat she wants from me? She buried him already with the lions on a hill, I'm supposed to find him? Vot a pair of *mashuggeners*. Her and her lover boy. She was vot? A baroness or something? Plenty it should cost her if I bring her Finch-Hatton back from the lions."

Madame Josefina took a drink of her special water.

"Thanks be to God for this grepps vasser." She gave a little belch. "Dot Mister Mooney Levine is a real *mensch*, he got for me a case of my special vater. Now with my bad leg, throbbing with sciatica, up on the cushion he got for me, already I feel better. My powers are coming back to me. So vot can I do for you young man?"

The Danish harem maiden stood at her side in the candlelight, her gaze falling on Jonny Levin, her nose twitching already at the scent he gave off, mixed in the tent with the odor of the chicken and the yellow tallow melting from the candle.

"Let me see your hand, mister. Give it over here to me."

Madame Josefina motioned to him to come closer.

"But first you give one-hundred kroner to Jenny Lind here."

He handed a hundred kroner bill to Jenny Lind and Madame Josefina snatched the bill away and held it over the candle. She squinted at the watermark, the shadowy profile of a young Queen Margrethe embedded in the bank note. She folded the bill and dropped it inside her toga.

"Gif to me your hand."

He put his hand in hers.

"Vot do you vant to know from me? Two questions. Two questions only."

She snapped her fingers at Jenny Lind and the handmaiden took the chicken out of its slotted cage and held it up to her breast.

"All right, go ahead and ask – question number 1."

"Madame Josefina, I've come to Denmark to write a novel. I'm a writer. Will I be able to write it? Can you help me?"

Her hooded eyes stared at him. "A writer? Every *putz* thinks he's a writer. Sit down in dot chair," she pointed to a stool. "Sit there. You vant to be a writer? Look vot happened to my darling Bruno Schulz. Dot fake, Cynthia Ozick, wrote about him in her 'The Messiah of Stockholm'. He never wrote such a novel vot name vas 'The Messiah' like Ozick said. There was no such book. I ought to know. I was with him every night in Drohobycz. Never was he writing on a novel. Day and night he was teaching carpentry to Polish kids in the high school. Teaching them to make birdhouses, chairs and tables. So now you say to me you vant to write a novel. Okay mister. Jenny Lind will hold dot white chicken over your head. *Shlogn Kapores* we call it. You know vot is *Shlogn Kapores?* On the night before Yom Kippur, a chicken is held over the head and your sins are transferred to the chicken and then its throat is slit and ve give it to the poorhouse. *Shlogn Kapores.* You vant this chicken's throat slit so you can become a writer? It's dot important to you dat you vant us to kill this poor chicken? No way. Ve don't slit our chicken's throat. Ve only got one chicken, so go ahead, Jenny Lind, twirl the chicken."

Jenny Lind twirled the chicken upside down, slowly over

Jonny Levin's head and covered him with a veil. He sensed her cheap adolescent orange blossom perfume. Its sickly sweet odor filled his nostrils. Then she plucked a white feather from the chicken and stuck it through his lapel.

"All right, now you got this white feather. Maybe you'll be a writer. Maybe you'll finish your novel. Maybe not? Only God and this chicken knows. The chicken can't talk. God can talk. Maybe he'll talk to you later. All right. So vhere is question #2?"

"Will I fall in love here in Denmark Madame Josefina? Will I find a woman here?"

"Let me look at your hand again."

She pulled his hand toward the candle and peered at it.

"Silky smooth. Never did any labor. Not a rough, working man's hand. No calluses. My Bruno had calluses from all the carpentry he made. The birdhouses, the rocking horses. He made me a magnificent dollhouse like a castle, vit a roof I could take off and tiny furniture in every room, even with a baby already in a cradle in our bedroom. It could have been our baby, like a tiny Jesus in a crèche. Only Jews don't believe in baby Jesus. Are you a Jewish man? A Yid? You got a yiddisher *punnim*. I say even with a hand like yours, silky smooth, never done no work, you, if you're a Jewish man, will find love in Denmark. Hamlet, that schmuck, found love here. So vhy not a yiddisher boy, can't he find his Ophelia? Only not quite so suicidal and so young with rocks already in her pocket. Maybe a nice Jewish woman wit a fish tank and colored pebbles in her fish tank, not a suicidal *shiksa*."

She snapped her fingers and Jenny Lind again took the chicken from its cage and held the chicken upside down over his head. She leaned toward him and whirled the chicken over him and covered him with her veils and pressed her breasts against his face.

"Oh my God," he thought lost in the sickly sweet odor of orange blossoms, a high school girl's fragrance.

"Okay, that's enough. Next," Madame Josefina held up her bottle of grepps water and took another swallow. "You're through, mister." She pointed to the opening of the canvas flap. "Enough already. Two questions. One hundred kroner. *Gai gesunt.* Go in good health."

As he turned to leave, Jenny Lind plucked another white chicken feather for his other lapel and thrust it through the fabric.

Enough already. Enough of Madame Josefina and her perfumed assistant. He walked away from the tent, the cheap orange blossom perfume in his nostrils. "Stay away from suicidal *shikshas*," she told him. How about apple-cheeked Danish hand maidens dressed as Arab odalisques? Enough already of séances and odalisques. He wouldn't stop at the shooting booth tonight. He'd go directly do his hotel room and work on his novel. "You want to be a writer? Every *putz* wants to be a writer." He headed down the flowered path that led to the main gate and walked past the tall guardsmen in their blue tunics and bearskin shakos. Before going back to his room, he'd pay a little visit to the Andersen statue. He'd spend a moment or two with Andersen. How did the old woman know of Bruno Schulz? Schulz, the tormented Polish Kafka. And how did she know Cythia Ozick? He loved Ozick. Her crazy Puttermesser character. Puttermesser, an exhausted single woman lawyer in New York working for some godforsaken city bureau makes a Golem out of her houseplant dirt to do her housework. The Golem arises from the dirt of the plant and takes over Puttermesser's life and Puttermesser runs for mayor. Ozick also wrote the great story "Envy; Or, Yiddish in America". Ozick, the mistress of *Yiddishkeit*, sometimes so impenetrable and magical that he can't understand what she's writing about. But her novel, "The Messiah of Stockholm", that was clear, a classic, easy, smooth Ozick read. The story of the lost son of Bruno Schulz working as a theater critic in Stockholm, living alone in a garret. Suddenly, the man's unknown sister appears in Stockholm clutching the manuscript of Schulz's lost novel, "The Messiah". Like Andersen's "Little Match Girl," standing barefoot in the snow. Supposedly "The Messiah" was Schulz's story of Sabbatai Zevi, the false 17th century messiah who started a messianic revolution among the Polish Hassidim. Singer wrote his first novel, "Satan in Goray", about Sabbatai Zevi. He was musing on all this in the Danish moonlight as he slowly approached the huge statue of Andersen in the square across the street, just outside the walls of Tivoli.

Should he give Andersen another little *shry* and tell him that his lost love, Jenny Lind, was back in town?

Should he tell the old Danish faery tale meister about Ozick's story of Bruno Schulz in Stockholm? Andersen, when he was dying, was befriended by a Jewish family in Denmark, the Melchior family. He was such a difficult and cranky old man living off the hospitality of his friends, most of his friends abandoned him. When Andersen was dying he made his last paper cut for the mother of the Melchior family. What was her name, the woman who nursed Andersen when he was dying? Dorothea Melchior. Dorothea and Moritz Melchior. Andersen made a beautiful paper cut for Dorothea. His final paper cut a gift to her. Marcus Melchior, maybe a grandson or other relative, was a rabbi in Copenhagen in 1943 when the Germans began their action against the Jews. He remembered a photograph of Marcus Melchior, the rabbi of Copenhagen, a tall slim professorial looking man riding a bicycle, wearing a wing collar and a foulard, a Prince Edward Hamburg and a black suit and vest.

As he stood before the statue of Andersen, he imagined Dorothea Melchior bending over the dying Danish writer, her black ringlets just touching his face, her breath, her dark eyes, infusing the old magician with another day of life. He had cut his last ballerinas for her. His last paper swans and then he cut a pair of leering skulls. He looked up at the statue of Andersen and reached out to him and touched Andersen's hand and turned and left the square and walked back to the hotel.

8

AN OLD MAN WAS BEHIND the front desk. Half asleep. He let him in the door. He didn't ask the old man if there were any messages. He took the elevator up to his room, untied his shoes and kicked them off. He hung his jacket up, sat in a chair and began to write, working on his cemetery again.

KAENE MAESCHE SWARTZSCHILD

My grandfather, Maesche Swartzschild. Maesche with the Masonic ring and the beautiful voice. He could have been a cantor. With a voice like that he could have been a *chazzan*. Instead he became a salesman. A wild, young, handsome salesman with a full head of black hair and his own carpet store at the corner of Wabash and Lake in Chicago when he was only 28. The New York Rug & Carpet Company. Maesche Swartzschild. They buried him with his Mason's ring on his ring finger, buried him beside his wife Brodie and his sister Sarah. Sarah with the round, pasty, moon face, who married a stooped, shy little man, Meier, a tailor.

What should I write about my grandfather Maesche Swartzschild? He'd lost all his money by the time the Depression hit in the early 1930s. The store, the buildings, everything. He lost it all buying Florida swamp land and then started over selling life insurance policies.

One day after he'd been remarried for two years, Maesche came to see me. I was in my carrel at the university, typing a paper. I could smell the cigar smoke that preceded him. How had he gotten in the building? He had $600 stuffed in an envelope that he handed me. "Here kid, keep this for me. It's my getaway money." "Getaway?" I asked him. "From her," his new wife, the widow he married after my grandmother Brodie was killed by a train in an accident hurrying home with the chicken dinner. Crossing an unmarked crossing in the old gray Dodge. I remember the tiny red glass jewel on the light knob on the dashboard that glowed when you pulled the lights on. I also remember an album with a photograph of Maesche and Brodie in a wicker chair in Palm Beach being pushed by a black chauffeur. Maesche, who had come from the steppes of Poland, who made a fortune and blew it all gambling it away on Florida swampland and losing Chicago apartment buildings in all night poker games. My sweet grandmother, Brodie Swartzschild, crushed beyond recognition by that train. And after Brodie died, Maesche married a slack-jawed, dog-faced widow from Skokie with dyed blonde hair, Madeline. She had a face like a prize fighter, but owned a neat little Skokie bungalow where she cooked for him, she did his laundry, and baked for him. No one could equal the bakery of my grandmother Brodie. I remember the folded white powdery pockets of apricot and raspberry or the date bars waiting and still warm under wax paper on the kitchen table when I came home from school. Brodie died in that car wreck, and Maesche found himself a peroxide blonde widow with a big mouth and a nutty family. They were all supposedly rich from some sort of diet drink. A chocolate milky drink that was a substitute for a meal. "Choco-Slim."

Another afternoon soon after his marriage to Madeline and

my first divorce, Maesche came up to my apartment and gave me an insurance policy with a brown savings passbook as a gift. He said he'd paid the first year's premium by forfeiting his first year's commission. After that I was to pay. If he sold enough of these he'd have a pension. He told me each year when I paid the premium I'd be adding to the cash value like a savings account. I paid the premium for three years and then I stopped. The last time I saw my grandfather, he came back to my office at the university and argued with me about my dropping the policy. His face turned red from shouting at me when I refused to renew the policy. He then asked for the $600 back which I gave to him. Six months later he was dead in a Miami hospital. Maesche, who'd get so excited he'd put his fist through his straw hat at Cub's games. He loved the Cubs and players like Ki Ki Cuyler, Tinkers to Evers to Chance. Frank Demaree. I remember my mother told me she often sat with Maesche as a little girl holding a spun sugar cone he'd bought just to keep her quiet. Maesche shouting at Billy Jurges, that anti-Semite. Hank Greenberg challenged Jurges to fight and Jurges, the coward, backed away. Kaene Maesche Swartzschild. Kaene Brodie Swartzschild. *Tak fir alt.* I was there when they lowered Maesche into his grave. The vault cover with the gold Star of David, falling into place. A miserable Chicago day of snow and ice. The rabbi handed each of us a rose to drop down into the grave. The rabbi recited the ancient Hebrew prayer, "El Moley Rachamim", and I watched a tiny old woman, huddled in her mink coat, crippled with osteoporosis, standing at graveside in her spiked heels. She fluttered some rose petals down into Maesche's grave. Who was she? A friend? An old girlfriend? Some cousin unknown to me? When was the last time I saw Maesche alive? Was it when he came for the $600? No, after that, he separated from the second wife for a few months and took a room in a run down hotel on Wilson Avenue. I met him there in his room, reading the Tribune stock market in his undershirt, tins of tuna and sardines out on the window sill. He had no refrigerator. He seemed happy. Maesche, who had the chauffeur wipe down the steering wheel of the car with alcohol in Palm Beach each time after the chauffeur drove it, now was alone again. From the steppes of Poland to Palm Beach to a flop house on Wilson Avenue. Can I remember the sound of his voice? No. Only one word. "Dassn't. You dassn't do that." An archaic word, "Dassn't". But I can hear Maesche instructing me and I see him pointing and instead of saying, "don't do that", "you dassn't do that." "You dassn't pick those dandelions." He was a city boy. He'd never lived in a house. Always apartments. He thought the dandelions on my front lawn were little yellow flowers. I do remember the sound of his singing voice, though. All the relatives at the Seder table, sipping wine and encouraging him, "Sing, Maesche, sing." He had a deep, mournful, cantorial voice. He'd hold up his wine glass and sing. He could have sung his own "El Moley Rachamim". I could just hear his voice. "Oh G-d, full of compassion, thou who dwellest on high. El Moley Rachamim. Shochem Bahromim." He would have done a better job than the bored young rabbi handing out roses under the sleet-filled canopy waiting for his $400 check.

KAENE MICKEY BERNSTEIN

I've left out a few more memories of my uncle Mickey Bernstein, pig eyed – shrewd Mickey Bernstein, with the mouth twisted to the right side, bullnecked, a gray fedora square on his head, the brim rolled down evenly all around. Married to my Aunt Rose, my father's sister. Heavy voiced, almost brutish, eye and mouth twisted by the stroke, stumbling as he walked away from another Seder table down Morse Avenue in the rain to a tavern. I was maybe nineteen. The family sent me after him to the tavern four blocks away to find him and bring him back. I found the tavern. He was on a bar stool watching a fight on TV. "Hit 'em in the kishkes," he was yelling up at the set and knocking down shots of bourbon. He stumbled out of the bar cursing at me. I pulled him by the arm. "You know, kid, when I die I'm gonna leave you somethin' in my will. You know what I'm gonna leave you kid?" "No Mickey." "You wanna know?" "No." "I'm gonna tell you anyway. I'm gonna leave you a concession." "A concession?" "Yeah, I'm gonna leave you the hot towel concession in a whorehouse. That's what I'm gonna leave you."

And so we made our way back through the rain, up the stairs and back to the Seder. Mickey and me. "El Moley Rachamim." Mickey Bernstein. *Tak fir alt.*

Enough of the novel. It isn't any good. Just ridiculous flashes of family memories. I should get out of the room. Call Elyse Friedberg. What's her room number? I should ask her down to the bar for a drink. Another flash of Cynthia Ozick, her story, "Envy; Or, Yiddish in America". The two old Yiddish poets, one was Edelshtein. Who was the other, Baumsweig? They were both jealous of Yankel Ostrover (Isaac Singer). They went to a lecture by Ostrover. He was a *Chazer*. His stories were translated into English. He had left the world of Yiddishkeit and now was worshipped by the *Goyim*. An international star. Edelshtein and Baumsweig were little nobodies. Little *pippuks* compared to Yankel Ostrover. Edelshtein was probably based on the modernist Yiddish poet, Jacob Glatstein – Yankev Glatshsteyn. Singer couldn't stand the Yiddish modernist poets of New York. He thought they were fakes. They thought he was a *goy*, a *Chazer* in the spotlight.

What was her room number?

9

HE CALLED ELYSE FRIEDBERG. She sounded happy to hear from him and told him she'd meet him in the lobby bar in ten minutes. He went downstairs and got a table away from the television set. They were still showing soccer, interviewing Danish and Dutch players from the afternoon's match. The bartender was an African-American who said there weren't many Americans in Copenhagen this year. He'd been in Copenhagen for two years and was from L.A. and liked it here and thought maybe he'd stay. He was living with a Danish woman and trying to paint.

He ordered another Carlsberg, but instead of Aquavit, he ordered a shot of bourbon, "Old Forester".

"A boilermaker," the bartender said to him smiling. "I don't serve many of these."

"Occasionally I like them."

"A real working man's drink."

He sipped some of the bourbon and went back and sat down. He thought about Elyse Friedberg. She was a refined, elegant woman, close to his age. He was tired of playing games with nymphets. He'd gotten himself involved in some kind of farcical, literary maze like a Nabokov character, and he wanted out. This woman could help lead him out. He had come to Denmark to do some serious work. The swan boat excursion and the séance were filled with grotesqueries. Leda, Mooney Levine, Madame Josefina, the bucolic harem dancer, all still whirling around in his head. They did nothing to advance his novel. He supposedly was a serious scholar. Maybe though, the construction of the little cemetery wasn't so foolish after all. He loved the cheerful little doves the Danes put on their headstones. He had another colorful postcard that he found lying on one of the gravel paths of Tivoli. A postcard of a little smiling Danish boy dressed as a gate attendant at Tivoli in an oversized black uniform. He wore a long double-breasted coat with brass buttons and a black peaked cap with a red Tivoli hat band. Red birds were whirling around his head. Three red and orange tiny birds. Each with a sprig of a flower in their beaks. The postcard had a legend, "Det gamle trykkeri smogen Tivoli". Probably "The Little Bird Man of Tivoli". Better the three red birds whirling than the sad white chicken of *Shlogen Kapores.*

Elyse Friedberg suddenly appeared at his table and reached out and touched his hand. He could sense her perfume as she sat down.

"Hello John," she said to him.

He was drawing on a cocktail napkin.

"What would you like to drink, Elyse?"

"I'll have some white wine. Ask him if they have a pinot grigio." She looked up at the bartender. "Do you have any pinot grigio?" She had a soft, gentle manner making a request. An absolute contrast from her friend Martha.

"We have a pinot grigio from Venice."

"I'll have a glass of that."

The bartender brought her a glass and a dish of peanuts and another of tiny black Italian olives.

"What are you drawing John? It looks like a circle full of dots."

"Actually it's an atom. It's a drawing of a single uranium atom and its nucleus. A U235 atom."

"Is that your field? Do you teach physics?"

He put the pen down and smiled at her. "No, I'm not in science. I teach English. I'm an English professor."

"At Northwestern?"

"How did you know?"

"You're a professor and you live in Evanston, you probably teach at Northwestern." She lifted her glass to him. "I actually went to Northwestern years ago. I have an English degree too, but I never did anything with it. I got married instead."

He raised his shot glass to her. He took a sip of the bourbon and washed it down with the Carlsberg.

"*Skål,*" she raised her wine glass. "Did you enjoy the séance?"

"I did. It was weird, but interesting."

"What happened?"

"Well, Madame Josefina had us all put our hands on a table and then she contacted some spirits. You know the Danish writer Isak Dinesen? She contacted her in the spirit world."

"I love Isak Dinesen. Did the Madame use a Ouija board?"

"No, she had a young woman assistant dressed in veils who would dance and twirl around to Arab music and then suddenly the voice of Isak Dinesen came into the room like a scratchy old record."

"Maybe it was a scratchy old record."

"It could have been an old phonograph hidden behind the curtain."

"What did she say?"

"She said she was looking for her lover Denys Finch-Hatton."

"I remember him in the film 'Out of Africa', Robert Redford. He flew away from her in that old biplane and tipped his wings goodbye to her. Later he crashed into a mountain."

"Right and she buried him high on a hill where the lions he loved would come to visit him. Tomorrow night Josefina promises to bring Finch-Hatton back for Isak Dinesen if she'll bring back Hans Christian Andersen to the séance from the spirit world."

"Oh, I love him too. Hans Christian Andersen, 'The Little Match Girl', 'The Princess and the Pea', 'The Little Mermaid'. We went out to the harbor and saw The Little Mermaid, "Den lille Haufrue."

"I haven't seen her yet. Come tomorrow night and leave your friend Martha at home. You can witness all these reunions."

"I'd love to," she said, shaking her hair away from her face, "but we're leaving early in the morning. Martha has an appointment in Stockholm with an orthopedic surgeon. She's certain that she has a torn rotor cuff and she was referred to this doctor by her doctor in Chicago. I can't stop her. She's like a bull in a china shop when she gets going. But she's one of my oldest friends. I've known her forever – grade school, high school, camp together as children."

"You've barely seen Copenhagen."

"I know. We've been here only two days and have just been shopping."

"Do you know what happened here with the Jews during the war?"

"I really don't know. Something awful I suppose."

"The Danes saved almost their entire Jewish population. There were seven thousand Jews in Denmark. They smuggled them out in fishing boats across to Sweden. Almost all of them were saved. Only five hundred were taken by the Germans. The Danes are a wonderful people. Denmark was the only country in Europe that refused to turn over its Jews to the Germans."

"I really don't know much about the history of the Holocaust. I know about Auschwitz and the concentration camps in Poland. I haven't heard the story about the Danes."

"One of the Jews rescued was Niels Bohr, who was part Jewish, the physicist who won the Nobel Prize. He was rescued and taken to the U.S. and worked on the atomic bomb at Los Alamos. He worked on the controlled chain reaction of fission."

"So you were thinking about him when you were drawing the circle with the tiny dots."

"I was."

"Was he saved by the Danes?"

"Yes, he was taken out of Denmark across to Sweden. Then he went to the Swedish king and got him to grant asylum to all the Jews who would come to Sweden."

"I feel foolish not knowing these things. I wish I had more time here. I don't think much about the Holocaust. I think more about Israel and the Palestinians."

"Before I leave Denmark I want to go up the coast and visit the harbors where the Jews boarded the fishing boats. Some of the boats have been preserved."

"If I were here and didn't have Martha in tow, I'd like to go with you." She drank more of her wine and her eyes flashed at him. Then she took his pen and a small notebook from her purse and wrote the letter of his first name "J" on a sheet of paper. "I do acrostics. I make poems out of the letters of your name. One line from each letter. I learned how to do it by watching these old men in a plaza in a town in Mexico. People would come to them for poems, for marriages, birthdays, burials or just for advice. This sweet old man had an old typewriter. The keys were bound with rubber bands. He taught me how to do it."

"J," she said, "I'll do your name Do you want 'John" or the diminutive 'Johnny?'"

"Do the diminutive but I call myself 'Jonny'"

"OK" J-O-N-N-Y."

"J – Just because we have only one night"

"Porque solo tenemos una noche"

"O – Only this one night"

"Solo esta noche"

"N – Never perhaps to meet again"

"Tal vez no volveremos a vernos"

"N – Never can the words be said"

"Las palabras nunca son suficientes"

"Y – I can't think of anything for 'Y'. Yet. Okay."

"No me viene a la mente nada con 'Y'. Al menos por ahora. Esta bien."

"Yet I'm happy that we met, Jonny Levin."

"De todos modos me dá gusto que nos hayamos conocido, Jonny Levin."

She tore the sheet from her notebook and handed it to him. His glasses were down on his nose. He read it and smiled up at her.

"Where did you learn to speak Spanish like that?"

"At Northwestern. I had three years. I love Spanish culture. In fact, Martha and I just visited Madrid."

"Madrid."

"I just love it there. We went to the bullfights, the Plaza del Toros. I think if I could be born again I'd come back as a Spaniard. I love the bullfighters. The matadors' faces. The high dark planes of their faces. I thought I'd be repelled by the killing of the bull, but I wasn't. Vaqueros, the picadors, the thrusting of the banderillos, the thrust of the matador's sword, I wasn't repelled, I was fascinated."

"I've never seen a bullfight. I don't think I want to see one."

"It's full of pageantry. I even bought these stockings there at the corrida." She was wearing a long black skirt and she lifted it and displayed her pink stockings.

"You could be the first Jewish woman matador."

"Why not? Do you know that I was once Miss National Zeta Beta Tau? Why not a matadora?"

"Miss National ZBT? That means you were voted the most beautiful Jewish college girl in the country."

"I was never that attractive. My father was president of the fraternity's board of directors. The election was rigged."

She smiled up at him.

"Jonny. Believe me, that was another life ago. I wonder if the bartender knows how to mix a pitcher of sangria? If I order one would you have some with me?"

"Sangria, why not?"

She went over to the bar and began an animated conversation with the bartender. He couldn't hear her, but he watched her gesticulating and giving directions.

She came back and sat down.

"He'll make us a pitcher. He's got the ingredients, he's just a little rusty. He's from L.A. He said sangria's very popular in L.A."

"There must be a lot of matadoras in L.A. Do you know about Sydney Franklin? Have you ever heard of him?"

"Sydney Franklin? No, I've never heard of him."

"He was a Jewish boy from Brooklyn. His real name was Sydney Frumkin. He was the first American to be given the title of Matador in Spain."

"Really? How marvelous."

"Maybe you'll be the second."

"I don't think I could actually kill a bull. There's just a teeny little spot on the bull's shoulder where you thrust the sword. I don't think I could do it or if I tried I'd miss and the bull would kill me. Anyway, I'm too much of a coward. I've read about the great Spanish matadors like Dominguin and Manolete. I just love their faces, their sad eyes. The way they tie their hair back. The golden suits they wear. The Suit of Lights. The way they arch their backs when they thrust their swords."

The bartender brought the pitcher of sangria and set it

down on the table. "It's been a long time," he said to her, "but I think I got it right." He poured them each a glass and put a slice of orange in both glasses.

"It's delicious, just right. There's a trick to drinking it Jonny. First you taste it and swish it around your mouth and hold it in your cheeks. Some people like to drink it when they make love and then spit it at each other and pretend it's blood."

"Spit blood at each other?"

"Right. If a matador is wounded by a bull, he'll suck his wound and spit his own blood back at the bull and dare him to come at him again. When the bull does, the matador has his sword hidden and thrusts for the kill. He lures the bull by spitting blood at him."

"I could ask you if you've ever done this?"

"You mean spit blood on a lover? No, but I have a friend who tied her husband to their headboard with his ties. They drank a pitcher of sangria and she pretended to spit her blood on him."

"Then she killed him?"

"No, silly. She didn't kill him. She tied him up and they made love."

"Elyse, what do you do in Chicago? Do you work?"

"Work. Oh god no. I haven't had a job in years. I taught school for awhile. And then I quit and married a very wealthy man. About ten years ago he left me for a younger woman, a trophy wife. I'm happy to be single. I travel, I take classes. I have a good life. I have a good time."

She reached into her purse and brought out what looked like a pair of black plastic scarabs. "Do you know what these are?"

"What are they, castanets?"

"Yes, castanets. I bought them in Madrid when I bought the stockings."

"You know Madame Josefina's assistant at the séance had a pair of golden castanets. She clicked them while she danced."

"Did she really?"

"Can you do anything with them? Play the castanets?"

"I've been practicing. I can do the beat of the Spanish dance Tchaikovsky wrote for 'Swan Lake'. Do you know the Spanish dance?"

"I know 'Swan Lake'. I saw it once in London in Albert Hall, the English National Ballet." He caught himself using the swan allegy again. Leda, the Swan Boat, the inn in Holland, "The White Swan," and now "Swan Lake".

"Drink your sangria Jonny. I can play these. I'll show you. I have to sit up very straight, very, very straight. Then you pull your skirt up to your knees, arch your back like a matador and close your eyes. Just cup your hand." She began to click the castanets and stamp her feet as if Tchaikovsky's Spanish dance was buzzing through her head and just then her cell phone began to vibrate on her belt.

"Oh my god, it's Martha." She playfully pinched his nose with the castanets and then reached for her cell phone which had begun chiming.

"What now?" she said into the phone.

"No, you're not having a heart attack."

"How do I know? Martha, it's just a muscle pull. Tell the doctor in Stockholm about it tomorrow and go back to sleep."

"No, I won't call an ambulance. You call the ambulance yourself Martha. Martha – answer me. Are you really in pain down your left arm? All right, all right, call the ambulance."

She hung up and now she was angry. "Oh shit, John. She's calling an ambulance. I have to go. She just drives me crazy. I should have never traveled with her. I always feel sorry for her and give in to her. I have to help her. If she's really having a heart attack, I'd never forgive myself."

"John, I'll give you my card and when you're back in Chicago please call me. I'd really like to see you again. You seem like such a nice man. I wish I'd gone to the séance with you. Also, I would have liked to have seen those fishing boats you told me about. There'll be no Martha in Chicago. I promise." She leaned over him and kissed his cheek. She pressed her cheek against his face, and in a moment she was gone.

He looked at her card.

Elyse Friedberg
143 Harbor Drive
Chicago, IL 60601

773-861-1421 Apt. 56-H

She'd forgotten her castanets. He could run after her and give them to her. Instead he'd just keep them and maybe return them to her in Chicago. He stuffed them into his jacket pocket.

10

He went back up to the room. His face in the elevator mirror seemed mottled and scabrous. Maybe it was just the dim light of the elevator or the blacking of the mirror had begun to fleck away. He took the castanets from his pocket and posed in front of the elevator mirror. "Just arch your back," she'd said. He tried a few clicks as the elevator ascended. He could combine them with a few Zulu tongue clicks, or better yet, some of Borge's tongue clicks. What would Victor Borge do with a pair of castanets? He'd build a whole act around them. The elevator door opened and he found his key and opened the door to his room.

The light was on. Leda was lying on his bed reading one of his books.

"Leda, how did you get in here?"

"The old man at the desk let me in. I told him I was your daughter."

"Well, get out. Get out now. I don't want you in here. I want you to leave."

"Where can I go? My landlady won't let me back in. I gave her the 300 kroner you gave me and she still won't let me in. She wants 4,000 kroner. She's got all my things locked up. Even my bird is locked away in my room. She's got a brute of a half-wit son, Mikos. He's locked up all my things, my clothes, my bird, my dishes, all my paints and brushes and my massage oils. Jonny, please help me. Jonny, give me another 3,700 kroner. I'll pay you back in a week, I promise. You can't be poor if you can afford to stay in this hotel and you have all these books and clothes."

"Give me that book, Leda." He reached for it and she held it away from him.

"No, it's very interesting to me. You have this page marked at this photo. I know this photo. My friend Iphigenia's father has the same photo in their home. This man here," she pointed to a figure of a young man holding a rifle in the photograph, "that's Iphigenia's father. He was a partisan in the last war." She pointed to the photograph of a young man wearing an armband guarding a group of women, moving them down the street. There were several men in the photo with rifles, all wearing the same armband. "Where did you get this book, Jonny? I swear this photo is the same photo. That man is Iphigenia's father. He has the photo framed on their mantelpiece."

He took the book out of her hands.

"What do you mean that man's your friend's father?"

"It's him, Iphigenia's father. Simon Braucivius. A very bad man. A drinker. A wife beater. He beat all of his children until one night Iphigenia attacked him with a heated rod from their fireplace. He left her alone after that. She took off as soon as she graduated from the gymnasium. Now she's in Riga with a husband and two children. Simon Braucivius lives across the street in Kaunas from my parents. Iphigenia's mother is gone, dead for years. Her sisters live in Poland. He lives there with some young whore who helps him drink up his pension and has a lover who is a police officer."

"Leda, I think you spin these fables like a little spider. You just exude this thread of fantasy and wrap it around everybody and everything at your will."

"Exude? What is that? Spin fables like a spider? I don't know what you mean."

"Iphigenia is a name right out of Euripides. You're a story teller."

"Thank you. To me, that is a compliment. We studied Euripides and now, I remember, we teased Iphigenia about her name. Her mother gave it to her. It's a beautiful name."

"This man, you say his name is Simon? He's still alive?"

"I don't know if he's still alive. I haven't been home for three years. He was alive when I left. He was just an awful man. I never spoke to him. Neither did my parents. When I was a child I was in Iphigenia's house all the time. We avoided him. He stayed mostly in his basement in his workshop with his shortwave radio. But the photograph of him is as a young soldier, a partisan. He was very proud of it. I'm amazed that you have it in your book. Where did you get such a book? A collection of photographs like that?"

"These men weren't Lithuanian partisans Leda. They were killers. Jew killers. The women they're herding down the street are Jewish women. They're leading them to their death. Probably to trucks that will take them to the Ninth Fort (IX Fort) or the Seventh Fort (VII Fort), the old czarist forts in Kaunas where the Jews were executed by the Germans and their Lithuanian helpers. Or maybe to Ponar, the forest outside of Vilnius. Probably not to Ponar. It would be too far. Do you know Ponar? Have you been there? Do you know the Seventh or Ninth Forts?"

She looked at the photograph again. "I know of the Ninth Fort. Everyone in Kaunas knows of that fort. I've heard of Ponar but I've never visited the forest there. Oh no, we went there once in a bus from the school. I remember now. You say these are Jewish women? That these Lithuanian men killed them? That is untrue."

"It is very true."

"There is a plaque at the forest in Ponar, I remember it, but it is in memory of those killed by the Communists, not in memory of Jews."

"So you don't think Lithuanians killed Jews? Who do you think these women in the photograph are?"

She held the photograph up to the lamp beside the bed.

"They are Lithuanian women. These men are saving them from the Germans. They're leading them to safety."

"That's what the man Simon told you? Your friend's father told you that?"

"Yes, he had a medal for that. Also in a case on the mantel. He and his fellow partisans. See the man in the beret standing beside the women directing them? I also knew him. He is dead, though. I know him to be dead. He was a friend of my father and taught English at the gymnasium. He taught me English. My father drank with him at the same tavern. He was a good man, a very kind man. He would never kill people. He would never hurt anyone."

"Do you see the armbands all the men are wearing?"

"Yes."

"They're all wearing the same armband, a tri-color. Perhaps the colors of Lithuania's flag. What are those colors?"

"Yellow, red and green, but I cannot tell. It's all gray in the photo."

He put the book back down on his dresser and pointed to the door.

"All right Leda, get out. Enough of the history lesson. These men weren't Jew killers, they were brave Lithuanian partisans. I want to go to bed and I want you out of here now."

"I won't go. I will only go if you give me 3,700 kroner. Give it to me as a loan or as a fee. I will even take you to Lithuania to Kaunas as your guide. I will show you where Simon Braucivius lives. I will introduce you to him if he's still alive."

"Leave before I pick you up and throw you out."

"Jonny, you would not do that to me," she laughed at him. "You're too much of a gentleman. Please give me the money. I will pay you. I promise. I swear I will repay you."

He thought of grabbing her ankles and pulling her off the bed and he put his hands around her ankles, but she kicked free and held onto the headboard and laughed again.

"You're not strong enough Jonny. No man is strong enough to push me around if I don't want to go. Except perhaps Mikos, the landlady's son. He's a moron and a real brute. You're not a brute. Also, you're not a moron."

He looked at her and decided she was right. If she resisted him there would be no way he could pull her off the bed and force her out of the room. But it would be worth 3,700 kroner just to get her out of his room.

"I'll give you the money," he said. "Stand up."

"I won't stand until you hand me the money. Put it in my hands."

He went to his suitcase and unzipped the compartment where he'd put the Danish money he'd changed. He'd changed $750 and he still had almost $600 in Danish currency. He counted out 3,700 kroner and dropped the bills down on her hands. She watched him drop the notes and when he finished she pulled his head down and kissed him full on the lips.

"Go now," he said to her. "Go."

"Don't be so harsh, Jonny Levine. See, I remember your name. I will go. I will contact you tomorrow though. I will make further arrangements with you. You will be paid."

She got up and walked to the door and she turned back to him and put her arms around him.

"You know, you still have that delicious scent, Jonny Levine. The odor of America. The allure of wealth, capitalism and great power. I am leaving. You will see. I will repay you. We will become great friends. You will learn to trust me." She stood in the corridor for a moment and then she was gone down the stairs.

Yes, he was a moron, a fool to have given her the money. He

turned all the lights out except the reading lamp over his bed and kicked his shoes off. He took the book and opened it to the marked photograph. The one of Jewish women being herded down the street by armed Lithuanian men. There was another photo of Jewish men being beaten to death by Lithuanian thugs wielding iron bars in a square in Kaunas. A crowd of Lithuanians and German soldiers were watching and laughing. There was another of Jewish men at the old fort in Kaunas. The Jewish men were standing in line on the abutments of the fort, pressed up against each other, their undershirts pulled up over their heads as hoods, moving forward toward a killing squad. He'd become obsessed with these photographs. He looked at the photograph of the women. There were about six Lithuanian men with rifles standing beside them. The man with the beret was the leader. He was the one Leda said had been her English teacher. He was holding a stick, like a whip, and was bending forward shouting orders at the women. The women were of all ages, young girls, mothers, grandmothers, children, simply dressed. The man she called Simon was to the right. He looked about twenty and he wore riding boots and an open-throated white shirt. It was summertime. The sun was on his face. A perfect, bland Slavic face. High cheekbones, Mongol eyes and showing no expression.

All the men with rifles seemed easily identifiable. He'd written several letters, one to his senator, another to his congressman, another to the American ambassador to NATO. A kind of Bellowian collection of letters. Right out of Herzog. Each of them answered him politely. Had these men ever been arrested and prosecuted, he'd asked in each letter. Had they ever been identified and made to stand trial for their crimes? Why admit Lithuania to NATO and to the European Union with these men, these killers of Jewish women, still walking around free? Why? The answers were all polite. Bureaucratic politesse. Inquiries would be made. He would be advised. Identities would have to be confirmed. These were events of over sixty years ago. Many of the accused were probably dead. Proofs would have to be established. His letter to the Simon Wiesenthal Foundation enclosing copies of each photograph was unanswered. He'd kept a copy of his letter in the book.

No answer. No response from Simon Wiesenthal. Only more solicitations for contributions from the Simon Wiesenthal Center. He'd sent them $100 with the photographs.

He'd tried to reach the president of Lithuania, Valdas Adamkus, a Chicagoan who'd returned to Lithuania after many years in America and was elected president. One of the professors in the history department, his friend, Marty Feinberg, went to a dinner in honor of Adamkus, but Marty, self-promoting Marty, did nothing. "It really wasn't possible, John," "It really wasn't propitious." Marty remained silent. Marty was a bull-shitter.

There was another photograph that he'd marked, but Leda had missed it. It was in a collection of pre-Holocaust photographs of Jewish children in Poland and Lithuania by the photographer Roman Vishniac. A photograph of a group of young Jewish boys and girls ages about twelve or thirteen, a group of young students standing in a doorway waiting for the school doors to open. They were all well-dressed. The girls wore dresses and knee stockings with sandals. Some had fashionable haircuts, mostly shorn on the neck and worn in a bob in the back. The boys wore shirts and ties. All the students were frozen in a moment, eating, talking, gossiping, waiting for the school to open. He would summon forth the photograph and the faces of the young students would be with him as he searched for sleep. Had they survived the holocaust? Was the photograph taken in Poland or Lithuania? What had happened to all these young Jewish students? Had they been killed? He would never know. But he had also brought the Vishniac book of photographs with him to Denmark. The two photographs were secretly etched into his memory, almost like crystalline etchings. The group of young students and the bland, remorseless, dead expression of the young Lithuanian man with the rifle.

It would be difficult, but tonight he would expunge the face of the man and call forth only the faces of the young students and try for sleep with only their faces haunting him. He would expunge Leda, Elyse Friedberg, the whirling dancer of the séance, Madame Josefina, Mooney Levine, the few paragraphs of his novel, the man in the beret, and the man with the rifle. He'd find the faces of the students standing on the stairs and they would remain with him and hopefully he would weave them into a dream where they would still be alive.

11

IN THE MORNING HE DRESSED and went down to the restaurant. It was empty except for one young waitress. He could smell the acrid odor of smoke.

She smiled at him and gestured to him to sit down and began to speak to him in Danish.

"I'm sorry I don't speak Danish. I'm American."

She immediately switched to English, but she had a Spanish accent.

"Sir, there was a small fire in the kitchen this morning. We are closed. I can only offer you coffee, tea, or toast."

She was quite lovely, slim with long dark hair. About twenty-five. Obviously not Danish.

"Where are you from?" he asked her.

"I'm from Argentina."

"Argentina?"

"Yes. Buenos Aires."

"What are you doing in Copenhagen?"

"My husband is here in medical school."

"Buenos Aires," he said. "I would love to go there.

"Yes, it is a beautiful city. May I help you sir? Tea or coffee?"

"Tea, please."

She poured gracefully. She wore a long black tapered skirt, a long black apron and had a silver cord attached to a cell phone sticking out of her rear pocket.

"Was anyone hurt? I didn't hear sirens or fire trucks."

"No. We did not want to alarm the guests. It was just a small kitchen fire, but it has shut down the kitchen. We are giving all guests a credit for breakfast. They have all gone off elsewhere."

"What did you do in Buenos Aires?"

"I am a musician. A pianist."

"And you play here?"

"No, I have no place to play. We have no piano in our flat. I go to concerts. Jeremy Menuhin, the son of Yehudi Menuhin, is quite a wonderful pianist. He is here this weekend in concert at the Tivoli Concert Hall."

"So you will go?"

"Yes, my husband and I have tickets."

"Is there someplace for breakfast around here that you could recommend?"

"I do not know. I'm not familiar with the neighborhood. I just come and go on my bicycle."

She reached into her apron pocket and unfolded a note. "Are you perhaps Professor J. Levin?"

"Yes."

"Well, then, this note is for you."

It was written in the neatly formed, looped calligraphy of a schoolgirl.

Professor J. Levin,

Sir, you are asked by your friend Mr. M. Levine that you be invited to be his guest for a breakfast at Y. Rabinowitz Delicatessen. Kindly go two blocks east, turn to your right on Hambrosgade. You will there see a portrait of a large fish in the window. That is indeed the place.

He took the note from her and her hand brushed his fingers. Should he add that to his list of hand-touchings? Why not a beautiful Argentine woman added to his list?

"Thank you," he told her, finishing the tea. I hope you get to play the piano again soon."

"I do too, sir. But even without the piano, Denmark is a lovely country. If I do not play here, still I can walk along the seaside and listen to the ocean. It makes music as it crashes against the rocks. I love to walk by the sea and listen. Those walks are my afternoon concerts."

"Thank you, *buena suerte*. Good luck," he said to her.

"Yes, *buena suerte*, it means have a good fortune. Thank you very much sir."

He glanced at the note and set it aside.

She returned to her station and picked up a newspaper and smiled again at him as he left. It was a Spanish-language newspaper, probably from Buenos Aires. He didn't notice the name. "La Prensa," was that a newspaper from Buenos Aires or perhaps Madrid? What did it mean, "La Prensa"? Could he name one Argentine writer? She was very beautiful. He was a soft touch for all these young women with their slim waists and graceful walks. She had a laughing melodic lilt to her speech. Jorge Luis Borges. He smiled. That was his Argentine writer. The poet, Jorge Luis Borges. Blind in his late years, he married a beautiful young woman. She was his consort, his escort, his helpmate, more than that she was his lover.

Borges lived in his ancient family home in Buenos Aires with his mother. The young beauty pulled him away from the old lady. Same as Chekhov who lived with his sister. Olga Knepper, the Moscow actress, pulled Chekhov out of that household. He read yesterday that Arthur Miller had died. Arthur Miller, 89? 90? Living with a beautiful 35-year-old, Bellow, how old was his muse, his wife, a former student. He wrote "Ravelstein" for her, one last burst of creative energy for his lovely young wife. And Jon Levin, alone in Denmark without a muse. Although, maybe he'd found one, Leda, the beautiful but crazy young swan who so adroitly separated him from his 2,700 kroner last night. He folded the note and put it in his pocket. He'd have to look her up and claim his massage. He walked out of the breakfast room through the lobby. No Dagne or Karen at the front desk to give him a white carnation. What would it be like to live each day with a Dagne or Karen? It would be extremely boring. They would soon stop handing him carnations. He had depleted his *pushkeh* last night by 2,700 kroner. He was becoming a foolish old man.

How old is Leda? Had she told him how old she was? 24, 26? The young women in the photograph on the staircase of the school. How old were they? The beautiful young women. The young women in that photograph standing on the front stairs of the school reading, gossiping, talking to the young men, waiting for the school doors to open, they were probably all in the ash. Or they were herded to some forest like Ponar and shot by drunken Lithuanian partisans after being forced to strip naked. So was he their redeemer? Should he go to Lithuania to find Simon Braucivius? Should he take a rifle from the shooting booth here in Copenhagen and with Leda as his companion, impress her with his shooting skill and put a bullet through the forehead of Simon Braucivius. He would wait for him outside the tavern, and as he staggered home, put two shots into his heart and one into his forehead. What was the Lithuanian word for Jew? *Zydu*? He knew it in Polish, *Zyd*. It would suffice. "*Ja jestem Zyd.*" "I am a Jew." He would stand up in the roadway as Braucivius staggered toward him, "*Ja jestem Zyd*," he would call quietly out to him and then slowly squeeze the trigger, two to the heart, one to the brain. There would be no prize, no wooden Royal Guardsman, no bust of Queen Margrethe. Maybe a feather. A red feather. He remembered another photograph. This one from the Holocaust museum's collection of photographs of the atrocities in Lithuania. It showed the scrawled word in Yiddish on a door in Kaunas. Just one word in Yiddish scrawled in the person's blood, "Revenge."

So instead of writing more letters to officials, he would simply go to Vilnius on SAS and then take a train to Kaunas. It wouldn't be that difficult.

12

HE FOUND THE DELICATESSEN with the inverted painted fish on the window on Hambrosgade. Y. Rabinowitz, Prop. 1953. Eight years after the war ended. A long counter, a short bucolic red-faced man arguing with a little old lady on her cell phone, ordering slices of corned beef. Was it Mr. Y. Rabinowitz who was muttering and slicing? The pungent odors of salami, tongue, corned beef, lox. There were even bricks of halvah. Mooney was right. A halvah emporium in Copenhagen only a few steps from the hotel.

"Professor," Mooney swiveled in his seat and called out to him. "Good to see you Professor. Sit down, join us. You're my guest. You know these two ladies."

One was Madame Josefina, dressed in her saffron Mother Theresa burka. The other was the bucolic angel-faced young Danish harem dancer who'd held the white chicken over his head.

"Madame, meet Professor Jonny Levin from Chicago. Same name as mine only without the 'e' at the end."

She looked up from her piece of smoked fish suspiciously. "I already met dot gentleman."

"And this young lady is Adelaide, my secretary and Madame's assistant."

Adelaide nodded shyly and replied in English, "How do you do, sir."

"You were the dancer last night," Jonny Levin said to her.

She blushed and looked down at her plate. She was eating a piece of smoked fish. Madame Josefina had finished her piece and only a fragile skeleton of the fish remained. Madame was wearing one silk glove on her right hand and she held the smoked fish skeleton up disdainfully and shook it. "You call this a smoked fish? A puny little piece of fish like dot? I call this *bupkes.* Not even enough to pick out your teeth with. This Y. Rabinowitz must be some kind of *gonif,*" she said looking over at the red-faced man in the yarmulke behind the counter. "If you want real smoked fish, come to Jerusalem. You'll see real smoked fish, not tiny little fake imposters so skinny they could hardly swim."

Mooney grabbed Jonny's arm, "Professor, I've got a deli joke for you." Mooney nodded at the little old lady on her cell phone pointing at cuts of meat.

"A little old lady comes to the butcher, 'I vant some corned beef.'

"The butcher stands in his apron holding the beef.

"How much, madam?'

"'Cut,' she said pointing to the side of the corned beef.

"He starts slicing and looks at her.

"'Cut,' she says again.

"He keeps slicing.

"'That one,' she says finally pointing.

"'That one slice? You want only one slice?'

"'I only want one slice from the middle. That one,' she said pointing and jabbing her finger.

"'Oy. *Gevalt,*' the butcher says.

"'One slice, that's all?'

"'One slice.'"

"How do you like that one Jonny? 'Cut,' she said."

"That's a good joke Mooney."

"How about this place, Professor? A real deli in Copenhagen. I told you, get yourself some halvah, maybe a piece of lox, bagels, cream cheese, wash it down with a chocolate phosphate."

"*Grepsvasser*," Madame Josefina said. "Only in chocolate yet. In Jerusalem, the *grepsvasser* is not drowned in chocolate."

Adelaide, the Madame's assistant, said nothing and ate nothing. She kept her eyes down and remained silent.

"Eat. *Fress* a little Adelaide. A young woman needs her energy. Butter a bagel. Have some cream cheese. Tonight we vill bring back Hans Christian Andersen and you will dance for him Adelaide."

"You will bring him back tonight? Hans Christian Andersen?" Jonny Levin asked her.

"Sure, vhy not? Hans Christian himself and maybe Jenny Lind vill sing for him. But dot Isak Dinesen is such a crybaby, always crying for her lost lover who smashed his airplane into the side of a mountain. Finch-Hatton. If her crying interferes, I won't find Finch-Hatton and she won't find the man with the big schnozz, Hans Christian. But maybe Jenny Lind, she will sing and find him." She buttered a miniature bagel for Adelaide and covered it with cream cheese. "*Fress* a little Adelaide. You will dance tonight like an angel. And maybe you will sing tonight too, like Jenny Lind. Drink some chocolate *grepsvasser*."

"Madame, I am a Professor of English literature in the United States. You spoke about the Singers, Isaac Bashevis and his brother Israel Joshua."

"Oy. The Singers. Vot a pair. They should have given the Nobel to my love Bruno Schulz, not to Bashevis. Dot Bashevis and his brother who used to sit up in the trees in Swider in Poland and write meshugana stories about yeshiva bochers. For that falafel they give the Nobel? What about his sister Hinde Esther? She vas the real writer in the family. Have you ever read her novel 'Deborah'? They did nothing for her, their sister, the Singer brothers. Nothing. Hinde Esther Kreitman. Vot a genius. No recognition. The vorld knows nothing about her. Only the two meshugana brothers, but Hinde Esther—ptuii," she spat a smoked fishbone into her plate. "*Bupkes*," she said. "*Bupkes* about Hinde Esther dot marvel of a woman writer of blessed memory."

"I read 'Deborah' and I don't think it's so great," Jonny Levin said to her. "It's the biography of her marriage. Rather crude, uneven, a typical first novel."

"Vot are you, some kind of literary critic? Vot do you know of the suffering of dot poor woman Hinde Esther? A forced marriage to some little diamond cutter from Amsterdam who took her to London and dumped her. There alone with her little boy she did needlework for rich English ladies to make a living and wrote her novel at night – 'Deborah' a masterpiece. Crude? Uneven? You sound like dot Cynthia Ozick who stole my Bruno's masterpiece and ripped the flesh from its bones and left only this," she held up the smoked fish skeleton. "May she choke on it, dot Ozick woman."

"You compare Hinde Esther Kreitman to Cynthia Ozick? Ozick is a great writer," Jonny Levin laughed. "No comparison." He remembered when Ozick came to Chicago last year with her husband Bernie. She read at Northwestern downtown from her new novel "Heir to a Glimmering World." He remembered sitting in the lecture hall listening to her, marveling at her ability, her magic with words.

"Professor, I've got news for you. Ozick thinks she stole Bruno's masterpiece, but he never wrote such a book, 'The Messiah'. Never. Ozick came to Jerusalem last year. Her audience even in Israel, a room full of yentas. Dot should be the title of her next book, 'A Room Full of Yentas', not 'The Messiah of Stockholm'. Vhich 'Messiah' she stole from my Bruno. How could he write 'The Messiah' when he was all the time teaching Polish children how to make furniture and birdhouses? After her marriage, Hinde Esther came to Swider from London with her baby boy to visit her parents and her brothers at the seaside. No one even spoke to her. The two brothers just stayed up in the trees like monkeys writing feuilletons. A monkey writing with a quill pen, not even a typewriter yet, could write better feuilletons than Bashevis or Israel Joshua. They did nothing for their sister and her baby boy. Nothing. They treated her like she was *trafe*."

Mooney Levine paid no attention to this literary discussion. He was busy cutting slices of halvah from a large beige brown block studded with nougats and he put a piece on each of their plates. "Ladies, and Professor, have some delicious halvah."

The Madame reached for a piece with a talon-like finger shooting out from her burka sleeve. "Not bad. Nice and smooth even with nuts yet. Give some to Adelaide."

"Here Adelaide dear," Mooney said to her, "it's like a Jewish sugar candy."

Adelaide daintily took a piece.

Madame Josefina suddenly stood up and daubed the crumbs of halvah from the corner of her mouth.

"Oy, my leg is throbbing so with sciatica. I see a taxi stand outside across the street. Adelaide, angel, go get us a taxi. Gentlemen, I vill see you tonight. Ve will unite Hans Christian with his lost love Jenny Lind and do more Shlogn Kapores with the white chicken which we have left in his cage back at the hotel with the drapes drawn. But I vill take the chicken some halvah. She reached for several pieces and wrapped them in a napkin.

She shook hands with each of them and took her cane and headed toward the doorway. Then she came back to the table and took two bagels from the bread basket and put them in her purse and left again calling, "Taxi, taxi."

"She's quite a lady," Jonny Levin said to Mooney.

"How did you like the séance last night professor?"

"The Madame is an actress and the young Danish woman who doesn't talk is a very talented dancer."

"No, she talks. She sings. She has a beautiful voice. She

speaks English. She's from the Danish academy. She's a country girl studying in Copenhagen. She's from Hans Christian Andersen's hometown, Odense. I got her as a part-time secretary for almost nothing. She's a dancer and chanteuse."

"You're like a father to her Mooney."

"You'd be more than a father to some of these Danish women, professor, if you'd spritz yourself with some of my cologne."

"She's the one who held the chicken over my head."

"That's not a real chicken professor."

"It has feathers. She gave me two white feathers."

"It's a rubber chicken with feathers. I bring them here from Coney. Every year I bring the Madame a rubber chicken with feathers for Shlogn Kapores."

"So who eats the halvah Madame brings to the hotel."

"Who do you think? Madame eats the halvah. A rubber chicken don't eat halvah."

"How can you transfer your sins to a rubber chicken?"

"You can't," Mooney said snapping his fingers for the check. When Y. Rabinowitz behind the counter paid no attention, Mooney caught a streak of sunshine coming through the window image of the inverted fish and flashed it with his ring into his eyes.

"You can't transfer your sins to a rubber chicken, professor."

13

THAT AFTERNOON JONNY LEVIN RENTED another bicycle and visited Constanza's house on Lakesgade (Mozart's wife Costanza married a diplomat after Mozart's death and lived in Copenhagen). He couldn't go inside, he just looked at the facade. It was a beautiful solid gray-stone home built like a London townhouse. It seemed that Costanza lived like a burgher while Mozart was left in a pauper's grave and forgotten. He rode back through Radhus Pladsen, the city hall square, and returned the bike. After lunch he took a tram out to the harbor to see The Little Mermaid. He got off at the Danish Resistance Museum, bought a ticket, went in, and looked at the exhibits and saw a display of the execution posts the Germans had used to execute members of the Danish Resistance. There were three wooden posts splintered at the tops by bullets. Also a glass case of letters written by 19 and 20 year olds to their mothers, "Dear Mother. Tomorrow I die at dawn for Denmark. I am not afraid."

Up the hill along the sea he walked to The Little Mermaid away from the Resistance Museum and stood at the edge of the harbor and watched the sun glisten off the statue. She was a sad, lonely figure. Alone on the rocks, welcoming ships into the harbor waiting for her love. His head was still filled with the voices of the young men in the letters, "Tomorrow I shall die at dawn. I am not afraid mother." He walked back down the hill. Far in the distance he saw the large gray building that had been the Gestapo headquarters. The British had bombed it during the war. He thought of walking all the way back to the hotel and began walking along Bredgade, the street of the tramline. He stopped at an art gallery. A smiling Danish woman artist greeted him in a full-flowered skirt and thong sandals. Her English was hesitant, but her abstract paintings were large acrylics with bursts of color. He felt better as he looked at the paintings. The voices of the young men gradually receded as he opened himself to the warmth of the colors of the paintings. He decided to eat an early dinner and return to the séance at eight to see if Madame Josefina could produce Hans Christian Andersen. He had nothing more compelling to do unless he would stay in the room to work on his novel. He thought of doing a section on Brodie Swartzschild, his grandmother, or he could eat dinner at Tivoli again and take a swan boat back to the same restaurant where he ate with Leda. He could order more herring with Carlsberg and Aquavit.

Instead he crossed Bredgade and ate his dinner at an old cellar restaurant named St. Petersburg. It was dark and there were only a few other customers, older couples. A woman owner, sad faced, hesitant, brought him a tankard of Carlsberg. He didn't ask for Aquavit. On the walls were photos in sepia of old Copenhagen scenes. Workers on the docks, horse and buggy traffic, large workhorses hauling barrels, sepia photographs of Tivoli dancing ladies in costume. After a dinner of Skate and boiled potatoes, he had coffee and then left the sad-faced woman owner a tip and gave up walking and took a tram back to the hotel.

At eight, he was seated in his navy blue jacket and an open throated white shirt at Madame Josefina's séance table.

14

AS HE SAT AT THE SÉANCE TABLE waiting for the Madame, he thought about the rubber chicken. Admittedly, one can't confess his sins to a rubber chicken and then slit its throat and give it away to the poor house. He'd seen the postcards from Warsaw of Orthodox Jews doing Shlogn Kapores with a white chicken over their heads on the eve of Yom Kippur. Also a photo in an album of Jerusalem photos, a photograph of a little girl grinning and covering her ears as her bearded father twirled a black chicken over her head at the poultry market.

Suddenly the lights dimmed, and the reedy, atonal Arab music began again. Adelaide entered the tent and whirled around the audience dressed as a harem dancer, barefoot with a silver bell anklet and arm bracelets and a tambourine that she was shaking. Again the essence of patouli filled the room. The music faded and Adelaide whirled back into the confession booth. The tent went dark and when the lights came up Madame Josefina was seated at the end of their table staring at them.

"Alright already," the Madame said thumping her cane once, "tonight we vill try again to contact the great Danish writer Hans Christian Andersen in the spirit vorld. Dot's assuming he vants to be contacted. And den ve will haf the beautiful Jenny Lind sing an aria to him, that's assuming her voice is recovered from the cold she has and a slight case of sinusitis.

"But all of this must be accomplished through the eyes of another medium and dot is the other great writer of Denmark, the woman writer, the Danish Hinde Esther Kreitman, the Baroness Blixen, Isak Dinesen." She thumped her cane twice.

"So hold your hands together and close your eyes. Spirits do not come to the table if anyone tries to peek at them. Close your eyes. Turn off your cell phones. Absolutely no cell phones. One cell phone buzzing or beeping and the séance will be ended. No cell phones in the spirit world.

"So now again, all eyes closed and I say – 'knock knock'.

"You say – 'who's dere?' and listen for a voice. All together now, 'knock knock'."

The people at the table answered "Who's there?"

She thumped her cane three times.

There was a voice, a tinny almost inaudible voice.

"Now all of you – say 'who's dere?' again. I hear a voice."

"Is that you again Bashevis? I hear you Bashevis. You should be ashamed to show your face here after vot you done to your poor sister Hinde Esther. Then you put a collection of your stories out dedicated to her. And the dedication reads 'to my beloved sister Minda Esther. You don't even get her name right. Such chutzpah. Four printings and still not correct. Vot a hypocrite. Chaim Grade's wife was right when she called you a writer who was writing only for dollars. In New York already, when Abraham Sutzkever was in Lithuania with the Jewish partisans in the woods writing his poems on birch bark.

"Knock, knock, I can't even hear you Bashevis –who - It's not Bashevis?

"'It's Henrik,' the voice said faintly.

"Henrik who? Speak up."

The scratchy whispered voice answered, "Henrik Ibsen."

"Henrik Ibsen who wrote 'A Doll's House', who vas in love with that housewife Nora dot he made a crazy woman?"

"The same."

"Henrik Ibsen, the Norseman?"

"That is me."

"Ve don't want no Norse writers here. Ve vant only Danes. Ve vant the greatest of all the Danes. Hans Christian Andersen. Have you seen him?"

"Yes I have seen him."

"Vhere?"

"With the Baroness Blixen at her grave at Helsingor behind her estate. They talk Danish together in the moonlight."

"Listen Henrik, ve have a deli here in Copenhagen. Ve can get you some good Norse lutefisk, the best. That dry fish, a real delicacy. It smells just like fjord moss. You tell us where to find Hans Christian. Ve don't vant the Baroness Blixen. Ve already dealt with her."

"In the same moonlight, you will find Hans Christian. My voice is fading. I am here with my darling Nora, but we have no glögg, no lutefisk, no fiske at all. Not even a tin of King Oscar sardines."

"Ve vill get you glögg, lutefisk, and King Oscar sardines."

"And open the tin for me? My fingers cannot roll the key to open the tin."

"Ve vill open the tin. Ve vill turn the key and open the King Oscar tin if you will open your mouth for us and tell us where to find Hans Christian."

No answer.

"Henrik?"

No answer.

"Henrik?"

Still no answer.

Madame Josefina thumped her cane four times.

"Henrik?"

Silence.

Music began to fill the tent and Adelaide appeared, slowly whirling while the Madame canted an ancient song in a language unknown and then the lights went up.

"Alright folks, dot's it. The best I could do. I got some mashugener Norseman, dot playwright Henrik Ibsen. A Norseman instead of a Dane and even with lutefisk and sardines promised to him I couldn't tempt him to bring to us Hans Christian Andersen from the spirit world. So my assistant Adelaide dances alone and the séance is now over. Those of you who vant a private session wit Madame, come to the tent over there and bring 200 kroner. And ve vill give you a private session. Und so, I say goodnight to all of you. Farewell to Denmark, a brave little country the only one who helped the Jewish people. May all your lives be filled with good fortune. If any of you come to Jerusalem, take one of my cards from my assistant and call my studio." She stood up. "And so to you and Copenhagen, I say *gai gesunt*. Go in good health. *Stark vi a hundt*. Stay as strong as a dog."

The lights went down and Madame Josefina limped into her private confessional. Adelaide twirled in after her, stopping to face the audience and in her soft voice, translated Madame Josefina's farewell message into Danish.

Mooney came over to the table, "Professor, you're number one, get in line."

The line was already forming of ruddy-cheeked Danish families, some of the men in shorts and sandals. The women wearing cable-knit sweaters.

"I forgot to ask you Mooney, did the two girls at the desk show at the casino?"

"Dagne and Karen? No, they didn't show. They both sing in a church choir and last night they had some kind of concert. They should have come because I was a big winner at blackjack." He reached into his pocket and showed Jonny a large roll of Danish kroner bills. "I think I'm up at least a thousand US. I don't know because I just put some of it down on two horses at Gulfstream and Hialeah. I've got two beauties running there today. I own and train horses Jonny, and name them after my carousel horses. I've got Hamlet and Ophelia running today. Hamlet at Gulfstream and Ophelia at Hialeah. Each at 8-to-1 and I'm down on both of them probably for 500 on the nose each. I've got my laptop in the room and I place my bets through a consortium in the Bahamas."

Adelaide appeared before them and touched Jonny on the shoulder, "The Madame will see you now sir."

"Listen Burchik, you want part of the action? I'll put a C-note on each of them for you. You're a professor of literature. Bet on the names. I'll lay off 200 on you."

Why not? 200 on two doomed lovers via the Internet. Maybe his luck would change. "Okay, Mooney, bet 200 I'll pay you at the hotel."

"You got it professor."

He walked into the tent and the Madame was again seated with her foot up on a cushion drinking water.

"Ah, the literary critic. The man who loves Ozick. You're number one in line again. Give your money to Adelaide and give me your right hand. I already know you've got a head full of nonsense."

"No I don't want my fortune told. You've already told my fortune, Madame."

"I remember your hand, so silky smooth. Not a working man's hand. My Bruno's hands were calloused, that's why he was such a great writer. He knew vot it was to labor with his hands, to build things, little tables with the children in his class, chests of drawers, mitred so tightly they were like treasure chests. Drawers that closed so smoothly like Pandora's box. So you're a writer, but not with these hands. Go out and plant something, like wildflowers. Something beautiful. You can make headbands of wildflowers, sell them from a little stand in front of your house with your books. Where do you live in America? People don't buy books no more in America, but they still may buy flowers."

"I live in Chicago, but I have only one request. I think you did find Hans Christian Andersen tonight. I think I know where he is. If you let Adelaide come with me for only half an hour I'll take her to him and she can sing Jenny Lind's aria for him."

"Adelaide has a cold tonight. She don't sing so well. She looks just like Jenny Lind, though. Look at that blonde *punnim.* Those braids. How she blushes. She is a double for Jenny Lind. Maybe if I gif Adelaide some lingonberry tea she will sing tonight, but if you vant Adelaide, mister, you must pay rent for her."

"Rent?"

"Sure rent. You think I let Adelaide out at night to take a walk with you for nothing? Five hundred kroner for thirty minutes of Adelaide."

Did he have five hundred kroner left in his *pushkeh*? "Do you take dollars?"

"Sure I take dollars, but they're not so good anymore. Too many wars you Americans make. Too many bombs you drop. War and bombs cost money."

"Five hundred kroner is fifty dollars. Here's fifty dollars." He removed a crinkled folded bill from his *pushkeh.* The Madame held the bill up to the candlelight and inspected it. "U.S. Grant looks Jewish, I heard he vas a Jewish general like Sharon but not so fat, skinny and mean."

"Okay mister, Adelaide, honey, go with this gentleman from America." She shot her watch out from under her sleeve. "Thirty minutes only Adelaide. Drink some more lingonberry tea from dot teapot and go with that gentleman. If he's a friend of Mr. M. Levine's he must be okay. But don't vorry, honey, I vill haf one of the guardsmen follow you and stand always in the shadows behind both of you – go already. Tell the next person in line to come in and turn that Arab music off. It's making me crazy."

Adelaide and Jonny Levin made an unusual twosome as he led her down the flowered paths of Tivoli to the main gate. She shyly told one of the guardsmen that the Madame requested that he follow them. When this was confirmed, a very polite, tall young Danish guardsman in a bearskin shako and with crossed white belts on his coat followed them as they crossed Hans Christian Andersen Boulevard.

"Where are you taking me sir?"

"I am taking you to meet Hans Christian Andersen."

"Do you know where he is?"

"Yes."

"And where is that?"

"Henrik Ibsen said Hans Christian Andersen would be waiting in the moonlight."

"Yes."

"So if you will just follow me Adelaide, I'll lead you to him."

She walked a pace behind him. "Do you know sir that I am also from Odense, the birthplace of Hans Christian Andersen? I am just a country girl trying to make my way in Copenhagen. A student at the dance academy. Andersen was a poor boy from Odense. He came to Copenhagen to become an actor."

He led her across the boulevard to the huge statue of Andersen. Andersen was seated with his head tilted toward Tivoli. He wore a top hat and held a Malacca cane on his lap.

"Adelaide, who is that man? Do you know who he is?"

"It is Hans Christian Andersen I believe sir. I have seen this sculpture from a distance, but I have never approached it."

"It's a wonderful portrait of Andersen. Now I'll leave you and stand back in the shadows with the guardsman. I want you to sing your Jenny Lind aria. She was his great love, The Swedish Nightingale. And you look just like her Adelaide. I want you to sing for him. I promised myself that I would bring Jenny Lind to him to sing in the moonlight." He left her and stepped back and stood in the shadows with the guardsman. Adelaide stood alone in front of Andersen. She slowly began to unpin her hair. It fell softly on her shoulders. She held her hands clasped down in front of her, looked up at Andersen and cleared her throat and then began to sing the Jenny Lind aria "Svenska Flicka". It was a story of a young Swedish girl in love. Her eyes were glistening and beginning to fill with tears and at the end of the aria, she bowed, holding the edges of her skirt and then went over to the statue and touched Andersen's hand.

So he had kept his promise and had brought Jenny Lind back for a moment to the great Danish faery tale-meister. He shook Adelaide's hand and bowed his head to her and the guardsman. "*Tak*, Adelaide," he said to her. "Thank you very much."

He then walked back to the hotel and sat on the edge of the bed with his notebook and added the following paragraph to his novel:

KAENE MAESCHE SWARTZSCHILD

> I've recently read Amos Oz's "A Tale of Love and Darkness" and he spent pages and pages on his grandfather. Oz describes his grandfather's clothes, the details of his childhood, his old loves, his voice, his speech patterns, even that the grandfather often called Oz as a young boy, "Bed-wetter." My work seems weak compared to Oz. I haven't really captured my grandfather Maesche Swartzschild. The blue Masonic ring he wore, it was enameled blue on the sides with

a large diamond inset in gold in front. The Masonic emblems were etched on the sides. Did the second wife really bury him wearing his Mason's ring or did she take it off his finger? I don't know. The ring disappeared with Maesche. And his hair. I know I really haven't described his hair. Maesche had a full head of white hair, even into his eighties. It was dark brown or black when he was young. He was very proud of his hair. It was healthy, lustrous hair. He washed it all the time, shampooed it, and conditioned it with fragrant oils. He had a healthy pink scalp line. He looked like a banker or professor. He wore gray suits, always a white handkerchief in the breast pocket. He wore glasses, usually metal framed or framed with a natural clear plastic. He always smelled of cigars. He insisted on a schnapps the moment he came home from work. A shot glass of schnapps and a glass of water. When he finished you never knew if he would be pleasant or in a dark angry mood shouting orders at everyone. Most of all he was a salesman, a bulldog of a salesman from the old school who would harass and annoy his customers until they bought. They feared his coming. He was a pest. He wouldn't take no for an answer. And he was a gambler in business and in life. A winner and a loser, a streak gambler. When he won he took his family to the Roney Plaza in Miami Beach or to the Ambassador in Los Angeles. This was in the '20s and early '30s before the Depression. They all rode the 20th Century Limited to New York. His wife and children were always beautifully dressed. They had servants and owned buildings. This poor boy from Poland with the beautiful voice of a cantor, this Maesche, this wild, wild Maesche, who as he grew old had lost everything, but never quit on his American dream. Who was buried, who knows, with his Masonic ring on or off his finger? El Moley Rachamim. Kaene Maesche Swartzschild.

15

Before going down for breakfast in the morning, I read my work from last night. It wasn't so bad. Certainly not as descriptive as Oz's work, but not too bad. I'm beginning to actually hear Maesche's voice. I can hear him saying other words than "dassn't", but I can't make them out. I can hear his voice, but I can't make out the words. I can even hear him singing at the Seder table, holding up his wine glass, and beginning to sway and sing. I hear him singing in a low mournful voice, the wine glass glistening in the candlelight. I hear the words forming in Hebrew, a solemn cantorial prayer, Maesche toasting all the relatives at the table as he sings, bowing his head and lifting his glass to each of them.

What I wrote last night was about as good as I can do. I'm definitely not in Oz's league. There's another Israeli writer, David Grossman, *See Under: Love.* Grossman is younger than Oz. If he was thirty-five in 1989 when *See Under: Love* was published, "the leading Israeli writer of his generation" (or something like that) on the back cover flap, he must be in his early fifties now. Not so bad at thirty-five to have a Farrar, Straus & Giroux novel in English translated from Hebrew. On the back cover, a full photo of Grossman covering the entire back cover. He's wearing a sports coat and a polo shirt. A very sad face, almost no expression, curly dark hair, very studious looking and bland. With the large glasses he looks like a young version of Menachem Begin if Begin had curly hair. Begin at thirty-five with curly hair and a magical novel under his belt instead of a pistol.

Momik, a nine-year-old boy is the narrator of Grossman's *See Under: Love.* Momik Neuman, the only child of Holocaust survivors, very much a precocious, shy, literary child like Oz's child narrator. Momik's grandfather, Anshel Wasserman is a little bearded old man suddenly delivered by an Israeli ambulance service to the doorstep of Momik's family in Jerusalem. They thought he was long dead in the camps. Momik is entrusted with his care after school while Momik's parents run a lottery booth a few blocks away from which they barely make a living. Momik is determined to make Grandfather Wasserman speak and tell about his life. He does speak, but only in constant gibberish, no one can understand him. He has a number tattooed on his arm and Momik tries to use cabalistic combinations of the numbers that he calls out in different sequences to unlock his grandfather's secrets. He wants a younger, vital grandfather to appear to tell his grandson the story of his life, so he chants the number combinations of his grandfather's tattoo hoping that his grandfather's body will unzip and a younger, refreshed man, a new grandfather, will step out of the frame of his ancient grandfather and tell Momik about his life. But it doesn't happen. The old man only responds with more gibberish.

David Grossman also writes a chapter in the novel on Bruno Schulz that he calls "Bruno." I should have remembered that and offered up Grossman's version of Schulz to Madame Josefina when she was berating Cynthia Ozick. Grossman's Schulz escapes Drohobycz and makes his way to Gdansk on a train that is forbidden to Jews. He has his novel *The Messiah* hidden in a suitcase. On the run from the Gestapo, he walks out on a pier in Gdansk and sheds his clothes, leaves his suitcase with *The Messiah* on the pier and gently lowers himself into the sea. He begins swimming and when a patrol boat spots him and turns to come after him, he transmogrifies into a fish. Grossman turns Bruno Schulz into a fish that loses itself forever in the cosmos of the ocean. A fish that later reappears on land and produces for Momik not the lost novel but the real Messiah who suddenly magically appears riding a gray donkey down the street. Momik the child narrator witnesses all of this.

I didn't turn my grandfather Maesche Swartzschild into a fish. Maybe I should have. I remember he was a great lover of gefilte fish with purple horseradish. If he had met Bruno Schulz or even the Messiah riding on a gray donkey he would have tried to sell each of them an insurance policy. The only person who could calm Maesche Swartzschild, either with her soothing voice or the touch of her hand brushing a lock of his hair off his forehead or by offering schnapps, or by a folded apricot powdered sugar pocket, or by a helping of gefilte fish with the purple horseradish, that person was my grandmother Brodie Swartzschild and before I go downstairs for breakfast this morning, I want to think about her for a moment.

KAENE BRODIE SWARTZSCHILD

Before I tell about Brodie Swartzschild I will make one other point. Both Oz and Grossman's grandparents spoke Yiddish. They also spoke Polish and in Oz's novel the grandfather also spoke Russian. Both writers interspersed their dialogue with Yiddishkeit like "*nu* and *choloria*" and "*nebuch*" or "*pshakrev*". I have no idea what "*nebuch*" or "*pshakrev*" means. I think "*choloria*" may mean "bad omen". Grossman will write a piece of dialogue, "I remember the marble statue of Jagiello in the square in Kirov, *nebuch,*" or "he died in the camps, killed by the Nazi's (may their names be blotted out), *choloria* and his son moved to Haifa and, *nu*, became a candymaker." My grandparents didn't talk like that. They didn't speak Yiddish. If they spoke any other language than English I wasn't aware of it. Brodie, my grandmother, was born in Chicago. Maesche was born in Poland, but was brought here as an infant. I know nothing about their parents, who they were, when they came here, or what their names were.

My grandmother, Brodie, did occasionally embellish her speech with two Yiddishisms. One was *umbeshrien* which means "G-d forbid." The other was *Gutenkeh* (phonetic). I don't know what it means. It may be German, it may mean "G-d in heaven." "He should only grow up to be a professor, *Gutenkeh*, and not get married *umbeshrien* before he finishes school." I only remember those two phrases. No, one more, *Keppe* or *Keppeleh*. "Did you hurt your poor little *Keppe* (head)," usually accompanied with a kiss to the forehead or with a cold, wet washcloth.

KAENE BRODIE SWARTZSCHILD

Okay. No. I've changed my mind. I'll do a paragraph on Brodie later. Also some of the faces of my young loves are beginning to appear. I can't deal with them before breakfast. I haven't even showered. I don't think I can build a novel by trying to recreate my grandparents. Oz and Grossman can do it, even in translated Hebrew. I can't do it. I should stop trying.

But before I leave I want to add one more item. Grossman didn't have Bruno Schulz leave the manuscript of *The Messiah* on the pier in Gdansk. I was wrong about that. Before Bruno went out on the pier, he'd been to an art gallery to see a Munch exhibition. He wanted to see Munch's famous painting "The Scream" so he walked into the exhibition, also strictly forbidden, a Jew attending an art exhibition. Grossman's Bruno was so overcome viewing the painting he in a sense became the figure in the painting and as he approached the pier and the ocean he became the figure in "The Scream". It is in this state of frenzy that he undresses and lowers himself into the sea. Almost as if the whirling figure of "The Scream" had developed scales and merged with him to enter the sea. The manuscript of *The Messiah* wasn't left on the pier in Gdansk, it was left in the cloakroom of the art gallery. Whether he'd forgotten about it or left it there intentionally, I don't know.

16

HE WENT DOWNSTAIRS FOR BREAKFAST. No one was in the breakfast room. No sign of the beautiful Argentine waitress, just a tall, apple-cheeked, young Danish man wearing a black bow tie who brought him tea, toast, and marmalade and brought him a tray of cheeses and cold fish, salmon and herring. The young man didn't speak English well, but gave him the Herald Tribune. On the first page both the Pope and Saul Bellow were dead. A photo showed the Pope's body being carried across St. Peter's Square. Bellow dead at 89. Now he felt sorry that he called Bellow a desiccated cocksman. Was that in his novel? He didn't think so, that was just in his head, a scrap of interior monologue. Interior monologue comparing Bellow and Singer, the two Nobelists, to Phillip Roth, who keeps rewriting "The Grapes of Roth" and will never win a

Nobel. Oh don't say that Jonny Levin. Don't speculate on what Roth might or might not do, he could surprise all of us. But Bellow dead at 89, who does that leave? Only Roth and Mailer of that generation. All the rest, dead. The Pope and Bellow, what a strange combination to be united in death.

What would he do today? He didn't know. He could rent another bicycle? It was a gray day. He could get on a train and visit Louisiana, the art museum up the coast up near Helsingor north of Copenhagen. It was supposed to have a very nice modern collection with Henry Moore sculptures in the courtyard. That was hardly a reason to get on a train, a courtyard full of elongated, pinhead torsos of Moore figures, but he could combine a trip to the gallery with a visit to Isak Dinesen's home and see her African paintings and visit her grave. Not really more compelling than the Moore figures. Or he could take the ferry from Helsingor across to Sweden and trace one of the routes the Danish fisherman took when they ferried the Jews out of Denmark to Sweden. He even thought of hiring a fishing boat and asking the captain to let him go down into the hold and go across with the hatch closed to see what it felt like. Or even ask the captain to cover him with a layer of fish and let him travel across under a covering of fish like some of the Jews. Why do it though? Why put himself through an ordeal like that? Why not just forget the bike, call a cab, and look for Leda's apartment and pay her a visit. Maybe collect on her promise of a massage. He had a massage promised for three hundred kroner. Now he had a credit with her of four thousand kroner. That would buy thirteen day's worth of massages and certainly would be better than covering himself with a layer of fish and hiring a boat to take him to Sweden. Although maybe one of the fish would know of Bruno Schulz and would let him in on the secret of where Bruno had hidden the manuscript of *The Messiah*.

All this amused him as he left the breakfast room and saw Mooney Levine and Madame Josefina seated in the lobby.

"Hey professor. Come say goodbye to the Madame. We're waiting for the airport limo. Your horses came in professor, both of them winners. Two little beauties. Both of them at 8-1, a C-note on each. I've got sixteen hundred in my pocket for you. A nice little score. I think I won almost 15 thousand American."

Madame Josefina barely extended her hand to him and immediately began talking. "So the Pope is dead. A nice man, the Pope, *avelesholem*, but I've got news for you. They'll blame his death on the Jews. They'll claim that Jewish Cardinal from Paris, Lustiger, poisoned the Pope. Put poison in his holy water. In his *grepsvasser*. Like they still blame the Jews for the death of *Jushke* (Jesus). Saul Bellow and the Pope. Both dead. Bellow vas such a little *pipek*. He liked his fancy clothes. A fancy man. Not a brave soldier like our Israeli writers. A man who bought his shirts in London, how can you compare such a fancy little man to Yehoshua, to Oz, to Yehuda Amichai? All soldiers, not little sissy boys vith a head full of *goyischer* philosophies. Like Nietzsche, like Heidegger, or like Kierkegaard, another Danish prune-face. No one understands or cares about them. They should just put Bellow in the wooden box instead of the Pope. *Avelesholem*. Then the world vill have a dead Jewish Pope and he vill be the messenger for *Jushke*. Bellow, the little *pipek*, vill be *Jushke*'s messenger like Peter, a Jew, vas the first Pope. A Jewish Pope. *Jushke* vas nothing but an ordinary Jewish boy who wore sandals and vas a carpenter like his father Joseph and like my Bruno who could make the mitred boxes. *Jushke* vas a good carpenter, but the Son of G-d, the Messiah, that he vasn't. It's all a fairy tale. The virgin birth, the Pope in his box with the red shoes and the pointed hat and the shepherd's crook. All fairy tales. Hans Christian Andersen wrote better fairy tales than the Jews who wrote the Bible. Peter, Paul, Matthew, and Luke, really just a bunch of Jewish fairy tale tellers like Bashevis and his brother. And look vot happened. The whole world believed them and six million were butchered because the *goyim* still believe *Jushke* was the Messiah and was crucified by the Jews. *Jushke* vas nothing but a poor Jewish boy from Nazareth. He couldn't even keep his pants up. He vas just a poor boy, not a *kopeck* to his name. He wore a dress, not even a girlfriend, unless you call that Mary Magdalene a girlfriend, the one who washed his feet with her hair. I've got more news for you. Come to Jerusalem and visit me in the Souk. Ve can have another séance. I'll really give you something to write about, mister. I'll bring back *Jushke* and Mary Magdalene and see what they have to say. Let them tell the world that they are lovers and have been together in the afterworld. That *Jushke* vas not the Son of G-d, he vas just a Jewish *nebbisher* vith long hair who vas skin and bones and who died. They made him say he vas the 'King of the Jews'. There vill never be a 'King of the Jews'. We, the Jews, don't vant no king. We don't want no queen, like Camilla. The Jews don't need a Camilla in Jerusalem. There's my limo. Mister Levine, carry my bag please and my *grepsvasser* and I'll say goodbye once and for all to Copenhagen. To you vith the silky smooth hand who vants to be a writer like Bellow and the Pope, look vot happened to them, they're both in boxes. Get out of Copenhagen, go find yourself a lady and have a good time, while you're still alive. If you can't find one here, come to Jerusalem and I'll send you to a matchmaker. A real *yenta*. She'll find you someone." She shook his hand and limped away to her limo.

Mooney Levine came back after seating her in the back seat.

"The Madame is one crazy chick, you don't need no *yenta*. Just give yourself a spritz of my after-shave. The Danish women will really be hot for you."

Madame Josefina suddenly got out of the car and limped back

into the lobby. Her eyes were glistening and she thumped her cane twice.

"Listen, before I leave, I got more news for you. That little *Schmendrick*, the shepherd from Mecca, Mohammed, he vas also a nothing. Vot kind of messenger rides a phony horse vit wings to heaven to meet Moses and Jesus and rides back down again? Son of Abraham? How old vas Abraham? 101? He had over a thousand sons, none named Mohammed. So maybe the Muslims in Jerusalem vill come to the Souk and slit my throat. I'm not afraid. Let them come. I'm an old lady. Did dey get that nutcase Salman Rushdie who dey put out a Fatwah on? Not a hair of his head vas touched. Rushdie is still walking around scribbling. Do you think those are the footsteps of Mohammed's winged horse by the name of Burak on the stone in the Dome of the Rock vot horse *Schmendrick* supposedly rode to heaven to consult with *Jushke* and Moses? Should ve fight a war over dot rock and dose footsteps? Let the Palestinians have dot rock. Vot do ve care about Allah and *Schmendrick*, all of which never happened and is just an excuse like *Jushke* for the whole world to make war on the Jews. Like Bellow, Mohammed vas just a little *pipek* and his horse didn't have no wings."

Madame limped back to the limo, got in the back without help and tapped on the driver's shoulder with her cane. She lifted her bottle of *grepsvasser* to her lips, waved goodbye, and was sped off to the airport.

"Well, we got another lecture, professor, from the Madame. I don't listen to her for a minute. She's great running a séance, but when she's off the stage, she's a pain in the *toches.*"

"She forgot the Buddhas the Taliban blew off the cliff walls in Afghanistan. She could have given us a little something on idols and graven images."

"I remember photos of those Buddhas, professor. They

looked like sumo wrestlers with no hands or feet. They just blew them off the walls. I think Bin Laden and his boys did it, then he went underground."

"The Madame and Osama would make an interesting pair. We could use her as a secret weapon. She'd nag him to death and he'd come out of hiding and surrender."

"Listen, I don't want to forget the money for you." Mooney reached into his pocket and flashed a large roll of hundred dollar bills. He wet his fingers and counted out sixteen and handed them to Jonny. "I've got two more little beauties running tonight, same tracks. Hialeah and Gulfstream. Desdemona and Romeo."

"An interesting combination."

"You should get down on them. They're each 15-1. I'm in for a grand on both of them. I'll lay off two hundred on you, just like last night. You'll pick up another three grand if they win. If you don't, you're still way ahead."

"I'll bet another two hundred, one hundred on each. Romeo and Desdemona."

"Listen, professor, you could hit big. I think you're a lucky guy. You bring me *mazel.* You know what I mean? Take your winnings from last night and blow it on some of these beautiful Danish broads. I've never seen so many gorgeous blonds in my life. Believe me, you don't need no *yenta.* I've got to go. I promised to meet some customers this morning. If you want to go to the casino tonight at the SAS Radisson, call me at my room about six. Anyway, *burchik*, it's a pleasure to give money to a winner like you. It's like a *mitzvah* for me to give money to an educated man. I never got past grammar school, but I'm good with money and horses. Also you bring me *mazel.* You know what *mazel* is, luck. You bring me luck. An educated man, a professor, as my partner. I can't believe it."

Mooney turned to leave then turned back. "Here's one more joke for you before I leave.

"Ira Gershwin and Michael Feinstein are having a rehearsal for a Broadway show.

"A young lady steps out on the stage and hands her music to the piano player.

"'Okay Miss Levine (Leveen), whenever you're ready,' Ira says to her. She nods at the piano man and looks out across the footlights and then begins to sing.

"'You say potato, and I say potato (both pronounced the same way).

"'You say tomato, and I say tomato (again, both pronounced the same way).

"'Potato – Tomato –'

"'All right Miss Levine (Leveen), all right,' Ira says to her, 'thank you very much Miss Levine. If we want anything further, we'll be in touch with you. Thank you Miss Levine (Leveen).'

"She turns and gets her music back from the piano man and stands and peers out again over the footlights.

"'That's LA-VINE,' she says and walks off the stage.

"How do you like that professor? 'That's LA-VINE', she says. I love that joke. It's a great joke. 'That's LA-VINE."

"That's a good one Mooney, but I don't think Michael Feinstein and Ira Gershwin ever worked together. They're different generations."

"Okay, professor, so I'm a *schmuck*. Maybe it was Bobby Short. Did you ever catch Bobby Short at the Carlisle? What a showman. I just heard he died. I used to drink at the bar at the Carlisle, Bemelman's. Next time you're in New York, I'll buy you a drink there. I'm out of here. You're down for a C note each on Romeo and Desdemona. If I can, I'll also bet them as a Double. I'll credit you for twenty percent of the Double or I'll wheel them and put you down for twenty percent of the wheel. I've got fifteen grand to play with. I'll be back at six. Come to the casino with me and we'll invest our winnings."

"Mooney, thanks for the money. If I can make the casino I'll be in the lobby at six, but don't wait for me, I've got some things I have to do. I don't want you to wait for me."

Mooney pressed his knuckles to Jonny's and headed toward Hans Christian Andersen Boulevard and Tivoli. Jonny sat down on a bench near the hotel in a spot of sunlight and half turned his back away from the street and counted his winnings. Sixteen new one hundred dollar bills. He folded over one edge of each bill so they wouldn't stick together. A trick he'd learned from his father. He then stuck the roll of bills deep into his right trouser pocket. His father always carried a roll of new hundreds. The salesmen who worked for his father also always carried their money the same way, but they didn't have hundreds. Only the top bill was a hundred. His father had a name for that kind of roll, a false roll. He couldn't remember the name. It was Chicago slang.

In the spot of sunlight he tried to see his father's face. He couldn't see him as clearly as Maesche. Maynard Levin, his father, a successful auto parts executive. Owner and founder of an auto supply company on the west side of Chicago. He smoked a pipe. He looked like a lawyer or a banker. Pale. Autocratic. A thin boned face, slight brown hair. He looked like a German or Austrian Jew, but he was actually Lithuanian, and had been educated by his parents at the University of Chicago as a pre-med student, but he dropped medicine for business. Maynard broke his father Meyer's heart when he took a job with Ford right out of the university. The first Jew hired by Ford in Chicago at its Torrence plant. He worked his way up to become the manager of parts inventory at Torrence and then he left and opened up his own small warehouse in Hammond. Later he moved to Chicago's West Side. He drove the expressway from Glencoe on the North Shore to the West Side every day of his working life. Twenty-five miles in and out in choked traffic. "Kaene Maynard Levin," his father, "*tak fir alt.*" He was always dressed in a dark suit, an expensive tailored suit, a daily brushed fedora, a beautiful silk tie usually from Brooks Brothers or Sulka. A strict, but elegant and circumspect man, who raised his son and daughter in a lovely home on the North Shore, two blocks off the lake in Glencoe. The daughter, Ruth Levin, ten years older, was an ivory-faced beauty like her mother, and a graduate of Scripps in California. She died at twenty-eight from a rare leukemia. She looked like a large porcelain doll in a silk dress in her casket. His parents were broken. Maynard and Elaine Levin, his beautiful graceful, artistic mother, "Kaene Elaine Levin, *tak fir alt.*" She was broken completely by her daughter's death. She changed from a vivacious woman into a sad, crumpled, silent figure who spent her mornings in bed in her dressing gown and drank wine alone in the evenings with TV, her husband always also alone in his den with his pipe and books and magazines. By then the house had emptied and eighteen year old John Levin was away first in Champaign studying in an honors English program, then in Ann Arbor in a Master's English Literature program. After that an instructor's position at Northwestern in Evanston that lead eventually to tenure and a full professorship.

Both of his parents were dead. The house in Glencoe sold long ago. His inheritance reduced by his first divorce and the education of his two daughters to less than three hundred thousand in a trust fund with a Chicago bank and provided only three percent annually, about nine thousand dollars. His salary as a professor was $95,000. Even with the additional income from his father's estate, after taxes and the girls' tuition loans which he was paying, it was hard for him to come out ahead though he was a good money manager. Sandra began at Stanford and then transferred to Berkeley; and Alysia, the younger daughter, went to Middlebury and then Yale. They were both fine students. Sandra was now in Los Angeles as an assistant curator at the Los Angeles Museum of Natural History. Alysia was in New York as an instructor in Women's Studies at NYU in the Village. Both of them were unmarried, but each was living with a man. He loved them both, but had seen each of them only once in the past year—once in LA for Sandra's birthday and another time in New York for a quick visit with Alysia. He'd promised them postcards from Denmark. Postcards to his daughters. He took a pen from his pocket and wrote that down on the first page of a small notebook—"Postcards to Sandra and Alysia", then he put his pen and notebook back and stood up from the bench and with the last vision of his father's face floating away from him, he started back to the hotel.

Why was he doing this to himself? Why was he constructing a family history? Was it really necessary for his novel? If he inserted each member of his family into the novel, he'd never finish. He'd just bore the readers, Kaene Maynard Levin, Kaene Elaine Levin, Kaene Ruth Levin, Kaene Sandra Levin, Kaene Alysia Levin. "*Tak fir alt.*" He could send a postcard to each daughter telling her that even though they were still alive he had constructed a small headstone for each of them in his bizarre little cemetery in Copenhagen. They would each have two tiny doves peeking over the corners of their gravestones. Beside them would be the stone he created for his sister, Ruth. Would his rather effete daughters consent to be buried in a small cemetery in Copenhagen with their grandparents and their Aunt Ruth? He could arrange that for them by postcard. But he would have to exhume his parents and his sister and bring them to Copenhagen. That would cost a fortune. What about his own stone? Kaene Jonny Levin. Where should he build that? Also in Copenhagen? Where else? He should put his own stone in Chicago., but the name would be John Levin, not Jonny Levin, and there'd be no "*tak fir alt*" and no trellis of doves, but in his novel, he'd set his stone in the little cemetery in Copenhagen with two tiny doves perched over him. "*Tak fir alt*, Jonny Levin." Why was he so busy constructing a cemetery? No one would want to read a novel about building a cemetery. What would his daughters say if he sent each of them a postcard, not about the cemetery, but about Leda? Should he tell them that their very careful sixty-two-year-old father with the secret, hidden *pushkeh* stuffed with Viagra and a package of French condoms was consorting with a brash, young Lithuanian prostitute? Of course she was a prostitute. How could she possibly make a living selling Royal Copenhagen birds and angels or bringing tourists in swan boats to restaurants?

Would Bellow or Roth have consorted with her? Would either or both of them been charmed by her? He'd once met Bellow's second or third wife, Susan Glassman, in Chicago at a cocktail party at the Canterbury Court on the near North Side on State Street. He remembered she had a nervous, fragile beauty. Should he have spoken to her and asked her for a date? She was a young, nervous, haughty, Chicago-German-Jewess. He had carefully watched her movements but had never spoken to her. She became the wife in *Herzog*. He tried to buy *Ravelstein* in Marshall Fields downtown before he left for Denmark. No *Ravelstein*. Only a new collection of Bellow's stories with a beautiful touching forward by his young window, Janis. She wrote that Bellow worked every day in Vermont in a small writer's annex in the back. Day in and out the typewriter clacking, sick and bleeding, but working every day. What would Bellow have said to him about Leda? "Go for it, *burchik*, it's much better than sitting naked in an orgone box doing Reichean scream therapy. Go for it, pal, while you're still alive. Stop building your goofy, little cemetery. Forget the doves. The reader doesn't want to hear about doves and grandparents and parents."

The first thing he did when he took off his shoes in the hotel room was look for Leda's card. Before he called her, though, he wrote the following paragraph about his grandfather, despite Bellow's advice. He wanted to get something down. It kept annoying him like a fly buzzing in the room.

KAENE MAESCHE SWARTZSCHILD

Maesche's trick with cigar smoke rings. First he'd ceremoniously hand you the band from the cigar as a ring for your finger when he lit up. Then he'd blow smoke rings at you so you could slip the finger with the cigar band into the smoke ring. Kaene Maesche Swartzschild, *tak fir alt.*

He picked up the phone and called Leda. He was fascinated by the throaty buzz of European phones. He rehearsed what he would say to her. "Hello Leda, this is Jonny Levin, your American friend from last night. I would like to come to see you. I want to make an appointment for a massage; my back is killing me. *Choloria.*"

17

HE WAS IN A TAXICAB ON HIS WAY to Leda's apartment. She'd sounded happy to hear from him and had given him a complicated set of directions to the apartment that he'd written down on a hotel tablet. The driver though, an old man with a scabbed red neck and woolen, peaked, dirty tweed cap and paper wound around the ear frames of his glasses, knew the street and didn't want directions.

So what did he want from Leda? Did he at his age really want to climb into bed with a twenty-something-year-old prostitute? Would it make any sense? No, it wouldn't make sense, despite his musings about Bellow and Bellow's admonition to "go for it while you're still alive." All the horny old Jewish writers had beautiful young women in their lives as their muses or even their lovers. He needed a muse. He deserved a beautiful young muse. Bellow had Janis, his lovely young wife. He probably died with her name on his lips. Roth had Claire Bloom, so beautiful when she was young – ivory-faced with an elegant English accent. When Roth was suicidal, Claire Bloom saved his ass. Singer, he was indeed, a crafty old cocksman. He lived with Alma in an old apartment on West 86th Street and she supported him for years with her job at Lord & Taylor. Late in his life, when he was really successful in his seventies, he met a twenty-one-year-old, Dvore Menashe, a student at Bard who used to pick him up and drive him to his lectures there. She was a young married woman. She was like another Shosha. She and Singer were together for years. She became his administrative assistant. He probably never touched her, but she brought the creative juices flowing again to the old man's fingers. There's a photo of them on Singer's balcony overlooking the ocean at his condo in Miami Beach. Her face almost touching his as they worked on a manuscript, his panama hat pushed back on his head. Just the two of them huddling over a manuscript. Salinger, what happened to him? He went underground and never published again. Some young woman surfaced who had lived with him and published a long narrative of their sex life. Arthur Miller, when he died in his eighties, was living with a woman in her thirties. What about Bernie Malamud? In "Dubin Lives" a young woman threads a wire stemmed rose around the stiff cock of Malamud's hero, Dubin. And the Goyim, ah, the Goyim. Hemingway had his Adriana Ivancich. She was Renata in "Across the River and Into the Trees." Did he ever touch her? Probably not. She was nineteen, an Italian-Venetian beauty living in a decaying palazzo when he met her. He was fifty. She became the muse for the novel. He became the foolish Colonel Cantwell. But Hemingway probably never touched her. She was only "Daughter" to his "Papa." But none of these women were prostitutes. Some were wives, some were secretaries or translators, but none were prostitutes. According to Singer's Jacques Kohn in "A Friend of Kafka," Jacques Kohn went one night to a brothel in Prague with Kafka who was so frightened, he became ill. But even Kafka had Hansi, his "Trocadero Valkerye." Kafka supposedly did frequently visit the brothels of Prague. There is a famous photo of Hansi and Kafka together, Kafka in a derby, Hansi in a tiny pillbox hat. They looked so young and innocent. At Jonny Levin's age, he certainly didn't need a sexually transmitted disease. Pushkeh full of unused French condoms or not, he wasn't about to take a chance of AIDS. So what did he really want from this beautiful, young wild woman? He wanted to find out about the man in Lithuania, the man in Kaunas, the father of her friend with the name from Euripides, Iphigenia's father. Was he really the man in the photograph, the young man with the rifle herding Jewish women out of trucks and down the street in Kaunas?

The cab driver stopped the cab about six blocks after they crossed a river and pointed to a small apartment building. He paid the man who showed no expression when he gave him a ten kroner tip, not a thank you, just a grunt and then he was alone in front of the building. It was an old four-story yellow and brown brick four-flat. She told him she lived on the top floor. He looked up to see if she was watching him through a window. He saw nothing at the fourth floor windows, except one window had a small red, yellow and green banner hanging from a window sash. He recognized it as the colors of the Lithuanian flag. He entered the first floor cautiously, afraid of being confronted by Mikos, the landlady's son she'd described as a half-witted brute. With his sense of guilt already pulsing in his ears, he didn't want an encounter with a half-witted brute. It would be like a sixty-year-old Jewish inept Ulysses meeting Cyclops. He poked his head in the front hall, mail scattered on the floor, it smelled of cabbage cooking, a radio was blaring, a baby crying. He could avoid all this. Avoidance was his métier. All he had to do now was turn around and leave, but he heard footsteps echoing in the concrete chamber of the stairwell and the lilting, challenging sound of Leda's voice calling to him. "Jonny Levine, I can't believe you've come to see me. *Labas*, that's hello in Lithuanian." She threw her arms around him and buried her face in his chest. "Can you say *labas* to me?"

"*Labas.*"

"No, say *labas*, Leda'."

"*Labas*, Leda."

"And you're wearing that beautiful blue American jacket.

The same blue jacket. How handsome you look. Like an American businessman visiting the slums of Copenhagen."

"But I am not an American businessman."

"No, you're not. You're quite different. Very different. And you're wearing that delicious cologne. I love it."

She took his hand and began to pull him up the stairwell.

He was out of breath when they reached the fourth floor and entered her apartment. There was music playing, a woman singing in a language he didn't recognize. She had a lovely voice, sounding like Lee Wiley singing "Manhattan," the same kind of sultry voice. The sun was shadowing her hanging plates. There were large paintings of flowers and a portrait of a fierce blue-eyed owl with tiny ink strokes of layers of feathers. Also artificial flowers, long stemmed lavender puffballs and the scent of oils and perfumes. A small kitchen behind beaded curtains and the smell of something baking. A large cat sat atop a bookcase, a brown and white cat with yellow eyes staring at him. More Lithuanian flag plaques were stuck on a wall cabinet, the yellow, red and green tri-color.

She pulled him over to the couch.

"Sit down Jonny Levine. You have saved my life. I gave the thirty-seven hundred kroner to the landlady and she gave me my keys back. I am brewing you some Lithuanian tea and I baked some cookies in honor of your coming to visit me."

"Actually Leda, I've come here for a purpose." He pointed to a chair gesturing for her to sit down.

"A purpose? What kind of purpose? You want your four thousand kroner back?" She dropped his hand and stood in front of him. "How can I give it back to you? I will over time, but not in twenty-four hours. It's impossible. I will give you several massages, every other day for two weeks. I will fix your back. You will be a new man and my debt will be paid."

"I haven't come for the money."

She began to tug at his coat.

"Take off your coat, Jonny Levine, and your shirt and go over to my massage table and lie flat. I don't want to injure your expensive clothes with my massage oil." She took his coat and hung it up on a wall screen of a huge painted red flower on a yellow background and walked back to the kitchen. "Do as I say, the tea is ready."

"I don't want a massage, Leda."

"Don't be stubborn, Jonny Levine. You'll love it."

She came back with a tray with a large white china teapot and cookies. "Give me a minute, I'll put on my smock. You lie over there, take your trousers off. I won't hurt you. Most men would jump on that table and lie naked. You Americans are so, how do you say, uptight. You make war, but not love. You don't know how to relax so you make war."

Suddenly the shriveled face of Bellow from his coffin was winking at him and then the whispered voice, "Don't be a schmuck. Do as she says."

"Do as I say. I will hang your trousers also on the same screen. Then I will pour you some tea in the Lithuanian manner. This is a famous Lithuanian tea 'Meskauoges Lapai'. It is very mild, a slight taste of cherries and flowers. Very slight. It is so relaxing and the cookies are my mother's recipe, raisins and almonds. You know my mother is Polish, I am half-Polish and I speak Polish. Now I will change the tape and play for you Eva Demarczyk. She is the Edith Piaf of Poland."

"I don't want a massage Leda."

"What do you want then? You want your money? I can't give it to you. Maybe later in the week I can give you something."

"The flower on the screen where you hung my jacket, it's quite striking. Are you the artist?"

"That is my flower. Yes. I am the artist. All those paintings of flowers and cats are mine. You want to buy one?"

"How much do you charge?"

"They are all four thousand kroner. Exactly what I owe you. Why don't you buy one?"

"What will I do with it, hang it in my hotel room?"

"No, you will ship it home. I have a friend who ships overseas. They will send it to the States. It will be waiting for you when you get home, but you will pay the shipping charges, maybe another five hundred kroner."

"I will consider it, but I have something else I want to talk to you about."

"I also have smaller paintings made of amber chips, amber from the seaside in Lithuania, and I model figures and animals, also flowers, with these chips." She brought out a small painting of a hill of crosses, pen and ink drawings of crosses outlined in amber chips of different colors. "It is a hill in Vilnius, a holy site that is filled with the ancient crosses and I have modeled it. I will sell it to you for three thousand kroner, three hundred dollars, if you also buy the flower for four thousand. They are together. It is an original, not a copy. I have signed it. I will also sign the back 'To my American friend Jonny Levin, Leda Renauskas Vicivious, Copenhagen artiste'."

"I don't think I'm in the market for a hill of crosses, even one made of amber chips."

"In the market? What does that mean? We are not in a market, we are sitting in my flat. It is a gallery and we are discussing art and drinking tea."

"It's an expression. Maybe I might be interested in another one of your amber pieces, but I have something first to discuss with you."

"Discuss? What is it you have come to discuss? Your face is so serious. What is so serious. Maybe if you have a massage and buy my paintings I might be interested in a serious discussion. What is it you want Jonny Levin?"

"I want to find out if that man in the photo, Simon, the father of your friend is still alive."

"Iphigenia's Father?"

"Yes."

"How would I know? I haven't been home in three years. I have no contact with Iphigenia."

"You could call your parents."

"Call my parents? You think I am a madwoman? I don't speak to my parents. Besides, they have no telephone."

"You could get word to them. You said they live across the street from Simon."

"It would be very difficult." She tucked her bare feet under her. She was dressed in jeans and a white shirt.

"Why are you so interested in Simon Braucivius? He is an old drunk. A woman beater. A liar. He's probably not alive. You're wasting your time trying to find him."

"I simply want to meet him."

"You would have to go to Kaunas to do that. I won't go with you as your guide, they won't let me into the country. They claim I left illegally. It is true, but I wanted to come here and study art and be free. I had no passport so I had a friend, another student, who helped me get out. Why am I telling you this Jonny Levin? You could try to blackmail me."

"Don't you have a friend in Kaunas you could put me in touch with who could lead me to Simon?"

"If you insist I think I could do this, but it can't be done without money. I have a friend, Dalia, she speaks English very well, better than I do. She would help you. She could act as your guide."

"Couldn't you just call her and ask her if Braucivius is still alive?"

"She has no phone. I would have to write to her. She would contact you at your hotel in Kaunas. If he is dead, so you would have wasted some money on your travel and hotel. If he is alive she will lead you to him, but this will cost money." She poured him some more tea and began to nibble on a cookie.

"How much?"

"I don't know. I'm a masseuse and an artist, not a spy."

"Alright. Maybe I'll have a massage and buy two paintings. I might even forgive the four thousand kroner. If I lie down you can work on my back, but I won't take my shirt and trousers off. I'll buy the flower and that small portrait of the cat over there for seven thousand kroner. Four thousand for the flower and three thousand for the cat. That's seven hundred dollars."

"And you will forgive the four thousand kroner debt."

"I will forgive it."

"And what about my friend Dalia? You must pay for her."

"I'll pay Dalia twenty-five hundred kroner when I meet her."

"Pay her four thousand and as you Americans say, 'you have a deal'. I don't understand 'deal' but I say it when I meet an American. And it's always a 'deal' and we slap hands." She came over to him and slapped his hand. "You don't have to take your clothes off Jonny Levin. I will walk on your back with my bare feet. I will manipulate you with my toes and heels. It will cost you one session and I will straighten you. But first I have to have the money in my hands. I have learned from harsh experience that if I embark on a business transaction I must be paid in advance. Eleven thousand kroner. Particularly with an American – they act like innocents, but they are very shrewd."

"I will give you seven thousand in advance, Leda, and I will give you the other four thousand when I meet your friend Dalia in Kaunas. That's eleven hundred dollars."

"Plus the four thousand you are forgiving. The money I gave to the landlady."

"That makes it fifteen hundred dollars."

He'd just spent almost all the money he had in his pocket from his bets with Mooney.

"Alright, it's agreed," she said smiling and shaking her hair back.

"I will pay you in dollars." He took Mooney's roll out and counted out seven one hundred dollar bills and put them on the coffee table in front of her.

She inspected the bills by holding each of them up to the sunlight filtering through the hanging plants and then stuck the bills into a glass jar and screwed the top back on and put the jar in her refrigerator.

"I use these Lithuanian jam jars for my paints. Now I'll use one as a place to keep my money. American one hundred dollar bills. I can't believe it. Get up on the table Jonny Levin and I will put a sheet over you. Lie on your stomach. I'm light as a feather. I am like the Firebird in Stravinsky's 'Suite'. You will not even feel me."

He wondered why he was doing this. He didn't have to include the massage in his package, but at least he'd be paying lip service to Bellow. He'd try just a little bit of adventure and romance. A *bissel.* What about Bellow's buddy, Richard Stern? He was still alive. Stern wrote "Other Men's Daughters". He left his wife and family for a young woman. So what else is new? A beautiful young woman with a cloud of black hair. Would Stern let Leda walk on his back? Stern was still teaching at the University of Chicago. Maybe when he returned home he would go down to Hyde Park and call on Stern. Tell him about Copenhagen and Leda. No. Why hand the material to Stern? He'd use it himself. Stick the massage somewhere into his own novel, but not into the chapters where he was constructing cemeteries.

"Now I spread the sheet over you. I will not soil your clothes. After we're through we will leave and call upon my friend who will mend the wings of the angels I shattered at Royal Copenhagen. Now that I have money in my jar I can get the angels fixed.

My friend, Marguerite, and her father are Jews. They're Lithuanian Jews from Vilnius. The old man raises pigeons in the back of their store and I help him once each week with the pigeons. I earn a small wage. He was a professor at the University of Vilnius so you may speak to him, an educated man, he may speak English, although he is very frail and old. Marguerite will mend my angels' wings and they will fly again. I will take them back to Royal Copenhagen and restore my reputation with them. They are an important customer to me as a guide."

She replaced the tape of Ewa Demarczyk and put on a woman reading a poem.

"It is me. That is my voice. That is me reading, 'Locomotywa'. It is in Polish by the poet, Julian Tuwim, a famous Polish poet and also a Jew. My mother used to recite this poem to me every night before I would go to sleep and rub my back in rhythm to the poem. It is a poem about a steam engine getting up steam to leave the station."

She hopped up and stood on his back. She was right, he hardly felt her.

"The train now is starting. It is leaving the station and I am speaking Polish which I will translate as I dance on your back."

"BUCH – JAK GORACO!"

"That is a puff. One puff."

"UCH – JAK GORACO!"

"Another stronger puff."

"PUFF – JAK GORACO!"

"Puff, puff," she swirled her hips and began dancing.

"UFF – JAC GORACO!"

"Puff, puff, puff."

"LOCOMOTYWA."

"Are you okay Jonny Levin?

"BUCH – JAC GORACO!"

"Now the train is going, going down the track.

"UCH – JAC GORACO!"

"NAGLE – SWIST!"

"KOLA – W SUCH!"

"NAGLE – QUIZD!"

"Toot, toot goes the horn."

"Clang, clang goes the bell."

"Jonny Levin, how do you feel? Have I fixed you? You are okay now. I am slowly hopping off."

"NAGLE – QUIZD!"

"NAGLE – SWIST!"

"Goodbye train, no more pain. You are cured, Jonny Levin – absolutely, absolutnaya. Tak."

She puffed her cheeks like a furious little bird, whirled on one foot like a ballerina and hopped off his back.

On the massage table he was lost in a dream of Kafka and Puah. Kafka had planned to go to Tel Aviv with Puah, an eighteen year old. There they would open a restaurant together. Kafka would be the cashier and waiter, Puah would cook. But Kafka was dying of tuberculosis and he never made it. Was Puah still alive? Did she make it to Israel? Behind the dream he felt the feathery movements of Leda dancing on his back. Leda the swan, the Firebird, ever so lightly in rhythm to Tuwim's "Locomotywa" and he felt better. He actually felt better. A two minute dance on his back by this beautiful, conniving Lithuanian masseuse and he really did feel some of the old ancient pain that always was with him float away.

18

IN THE CAB ON THE WAY to her friend Marguerite's store. She was giving the cab driver directions. She did look a little like Richard Stern's Adele. The same cloud of frizzed black hair. He wondered if Adele had also been a student of Stern's like Bellow's Janis. Those delicate Jewish beauties didn't know what they had elected when they walked into their professor's classes. There was a photo in Stern's "Sistermony," the little book about his sister's death, of Stern and Adele together. She was looking up at him adoringly, the same way Puah might have looked at Kafka. Except he was dead wrong about Puah. She was never in love with Kafka. She was his Hebrew teacher in Prague, a young woman from Palestine. She looked like a tough Jewish farmer. Her face, round as a dark, desert apple, braids pulled back around her head. She wanted nothing to do with Kafka as a lover. He was dying and she knew it. It was Dora who fell in love with Kafka. Dora Diamant, his last love. They ran away together from Prague to Berlin and lived in an apartment there. He was forty, Dora was nineteen, a young woman who adored Kafka, on the run from her strict Orthodox upbringing. It was their dream of going to Israel to open a restaurant. They had no money. They lived off of food parcels from Kafka's family. Dora truly loved him and refused to give up his manuscripts after his death. She clung to them as if Kafka was still alive. Maybe he and Leda could go together to Kaunas and open a restaurant there. He could probably get her back into the country, contact a few people he knew at the State Department, pull a few strings. But that would be ridiculous, a restaurant in

Lithuania. No, it would have to be in Israel, in Haifa perhaps. He had always wanted to visit Haifa and Mount Carmel. Maybe a little shop like a bakery up the mountainside near Haifa University. He would introduce himself to Yehoshua who was a professor there. He'd once seen Yehoshua speak in Tucson. He looked just like Ben Gurion, and he was an old-fashioned Zionist orator.

Leda was carrying two plastic bags and he asked her what was in them.

"Feed for the pigeons. Every week I buy special birdseed for the pigeons. They are champion pigeons, Pakistani pigeons. They fly very high, higher than any other breed, and they require a special type of seed."

He was still lost in his dream of Kafka and Dora together in Berlin. The dying, pale, autocratic face, the doctors were injecting camphor directly into his larynx. The pain was horrible. He had tubercular lesions on his larynx; he could only speak in whispers. Dora and his friend Klopstock, a young doctor, cared for him. He kept calling out for morphine. "Josephine the Singer, or the Mousefolk," his last story, was about a mouse who spoke only in whispers. He'd instructed his friend and editor Max Brod to burn almost everything he'd written. Brod refused to do it.

Suddenly the cab stopped and they were in front of a small shop with a sign that read:

Marguerite Berenstyn

24 Helgoland, Brunsdrata 24
Silhouette Artiste
Berenstyn Frame Shoppe & Antiquaries

"I know that woman," he said. "She gave me her card. She's a silhouette artist."

"She's a genius artist, Marguerite, she's also a dancer. I love her, my dearest friend. Come, you pay the cab. It is part of our deal, the American pays the cab fare."

"But you're a wealthy woman now, Leda."

"Because I have seven hundred dollars in a jar? That is not wealth. That will pay my rent and buy my food for one month."

He paid the driver who tipped his hat to him when he drove away.

She opened the door to the shop and bells tinkled. It was a musty old shop filled with antiques, furniture, paintings, china, old silver, drawings, very dark with the smell of old wood and leather. Just a slant of sunlight came through the heavy drapes over the window.

"Marguerite," Leda called, "where are you? Are you in the back?" She gave the door another shake and the bells tinkled again. "Marguerite."

Marguerite came from the back wiping her hands on her smock. He recognized her immediately. It was the same woman who had cut the silhouette, the profile of his face, the intricate swan, and the rabbit. She was quite lovely with a sad, ivory-skinned, smooth face and brown hair that fell softly to her shoulders. She barely glanced at him. The most striking feature of her face was her pale blue eyes. She looked like Modigliani's love, the woman in the painting, his mistress, the one who was pregnant with his child and who committed suicide after Modigliani died. Jeanne Hebuterne. This woman had the same air of sadness and striking, slanted blue eyes. He'd seen the painting in New York at The Met the last time he visited his daughter Alysia. He and Alysia had gone to The Met together and then had lunch at the outdoor café at the Stanhope across the street.

The two women embraced and Leda introduced him.

"Marguerite, I want you to meet my American friend, Jonny Levin. His family came from Lithuania, Mariampole, and he is a Jew."

Marguerite said nothing to him.

"I remember you Marguerite," he told her. "You were in the square. There was a woman playing the accordion and a dancer. You cut a beautiful silhouette of a swan and then a rabbit and you gave them to me."

He took out his wallet and removed the two figures and put them down on an oriental tapestry she had folded in a triangle over her counter.

She picked up the silhouettes and looked at him.

"Yes, I remember the American gentleman. I did your face."

"I have that silhouette in my room. You told me to come to your shop and buy a frame."

She smiled for the first time and the pale blue eyes flashed up at him. "Yes, you should buy. I am sorry for my English, though, I do not speak it well."

"He's a very wealthy man Marguerite, he could well afford to buy one of your frames, even several. Does your father speak English? I think he does. Most definitely he does if he is a professor. Jonny Levin is also a professor in America. We could show him the pigeons and introduce him to Emanuelis and if he bought a few things I would also receive a commission."

"And then you could put that money in your jar," he said to Leda.

"Yes, next to my jar of frozen eels. Have you ever caught an eel? If you go to Lithuania you must learn how to eat them, catch them and eat them."

Marguerite smiled at her friend.

"He does not have to eat eels to meet my father, Leda. Come, sir, come with me."

"I never said that Marguerite. Only if he goes to Lithuania. Then he will eat eels. Perhaps I will go with him after all. I was going to have my friend Dalia meet him in Kaunas, but for a decent price I can get a passport and visa from a friend. What do you think Marguerite? I haven't been home in over three years. They don't know if I'm dead or alive."

"You are alive Leda. Did you bring the jar of vitamins with the pigeons' seed? My father's been waiting all morning." Then she said something to Leda in Lithuanian.

"I have all the vitamins. Also protein oil and his special spices. These pigeons fly by their stomachs, Jonny Levin. Emanuelis has always told me that the pigeons fly by their stomachs. They're healthy only if their stomachs are healthy."

"Did you two know each other in Lithuania?" he asked Leda.

"No, Marguerite is from Vilnius. We met only here in Copenhagen. I am her commissionaire, just like I am a commissionaire for Royal Copenhagen, although Marguerite is much more talented than any of the artists at Royal Copenhagen. Marguerite I have brought you some angels to repair."

She reached into her large purse and brought out the pieces of the Italian earthenware sugar bowl and pitcher.

"Marguerite I have broken the wings of these angels. I was so clumsy in the aisles of Royal Copenhagen. I swung my purse and hit them off their stand to the floor. Now they are very angry with me because they no longer can fly, but I promised them I would take them to my talented artist friend Marguerite and she would mend their wings and they would fly again."

Marguerite carefully picked up the pieces and laid them on her tapestry countertop. She manipulated the pieces so that each fit together and held the angels' wings in place. "They will fly Leda. It is not such a bad fracture." She spoke quickly in Lithuanian and Leda's face brightened.

"She will fix them while we shall visit her father. Come along with me Jonny Levin. I want you to meet Emanuelis."

"Emanuelis," she called down the hallway. "I have everything for you Emanuelis."

She motioned to Jonny Levin to follow her, but she put her fingers to her lips to caution him to be quiet.

"Be very quiet because he may be asleep." She looked at her watch. "Marguerite, is Emanuelis sleeping?"

"No, he's up in the coop with his pigeons waiting for you. Here, please give him these cuttings I have made for him." She handed Leda a small brown paper bag.

They walked back in the hallway which led to the back yard and a door open to sunlight.

"Emanuelis."

A frail, elderly man stooped and dressed in a heavy khaki sweater and shorts, barefoot with sandals was feeding the pigeons from a small stepstool.

"Emanuelis, this is a Jewish gentleman who is a professor from America, Jonny Levin," she said to the old man in English. "You speak English do you not Emanuelis?"

"Yes, of course Leda. You know that. You're late. I've been waiting all morning. Bring the gentleman over here, I cannot see his face in the sunlight. My eyes are not strong enough."

"Professor Jonny Levin, this is Professor Emanuelis Berenstyn, my employer."

"How do you do Professor Levin?" The old man's face was seamed. He had a bulbous nose, white closely-cropped hair, and the same slanted blue eyes of his daughter, and a patch of white stubble on his chin where he had missed shaving.

"What brings you to our little establishment in Copenhagen, Professor Levin? Are you a pigeon fancier? These are Pakistani tipplers, the best of all breeds. They fly higher and farther than any."

"It's a pleasure to meet you sir."

"You are a professor? Where do you teach? What is your subject? Do you teach in America?"

"I teach at a university in Chicago, literature, English Literature is my field."

"So in America they permit Jews to teach literature. That is good, a free country. In Lithuania at the university in Vilna, I was not permitted to teach English Literature. Even though I had studied English all my life and had taught in London at London University. My field was Lithuanian and Polish Literature, but I have a large library in English Literature. Keats, Shelley, Shakespeare, Browning, Wordsworth, even some American writers like James Fenimore Cooper, Walt Whitman, Thoreau. What will I do with all these books? I bought all of them here in Denmark. I will leave them with the Danes. The Danes are a wonderful people. I intend to leave all my books to them, to the Danish people. Marguerite will see to it. They have allowed us to run our little shop and fly our pigeons without interfering. We do as we please. We are free here."

"Where do you race your pigeons Professor Berenstyn?"

"We do not race ever. These are not racers, they are flyers. We send them far far away. Every day a few go, a few return. They are very strong. They can fly great distances."

Leda had busied herself cleaning out the coops and putting fresh seed in the feeding trays.

"Actually sir, you see I am just an old Jew from Vilna with his pigeons and his books. I smoke my pipe at night and fall asleep in the chair."

"My family came from Mariampole. Although I am an American, I also am a Jew from Lithuania."

"Did any of your family come out alive from Mariampole? I know it well. It is outside Kovno. All the Jews from Mariampole were slaughtered in a forest outside the city."

"I don't know sir, I was told my mother wrote to her aunt who was a dentist in Mariampole. They corresponded often, but there was no more contact after the war. She never heard from her aunt again."

"That is typical, a black veil has been drawn over Lithuania and its Jews. Almost all were killed. I myself was just fortunate. I was with the Resistance in Vilna. We got out through the sewers into the forest and we survived there as partisans. That is where I send my pigeons every week, three or four back to Lithuania. I send them to honor the dead Jews there, the thousands who were killed. I am too old to go. Instead I go to the shul here and send my pigeons in my place. I am ninety years of age, almost in the grave, but the pigeons, they are young and strong. The strongest flyers in the world. Purebred Pakistani tipplers. They fly in my place. They perform aerial maneuvers over Lithuania that I have taught them. They are very good students, excellent students."

"Aerial maneuvers?"

"I will show you if you are interested, Professor Levin. First I send them to Bornholm. It is an island in the Baltic. I send them to Rønne, the city on Bornholm where I have a colleague who has a roost. They find that and spend the night and rest. Then my friend sends them on to Gdansk in Poland where I have another colleague with a roost. They spend the night there and will rest and are ready to fly as I direct them. I direct them to Lithuania."

"How do you direct them?"

"It is quite simple. Come I will show you." He reached into the coop and brought out a grey-breasted pigeon with white tail feathers and a white head. "This is my warrior, Joshua. He is one of the strongest. You see his collar? It has a tiny radio chip built into it and receives radio signals that I send from here. Each pigeon wears a small tube attached to its collar band. In that tube I insert the cuttings that Marguerite has made for me." He opened the small brown bag that Leda had brought to him and spread several of the paper cuttings on his hand. They were stars of various colors, red, green, and blue

"They look like miniature Stars of David."

"Exactly. That's what they are, tiny Mogen Davids. On signal, the tubes on the pigeon's collar holding them will open and the stars fall over Lithuania to the place I have directed them. Every week, they fall on the Lithuanian cities and forests. A few at a time fluttering down like a gentle rain on the Lithuanians to remind them of their dead Jews. Sometimes Marguerite will write a name on each of them. Sometimes she will cut out a Torah or a Menorah or biblical animals, but always we send the tiny stars, the Mogen Davids in memory of the Jews who were killed. Then the pigeons go to another roost in Lithuania to rest, but I cannot discuss that. It is a hidden roost. They spend the night, then they fly back to Gdansk, Bornholm and finally here. If you and Leda will stay with us until later this afternoon at dusk you will see them return. I will ask Marguerite; perhaps she will serve us a glass of wine and a small dinner. You and Leda will be our guests and we will all wait for the pigeons together. I don't often meet a professor from America. Go with Marguerite and Leda and I will join you."

19

Marguerite served him a glass of wine and he sat for her while she did another cutting of his face. Emanuelis and Leda eventually came back into the front room of the store from the coops and Marguerite locked the front door and hung the "closed" sign over the leaded glass insert in the front door. It was a blue leaded glass panel inset with Stars of David and a Lion of Judah in silhouette.

"I also cut figures of that lion in the door pane," she said. "I give them to Emanuelis, he showed you sir?" She quickly cut a miniature figure of a Lion of Judah and handed it to him. It took her only seconds.

"This is for you sir."

"Thank you Marguerite. I would like to buy some of your frames. I have two profiles of myself, a rabbit, a swan, and now this beautiful lion. Could you select the frames for me?"

She said nothing but quickly found a few frames and put them in a plastic shopping bag.

"How much do I owe you?"

"Nothing, sir. They are, as one says, a gift. We do not sell our gifts to our guests."

"I should fight with you, but I won't." For once he reached out and touched a woman's hand. She looked at him directly when he did that and didn't withdraw her hand. "Thank you Marguerite. I will have your gifts to remember this day."

"You are welcome. And now if you will excuse me sir I will prepare dinner. Emanuelis has told me you and Leda will stay.

Please." She looked at him one more time as if she were thinking of saying something more and then she went into the small kitchen.

Emanuelis came to the front room after washing up and sat and lit his pipe.

"You'll excuse my pipe Professor Levin, please. I seldom have someone to discuss literature with and I am looking forward to our discussion." Marguerite poured him a glass of wine. "This is an Italian Chianti. A very nice Chianti from Venezia. The Italians are good with wines. 'Chin chin and sköal'." He lifted his glass. "And of course l'chaim."

"Do you know at all of the university in Vilna? The Stefan Batory University? Stefan Batory was the king of Poland when the university was established in the mid sixteenth century. Our most famous graduate in the United States was Czeslaw Milosz who only recently died. I believe he had retired to Krakow, but he spent most of his literary career in the States at Berkeley in the state of California where he was a professor."

"Yes I know Milosz. In fact I met him once at a conference in Chicago. I've read his 'The Issa Valley,' about his student days at the University of Vilnius."

"Yes, yes. How nice. He won the Nobel prize you know. I knew Milosz when I was a youth. We were at the university together and I was in a philology class with him. I was obliged to work and earn my way to pay tuition. I was older than Milosz, but he was very kind to me. He was from a distinguished Lithuanian family of Polish origin. We Jewish students had very few friendships with Lithuanians. We were barred from their clubs and social organizations. But Milosz was a friend to me. We drank together; we would discuss poetry together. His uncle, Oscar Milosz, a strange man, was even then a well-known poet in Paris. I think the boy was under his uncle's influence, but I may have my years mixed up. During the war Milosz joined the Polish Resistance. He was a very courageous man and one of the first of the Polish intelligencia to speak out about the tragedy of the Jews. Do you know his poem 'Campo dei Fiori'?"

"No, I'm not familiar with it."

"Well it was written in 1943, when the ghetto in Warsaw was burning. The Germans had set it afire. It tells of a beautiful sunlit day in Warsaw. There was a carousel in the park. Women laughing in the sunlight as the carousel turned and the smoke of the burning ghetto carried black petals that landed on their skirts. The women kept on riding and laughing, whirling in the sunlight as if nothing were happening. He called them all to shame. It was the shame of the Polish nation and Milosz saw it in 1943 and recorded it forever."

Leda came out from the kitchen. She poured herself a glass of Chianti and set down a plate of cheese and crackers.

"Leda, *na zdrowie*," Emanuelis held up his glass. "I speak Polish to her. She is part Polish. I believe her mother is Polish. I always tease her by speaking Polish."

"Emanuelis, in the year I have been working for you this is the first time I've been asked for dinner so I say, *na zdrowie* to you and also to Professor Jonny Levin, our new friend from America." She lifted her glass to both of the men and touched each of their glasses. "Now like a good daughter of Poland I shall return to the kitchen. Do you know the story of 'Cinderella'? In Poland and in Lithuania her name in the fable is 'Kitchen-Cinders'. That is how we translate Cinderella." She laughed and began setting the table.

"Do you know of the American woman essayist Lucy Dawidowicz, Professor Levin?" Emanuelis asked.

"I know of her, but I haven't read her work."

"If you want to learn about Vilna before the war, read Dawidowicz, 'From That Place and Time, A Memoir'. She was sent to

Vilna on a grant from the YIVO. I think it was 1938, just a year before the Germans attacked Poland. She got out of Lithuania almost on the last train out. But she wrote about her experiences as a young woman, a young American Jewish woman in Vilna. It is very interesting. May I recommend it to you?"

"Tell me something about yourself in the Resistance. That is very interesting to me. You say you escaped from Vilnius through the sewers?"

"Oh, may I say, it is not so interesting. It was so very long ago, but still I remember it as if it was yesterday. It was September, 1943."

"How did you get out?"

"Get out? We had to go. We knew the Germans were going to burn down the ghetto in the morning. We'd heard they were going to transport Jews to camps in Estonia and Latvia. Others would be taken to Ponar and shot. If we wanted to survive, we had to escape that night. We found a route through the sewers that wound up in the back courtyard of their headquarters. The Germans would never imagine us there, so we went through the sewers. It was miserable, unbearable. A journey I won't describe to you. I have never forgotten that night." He wiped at his face and then removed his glasses. With his glasses off he looked like a man in his seventies. His face was beginning to color from the telling of the story and from the wine.

"Was it similar to the escape from the Warsaw ghetto? I know they also went through the sewers."

"In Warsaw I believe there was a truck waiting to take them to the forest. They had made certain arrangements. In Vilna we had no one. No means of transport. We hid in the Germans' basement and then one by one, two by two, we walked to the Rudnicki Forest, fifteen kilometers. There were perhaps twenty-five of us, men and women. We pretended we were hunters or peasants or lovers. We went separately because if some were captured, the others would still have a chance to get away."

"Your leader was Abba Kovner?"

"You know of Kovner?"

"Yes."

"Abba Kovner is dead. God rest his soul. He was a brave, courageous man. A splendid warrior, and so was his wife Vitka Kempner. The two of them survived and lived in Israel as husband and wife. He was a fighter, a poet, our leader. He testified at the Eichmann trial. We fought side-by-side. Abba was our commander. Vitka was always at his side. She blew up German trains with mines. And also there was Ruzka Korczak, a brave soldier. They were a threesome. Ruzka also survived and escaped to Israel. I was with them every day in the Rudnicki Forest until the Russians liberated Vilna. They were my comrades."

"I would like to go to Vilnius to see where the ghetto was and to the Ponar Forest."

"Go, people should go and witness. Tell the world to never forget these places. Many thousands of Jews were killed in Ponar by the Germans and Lithuanians. Their bodies were stacked in tiers and covered with sand. They were shot and dumped into the pits, one body falling on top of another. Many were buried alive. We knew what was going on in Ponar. We told the ghetto that the Germans were lying. The Jews were not being taken to Ponar for resettlement, they were taken to be shot. The Germans were brutal beyond human understanding. Then as the Russians advanced, the Germans tried to burn the bodies. Jews were shackled together as slaves to burn the bodies." He looked away and his eyes were glistening.

"Does Leda know what you're doing with the pigeons?"

"No, I tell you these things in confidence. Even though you are a stranger to me, I sense that I can talk to you as a fellow Jew and scholar. She does not know or care where the pigeons go. She does not think in that fashion. She thinks I am a pigeon fancier, a crazy old man, that I enter contests with colleagues to see how high the pigeons can fly. She is a typical young Lithuanian woman. She knows nothing about Jews. Nothing about what happened in her country."

"What about the cuttings in the tubes?"

"We tell her that the tubes are mezuzahs, Jewish good luck symbols."

"And you think this really happens each week, the pigeons are dropping tiny Mogen Davids on Lithuania?"

"Yes, my colleagues tell me that we are successful and quite accurate. If you visit Lithuania you can report back to me. I will tell you where I will send the pigeons. It would please me if you would go there to see them. Before you leave we will set a time and place. You will see that the pigeons will arrive at the appointed place approximately on time. In fact they are due back here now." He looked at his watch. "Let's go out to the coops and wait for them. Bring your glass of wine, please, and I will bring the bottle."

They walked back out to the coops and Emanuelis set the bottle down on a table. He gestured to Jonny Levin to sit on a small wire formed chair with a wooden seat, then he brought out a triangular wooden box inset with three car headlamps covered with red, green and blue clear plastic wrap. Each of the lights was tilted at a different angle.

"This is my lightboard, Professor Levin. I call it my landing board. It has a quite distinctive pattern of colored lights. I run them off an automobile battery, that way I don't have a long cord leading back into the house that Marguerite could possibly trip over. It's almost time for the birds to return. A little longer perhaps, we should wait. We should wait for the sun to go down, then I will call the birds and switch on the lights. We'll have some more wine, no?"

He filled each of their glasses.

"How do you call the pigeons?"

"Oh, I talk to them all the time in the coops. They know me very well. They know my voice. I make certain sounds that they recognize. Also they can pick out the lights. They are highly trained and are night flyers. In the city there is a multitude of lights, but they recognize the shape and color of my landing board, and when they hear my call they drop down quickly. I persuade them. They are always very hungry and want to be fed and watered immediately."

"They've come a long distance."

"Yes, from the island of Bornholm. A long journey and they will be tired and hungry. I give them a special water formula with phospherine. I also give each bird a combination of niger, canary seed and maple peas." He held up his wine glass. "So again I say to you 'l'chaim'." He lifted his glass and drank.

"I am sorry, Professor Levin, if I became somewhat emotional talking about the events in Vilna. The memories are, even at this day, still very painful. When I go back in my memory to that time, it is always difficult. There were only maybe twenty-five or thirty of us in the sewers. We were covered with filth. We hid in the basement of the German Security Police and then we walked to the Rudnicki Forest. When we finally arrived at Rudnicki we were confronted by Russian partisans. There were several different partisan groups in the forest, Russians, Poles, Lithuanians, and none of them wanted to permit a separate army of Jews as partisans. We had hardly any weapons. They all had an eye on our Jewish women fighters. They wanted us to merge with the Lithuanians. Abba Kovner refused. He insisted we retain our identity as Jews and he faced them down. We had our own camp.

Of course, they treated us not as comrades, but as Jews whom they despised. We were always last to receive any arms or food parcels. Russian planes would drop supplies into the forest by parachute, but we would not be permitted to retrieve them, so we lived off the countryside. We took from the peasants. We slaughtered their livestock, we found their caches of arms, and when necessary we killed. We did what we had to do to survive, and we succeeded. We blew up trains, more than fifty trains we blew up with our mines. We blew up trucks. By then there were as many as three hundred Jews hiding in the forest. Only a few of them were fighters. We had to feed all of them. Vitka Kempner had led them out of Vilna to the forest and we took on responsibility for them to keep them alive. How many Jews died in Vilna? I do not know. Perhaps seventy thousand were killed in Ponar. Later after the ghetto was burned, maybe another twenty thousand were killed."

He removed his glasses.

"So I send my pigeons each week. Is it a futile gesture of a silly old man? I don't think so. I think it has some meaning. It has some meaning at least to me and Marguerite and a few colleagues." He looked at his watch. "Come now, Professor Levin, I will call the birds." He switched on the landing board lights.

The blue, green and red lamps cast swaths of color in the approaching darkness and Emanuelis shielded his eyes and looked at the sky.

"I don't see them. I may be a bit early. I will keep the lights on and we will have more wine. They will be here soon. I won't call them yet."

He sat back down at the table and filled their glasses again.

"You know, Professor Levin, you and I could have a secret pact. When are you leaving for Lithuania and where will you be going?"

"I have no definite plans. SAS has a Copenhagen to Vilnius flight two flights a day."

"Yes, SAS, a good airline."

"I would stay in Vilnius for a day, maybe two days and then take a train or drive to Mariampole and stay one night."

"A train would be best. Driving may be difficult since you don't know the language."

"Then I would go to Kaunas by bus or train, one night in Kaunas and then back to Vilnius and SAS return to Copenhagen."

"So about four days, maybe five?" Emanuelis looked up at the sky.

"Four or five days."

"And you would leave when?"

"At any time. Tomorrow, the next day, next week. I have no schedule. I have nothing to keep me here."

"Leda would go with you?"

"I don't know. She could go or I might meet her friend in Kaunas."

"It would be much easier for you if she would go. She is a very smart young woman, very clever. She could make things much easier for you. The language is difficult for Americans. The young people know English, but remember they have been under the hands of the Russians for years so they have studied Russian and are not that proficient in English. The older generation, they speak of course Lithuanian, often Russian and Polish, but not English."

"Leda could be helpful, but it would really be a private journey. I'm not sure I would want her around. I would meet her in Kaunas. I don't want her with me in Vilnius or Mariampole."

"She's absolutely honest, very loyal. A very good young woman and clever in money matters, but it is true, she has a wild imagination. She will often exceed the truth."

"She lies?"

"No, she does not lie. She fabricates. Like most of us the

only lies she tells are to herself. For instance, she pretends not to know about what happened to the Jews in Lithuania. Of course she knows. They all know. But they are peasants at heart, very cunning, very stubborn, and as far as the Jews are concerned, they have no feeling, no pity, no *rachmones.* You know our Yiddish word *rachmones*?"

"Yes."

"Well you won't find it in the Lithuanians. Leda is perhaps too young to understand this, but she is so much kinder and more intelligent than Lithuanians her age. You should encourage her to meet you, if only in Kovno, she could be of great assistance. If you go, I want you to call me before you leave. I will give you one of Marguerite's cards."

"I have one of Marguerite's cards."

"I will give you another. You will tell me the day you will be in Kovno. I will send the pigeons to Kovno to meet you. You will go to Vilijampole, the Slobodka ghetto across the river. There you will go to the main square, Demokratu Square, a large, open square. It is place where the Jews of the Kovno ghetto were forced to assemble for the Germans *aktions.* The old, the sick, families with children, the entire ghetto in lines. All the men, all the able men and women, motioned one way, the elderly, sick, the children motioned the other way, that led to the Ninth Fort and death. It was like Mengele in Auschwitz, only in Kovno it was another German doing the selecting. You will stand there in Demokratu Square, the place where thousands were selected for death, and I will send the pigeons to you. You will see them and report back to me. It will be our quiet secret. Do not tell even Leda. She can stand with you if you meet her and she will see with her own eyes where her pigeons go each week. But you and I, we will have this secret pact. Do you agree, Professor Levin?"

"I agree."

"Good. Very good." Emanuelis stood up and looked up at the sky. "I will call them down now."

He began to make cooing sounds through his cupped hand pointed toward the sky.

"Did you feel rain?" he asked. "I think it's beginning to rain. It makes it more difficult. They don't hear as well through the rain."

He made the cooing sounds into his hands staring at the sky. "I think I saw them flying through the lights." He called to them again and interrupted the call with sharp whistles. "I don't think they'll come. It's the rain. I'll have to call Leda and she'll bring them down."

"Leda, come out here Leda, please," he called back into the corridor. "Leda do you hear me? Come and call the pigeons down."

She came through the door wearing an apron. "It's beginning to rain Emanuelis. You'll never get them that way. Just let them fly. Marguerite almost has our dinner ready."

"No, bring them down Leda. They'll catch cold if we leave them in the rain. Watch her, Professor, Leda will now perform her specialité."

She began beating on a garbage can lid with a wooden rod.

Suddenly four birds swooped down through the beams of light in the rain and landed.

"Ah, Leda, you are always marvelous. You have a magic touch."

She smiled and made a little bow and refilled the glass of wine she brought with her. "Yes, Emanuelis, I'm good at pounding on garbage lids. It is indeed my specialité. It is my Magic Flute."

"Ah, but you are an expert."

"Now excuse me again gentlemen. I will help with the dinner, unless you want help with the birds Emanuelis."

"No, go back to Marguerite. Now Professor, let me introduce you as I dry them off. I have this old towel they love. I warm each of them for a moment." He reached for one of the birds, a gray-breasted bird with white tail feathers.

"Welcome home Yitzhak. This is my friend Professor Levin all the way from America." He fed the bird a few seeds and smoothed its crown feathers and soothed it, occasionally cooing as he talked.

"Yitzhak is named for our first commander in Vilna, Yitzhak Wittenberg. Before Abba Kovner there was Yitzhak Wittenberg. He was taken prisoner by the Germans and murdered. They captured him, but as they were taking him out of the ghetto we freed him. Then they threatened to kill all the Jews in the ghetto if they did not turn him in, so he surrendered himself. He was our first commander and hero. We think he committed suicide before the Germans could torture him. He never revealed our secrets." He stroked the bird as he talked and placed it in a separate small coop and gave it water and more seed. "So that is Yitzhak, one of my warriors."

He held out his hand to a second bird and made the same cooing sounds and wrapped it in the towel. The bird's head was barely visible, just its beak and red eyes darting. "This is Shmerke, named after Shmerke Kaczerginski. He was another comrade in Vilna, a very brave fighter. He survived, but died in a plane crash in Argentina in 1954." He lowered the towel and exposed the tube around the bird's throat. "Here Shmerke, my dear little fellow, let me show Professor Levin your mezuzah. You see, it is empty, the contents have been delivered." He kissed Shmerke's crown feathers and placed him in his coop with seeds and water.

"And now the last two, Abba and Vitka." He reached for them and held them together in the towel. "Husband and wife. The Commander and his lovely wife, Abba Kovner and Vitka Kempner, woman of courage. You see their mezuzah tubes are also empty. They have delivered their contents to Lithuania and have completed their mission." He kissed both of their crowns. "I love all of these birds. They're my children." He gently set them into their coops.

"An old man, Professor, yes. Now you see me, but I am still in my own way a fighter. An old Jew who will never give up."

20

THEY SAT DOWN TO DINNER. Marguerite poured each of them another glass of wine and served them cabbage soup, hot borscht, with thick cabbage leaves and raisins. It was very sweet and she put some challah bread on the table on a silver platter and covered the bread with a pink napkin.

"This reminds me of the cabbage borscht my grandmother used to serve," Jonny Levin told them, "very sweet and thick with cabbage. Thank you, Marguerite, it's delicious."

"I think Marguerite is making us all drunk with this Italian Chianti." Leda held up her glass. "I can feel my mind filling with dreams of Italia, Venice, the Grand Canal, dreams of a handsome gondolier in a striped shirt and straw hat with a black ribbon singing to me."

"Leda. You are a born romantic. You are confusing the gondoliers of your dream with your friends at the Tivoli lagoon," Marguerite said to her, and both women laughed and teased each other in Lithuanian.

Emanuelis watched the women, his eyes dancing in the light of the candles Marguerite had lit and placed in two fluted silver candelabra. "Professor Levin, you must tell us something about

America," he said. "I've never been to the United States; neither has Marguerite."

"What shall I tell you?"

"Tell about the political situation. What do Americans really think about Bush and his war in Iraq?"

"I can't tell you what Americans think. I can tell you what I think. I think it's wrong. We don't belong in Iraq or the Mid East."

"Ah, yes" Emanuelis said, "But what are we to do about the terrorists? Certainly a small country like Denmark cannot fight them. The whole world turns to America."

"The Superpower," Leda said to him. "You have all the money and the power in the world."

"Are you of the party of Bush or Cheney, or are you of the other party?" Emanuelis asked.

"I am of the other party although I have occasionally voted Republican."

"He is a nice man," Leda said pointing her soup spoon at him. "I have met several Americans, but this man is the nicest. He is a gentleman."

The dinner continued in good spirits. All of them were flushed with wine and they ate a pasta and shrimp sweetened in tomato and red wine sauce. They finished with a dessert of tiny Danish cakes and coffee. When the two women left the room, Emanuelis spoke to him again about their pact. He leaned across the table.

"You will not forget our understanding, Professor Levin," he said taking his hand. "You will notify me what day you will be in Kovno."

"I will not forget."

"I think it will be interesting for you. Quite interesting."

When he and Leda said goodbye, Marguerite pushed a tiny mezuzah into his hand, a replica of the mezuzah the pigeons wore. She closed her hand over his, "You will keep this, Professor Levin."

"Another gift?"

"Yes, I have filled it with some of my cuttings, lambs and angels and tabernacles, profiles of Moses, and lions of Judah. Take them to America, it would make me very happy to know that my gifts will be with you and seen in America."

"Thank you, Marguerite." He reached out to her and kissed her on the cheek and put his arms around her. She had the scent of a sweet perfume and warm, smooth skin that he brushed with his lips.

"Emanuelis," he took her father's hand, "I know we shall meet again. It has been my pleasure to meet you, to talk with you, and to see the work of your talented daughter. You are a fine man, a man of courage that I will always remember."

He also put his arms around Emanuelis, another gesture of emotion that he wasn't used to making, but it explained his real feelings and his sadness at leaving both of them.

Out on the street, Leda began to pull him across the street where she said she knew there was an alley that led to the boulevard where they could find a taxi station. "We'll go back to my flat. Marguerite has made me drunk again. We will go to my flat and I will give you another massage. This time I will paint a flower on your stomach."

The mention of painting a flower on his stomach made him think of the beautiful white flower tinged with pink on the cover of Gabriel Garcia Marquez's novel "Memories of my Melancholy Whores". Marquez was one of his favorite writers whom he affectionately thought of by his nickname "Gabo." In his first work of fiction in ten years, Marquez created a ninety-year-old bachelor who had never been with a woman he had not paid. By the age of fifty, he'd been with 514 women and then he'd stopped keeping count. On his ninetieth birthday, as a gift for himself, he had his Madam friend procure a fourteen-year-old virgin. If "Gabo" can have a ninety-year-old cavorting with a fourteen-year-old, why not Jonny Levin and Leda? The flower on the cover of "Gabo's" novel just covered the nipple of her right breast, her eyes are closed, she's asleep.

But suddenly he heard himself saying, "No Leda, I don't want another massage."

"You are such a foolish man. I never had a man refuse an invitation to come to my flat."

"I'm not refusing the invitation. I have another engagement. I told a friend I would meet him at six o'clock at the hotel."

"And you find him more important than me?"

"Leda, you are a beautiful young woman. Full of life and passion. I am sixty-two years old, older than your father. As much as I am attracted to you I have no desire to have a flower painted on my stomach."

"Even if I sign the painting?"

He laughed and she took his hands and rested her head on his shoulder. "You have not made me drunk this time. Marguerite has done it. I am not used to Italian wine. Anyway, if you find me so beautiful, you should take me to Lithuania with you as your companion. I will protect you from the Lithuanians. You will need protection."

"I won't take you, but I will meet you there. I'll meet you in Kaunas. I'd much rather meet you than a stranger, your friend Dalia."

"You would then pay me the four thousand kroner that you would have paid Dalia?"

"Only if you produce Simon."

"Simon? I don't even know if he's alive. And how will I pay for my trip? I will have to pay again for a false passport. I might be caught. They could put me in a prison. It's too big a risk, even for a fool like me."

"I've already given you seven thousand kroner."

"But that was for my paintings. I would need at least another five thousand just to get a passport and pay for my airfare. The passport could be difficult, but if you give me another five thousand, I will come with you." Her face brightened and she suddenly broke away from him and twirled with her hands extended from her body like the wings of a bird. "Even though I am drunk and you will not come to my flat, I am still willing to negotiate with you. Americans love to negotiate and I am a willing partner."

"A very clever partner." He quickly calculated that he would have given her two thousand dollars total if she produced Simon and if not about sixteen hundred dollars.

"Alright," he said. "We've got a deal."

She laughed and came running toward him and slapped his hand. "Like the Americans do, another deal. How do you say it? Deal? I slapped your hand and now according to the Americans I've met, you must abide by it. We again have made a deal."

They then came out of the alley into the bright lights of the boulevard. There was a line of taxis exactly where she'd said.

He took her to the lead taxi and opened the door and pushed her in.

She held out her hand to him and instead of shaking it he kissed her hand.

"You are very gallant my dear mister American. That is so unlike most American men. Alright, I will meet you in Kaunas. Call my machine and leave a message. Tell me what day you'll be in Kaunas and where you'll be staying. I'll come to your room and paint a flower on your hand. You are such a gentleman. But you must deliver another five thousand kroner to me before you leave. I will put it in my jar with my other dollars."

"Goodnight, Leda, my beautiful little swan. I will contact you."

He decided to walk back to the hotel. Had he actually said to her "Goodnight, my beautiful little swan"? What would he do with her in Lithuania? She'd just be in the way. He wanted to be alone in Lithuania without any distractions, but he needed her to deliver Simon to him. Unless of course she could be lying. The whole concept of her friend Iphigenia's father being the man in the photograph was highly unlikely. How would he be able to verify that he was really the man? He would need Leda at his side to translate, ask the right questions and relay the answers to him. If he was really going to Lithuania, he would have to stop dreaming and book his airline ticket when he got back to his hotel and leave, just leave Denmark tomorrow morning. He'd have to shake all the literary allusions out of his head, even his friend "Gabo." They just enfeebled him. Also the novel. He'd have to stop writing the novel. All the references to Jewish writers, Bellow, Roth, Malamud, Stern, the Singer brothers and their sister, Esther Kreitman, Cynthia Ozick, he'd shake them all out of his head. Bruce Jay Friedman, Norman Mailer, Henry Roth. He'd have to compress them all, along with their books, into a huge cube, a mammoth cube of compressed literary scrap. All their writing compressed into indecipherable hieroglyphics and have a crane pick the cube up and dump it into some junkyard far away from his imagination. Maybe turn it into an abstract sculpture and stick it with the Henry Moores in the courtyard of the Louisiana Museum and leave it here in Denmark. Bellow the *pipek* in his wooden box. Mailer, the man who stabbed his wife. Henry Roth who screwed his sister (now that's real sistermony). Also, Philip Roth and his manic friends Portnoy and Zuckerman. Malamud and his friend Dubin and Bernie's Magic Barrel. He'd make a compression of all their writing and leave one huge cube in the Louisiana courtyard. His gift to Denmark. *Tak fir alt*, Jonny Levin. What about the Israeli writers? He'd also have to bundle them up too, compress all of them and their novels into another cube. Hebrew letters, mashed together until they were indecipherable Amos Oz, David Grossman, Yehuda Amichei, Aharon Appelfeld, Yael Dayan. What about Kovner? He'd read Abba Kovner's poems written in New York at Sloan Kettering just before Kovner had his cancerous larynx removed. No, he wouldn't include Kovner. Kovner would be with him in Lithuania. Kovner in spirit. Also Abraham Sutzkever, another partisan poet of Vilna and hero of the Resistance. He'd take both of them with him, Kovner and Sutzkever.

21

VILNIUS. HE'S IN HIS HOTEL ROOM IN VILNIUS. He has brought four photographs with him and the Jäger Report. First the photographs. He keeps looking at them, examining them for new details, anything he hasn't seen before. Two of the photographs have the image of the man he refers to as "Simon." The primary photograph, which he allegedly shares with Simon, shows a group of Jewish women in Kaunas being herded out of a truck into a square, the women are surrounded by Lithuanian guards holding rifles. There must be maybe fifty women and six Lithuanian men with rifles. The man at the right edge of the photo could be Simon. He wears riding britches and boots. There is a tri-color armband on his left arm. He's shown in profile, fully visible. None of the others except for the man in the beret are fully visible; they all have turned their backs to the camera. No one really is aware of the photographer. The man, who could be Simon, stands with his hands on his rifle, the rifle held vertically before him, its band slung over his shoulder. This man shows no expression. Nothing.

Not menace, not repose. He doesn't even seem to be watching the women. He's just staring into space, a typical Lithuanian blonde face, a touch of the Slav in his facial bones leading from the eyes, a military haircut, hair shorn at the sides, flaxen hair full on his crown. Where are they taking these women? To the Ninth Fort to be shot? Will he be one of their executioners? None of the women wear yellow stars on their breasts or on their backs. This must have been early in the occupation of Kaunas by the Germans. No Germans are shown present in the photo. The women are of all ages; a few even seem to be smiling slightly at the shouted orders. Apparently they've just been ordered to run by the man in the beret, the only other Lithuanian shown in profile. The man Leda said was her English teacher and a friend of her father's. One of the young women looks almost like one of my daughters, he thinks, and holds a magnifying glass up closer to the photograph.

He moves the magnifying glass over their faces. Yes, that's probably why some of them seem to have a trace of a nervous smile. They are being shouted at by the man in the beret and ordered to run. He stands splayfooted, shouting at them, erect and tense. He's taller than Simon. He has a cruel face and holds a stick or a crop as if about to flail at the women as they pass him. The trees along the edge of the street seem to be in flower. White flowering trees. Perhaps it's springtime or early summer. None of the women are wearing coats, a few carry coats. Some of the older women wear kerchiefs on their heads. Why are they being ordered to run and where are they being taken?

He puts this photo aside and examines a second photo of men being marched down a street in Kaunas. A group of perhaps about thirty men, again guarded by Lithuanians walking beside them with the same tri-color armband worn on their sleeves. There are perhaps four Lithuanians walking with rifles. The Lithuanian man on the left of the photo, he is certain, is Simon. He wears the same boots and tan riding britches as in the first photo. The same black shirt with the tri-color armband on the left arm, the same facial characteristics, blonde, high cheekbones, hair shorn at the sides, a full head of blond hair at the crown, only this man is angry. This man is menacing and strides at the side of the group of Jewish men. Again, none of the men wore Jewish stars as badges. This Simon looks like a man who could kill. The Jewish men at the left of the column seem to be in step, perhaps he's calling out a cadence. It's unlikely. The men at the center are all out of step and are being watched by an inordinately thin man in a white summer peaked cap, his head averted backwards towards the prisoners as they march behind him. The Jewish men in front, their faces contorted in fear, stare at the thin man in the white cap incredulously. Beside them another Jewish man, a big man who looks like he could overpower any of the guards, walks stolidly staring without expression.

The third photo is of Ponar, men being led toward the killing pits. They have their undershirts pulled up over their heads so they cannot see, a group of about ten men holding on to each other's waists and shoulders. There must be one hundred men in a pit below them surrounded by Lithuanian guards standing on a scaffold. Guards wearing the same armband as in the other photos. Each group of ten men is ordered to stand up and walk a ramp up out of the pit holding onto each other with their undershirts pulled over their heads, until they reach another pit on the other side of the scaffold which is the killing pit. There they are shot and fall on top of the bodies killed before them. They are then covered with a layer of sand. Then another group of ten men is ordered out of the holding pit up the ramp and then the men are led down the scaffold to the edge of the killing pit. No German soldiers are seen in the photo, only Lithuanians in various forms of military dress, all wearing armbands and holding rifles.

The fourth and last photo he also examines with his magnifying glass to see if he can find anything he hasn't seen before. It shows four Jewish men and one Jewish boy about eight or nine about to be shot. They're all at the edge of a pit, presumably it was also taken at Ponar, but it could have been at any one of the execution sites in Lithuania. There are three Lithuanian men with rifles again wearing the same tri-color armbands. Also, there are five Lithuanian men standing at the side of the executioners. These men are civilians dressed in suits, ties, overcoats, and hats. They look like businessmen or civil servants. Each of them is holding a pointed stick, not really a cane, but more like a pointer or a prod. The four Jewish men and the little boy are all naked. Two men stand naked at the edge of the pit, their hands folded in front of them, two men in their late forties or early fifties. They are seconds away from being shot and falling into the pit. A Lithuanian in uniform holding a rifle stands beside them. He is looking up at a man standing above them who appears to be a German officer, but he is in shadow and it is difficult to see him. He is pointing and giving orders. Behind the two naked Jewish men at the edge of the pit is an elderly man, naked, and standing with his arms folded in front of him. Behind him is the little boy. He is also naked, but has a cap on his head, a peaked cap and his hands are tied behind him. He has black curly hair and dark eyes. Walking behind him is a man who could be his brother, they look so much alike, but with the magnifying glass it seems that he's the boy's father, also naked, his hands tied in front of him. He's examined the photo many times, but now for the first time, he notices that the elderly man is wearing one sock.

So now that he's looked at the photos again, he carefully puts them and the magnifying glass back into his briefcase. He then turns off the lights in the room and stands at the window and looks out over the lights of Vilnius.

Where should he go? What should he do? He has a queasy feeling in his stomach and his legs feel weak. The photographs are too horrible to look at without feeling ill. Maybe if he went for a swim he'd feel better. The hotel has a swimming pool. He saw it advertised in a brochure, but does he have a suit? He has some boxer shorts that look like a suit. The hotel is the SAS Radisson Astorija. It's a beautiful old hotel, four stories, in the heart of Vilnius' Old Town. It's advertised in the brochure as being across the street from Saint Casimir's Church and only three blocks from the Old Town Market. Should he take a walk? He turns on the lamp at his bedside and sits on the bed and takes the Jäger Report out of his briefcase. It's a report from the Commander of the German Security Police in Kaunas, one Karl Jäger, dated December 1st, 1941. It lists the number of Jews killed in each Lithuanian city and village chronologically beginning July 4th, 1941. "Kauen (Kaunas) Fort VII, 416 Jews, 47 Jewesses – 463."

The Jäger Report ends November 25th, 1941. During that four-month period, the Germans and their Lithuanian partisan assistants executed 137,346 people, almost entirely Jewish men, women and children. It ends with this chilling statement:

> "Today I can confirm that our objective to solve the Jewish problem for Lithuania has been achieved by EK3. In Lithuania there are no more Jews apart from Jewish workers and their families.
>
> The distance between from the assembly point to the graves was on average 4-5 Km.
>
> I consider the Jewish action more or less terminated as far as Einsatzkommando 3 is concerned.
>
> (signed)
Jäger
SS-Standartenfuhrer"

There are several entries in the Jäger report for Jews that were executed in Mariampole.

> July 7th, 1941 – Mariampole – Jews – 32
> July 8th, 1941 – Mariampole – 14 Jews, 5 Comm. Officials – 19
> July 14th, 1941 – Mariampole – 21 Jews, 1 Russ., 9 Lith Comm – 31
> July 18th, 1941 – Mariampole – 39 Jews, 14 Jewesses – 53
> July 25th, 1941 – Mariampole – 90 Jews, 13 Jewesses – 103
> September 1, 1941 – Mariampole – 1763 Jews, 1812 Jewesses, 1404 Jewish children, 109 Mentally sick, 1 German subject (f) married to a Jew, 1 Russian (f) – 5,090.

He folded the Jäger Report and put it back in his briefcase with his other books. It was all too much for him and was beginning to engulf him. He turned the lamp off again and stood at the window. He saw no people on the streets, only the shadow of the old church across from the hotel. The numbers were too much for him. 137,000 Jewish men, women and children killed by the Germans and Lithuanians methodically listed city by city, town by town and village by village. These were defenseless people dumped into pits. 70,000 alone in Ponar. He'd go there tomorrow. He'd say a prayer in Ponar alone in the forest. That would be something he could do, stop there on his way to Mariampole and then spend the night in Mariampole or Kaunas. He'd left a message for Emanuelis that he'd be in Kaunas on the third night and at Demokratu Square at 4:00 p.m. He left the same message on Leda's machine, she should come to Demokratu Square at 4:00 p.m. on the third night and she should bring Simon Braucivius with her. If she did, what would he do to Braucivius? Shoot him in the head? One shot in the head and then two to the heart and say to him, "I am a Jew." One dead, drunken old

Lithuanian man in exchange for 137,000 Jews. Would that be a fair exchange? Could he actually pull the trigger and kill Braucivius? And if he could, where would he get a gun? Well, why not just beat him to death like the Jews were bludgeoned by Lithuanian thugs in a square in Kaunas while the Lithuanians and Germans watched. Could he beat a man to death? Carry an iron bar inside his jacket, confront Simon and say to him, "*As Zydu*" and beat him to death. And what about Leda? What would he do with her? Leda would be a witness. Would he have to kill her too, beautiful young Leda? The Lithuanian Swan, would he have to kill her because she was a witness? How could he do something like that? He couldn't. He could ask her to leave him and Simon alone, to walk away and go back to her house and leave the old man alone with him. There would just be the two of them. Still Leda would know what had happened when Simon's body was discovered. Or maybe he would burn the body, like they burned the bodies of the Jews and then dig a pit and burn Simon's bones. Would that be revenge? Would that atone for the dying man who in Kaunas had scrawled on the wall of his house in his own blood the Yiddish word for "revenge." How could he even think this way. He was a scholar, not a killer. He should leave the room and take a swim, go down to the pool and try to wash away the stench of death that was everywhere in Vilnius.

22

He's in the pool in his boxer shorts. There's no one else there but two boys and their mother. The boys are playing a diving game, the mother is stretched out on a lounge chair reading a magazine. She's slim and brown-haired, in her thirties, wearing a bikini, and smoking. He wanted to say something to her about smoking in the pool area but he didn't know how to ask her politely to put her cigarette out. Also he didn't want a scene so he just stayed at the deep end of the pool and tried to ignore her and the boys. The boys were hard to ignore, though. Each about eleven or twelve, water rats, skinny, and wrestling with each other until one would fall into the pool. They were playing a diving game, counting to three, *vienas, du, trys*, and then diving. One would dive and the other would dive in on three trying to tag the first boy, *vienas, du, trys,* the shrieking and laughter disturbed him. The mother paid absolutely no attention. What if he were to stand up and dive off the edge in his boxer shorts that would probably fall down? Would that get her attention? Would she look up from her magazine? He let go of the edge of the pool at the deep end and swam down deep toward the bottom, the sounds of the boys shrieking *vienas, du, trys*, and their laughter and the mother's smoke all dissolved into a deep cerulean blue.

He bumped his belly on the bottom of the pool. He felt like Bruno Schulz transmogrified into a fish in David Grossman's novel. He'd given up on literary allusions, though. Left them all in Denmark. He wasn't Bruno Schulz. He wasn't transmogrified, but he did feel covered with a slime, a kind of green jellied slime that had worked its way up from beneath his pores and was trying to choke him, moving into his nostrils and his eyes, a putrid slime that began to seep into him after looking at the photographs. Diving deep into the blue of the pool, clumsy in his boxer shorts, almost ridiculous, nevertheless he was cleansing himself. He could feel the slime washing away and when he popped up from the dive there was the mother, her hand over her breasts bending down toward him at pool's edge asking him something. What was she saying? She pointed to his watch. He was wearing his wristwatch; it's waterproof, he'd always worn it while swimming. She apparently wants to know what time it was. He held his left hand up to her; she squinted and took his wrist in her hand. His first Lithuanian woman wrist touching. She was nearsighted and as she bent toward him and took his wrist he could see a mole glistening on her right breast. *Aciu*, she said to him. Apparently "thank you," it sounded like "achoo." Like a sneeze. She went padding barefoot back to her chair and magazine and lit another cigarette.

So he'd at least partially removed the slime and a Lithuanian woman had touched his wrist. He would get out of the pool, put on the white terrycloth robe the hotel had provided, and go back to the room and dress for dinner. He'd seen the dining room, a glassed-in area in front of the hotel overlooking the street. He would go there and have a glass of wine and then perhaps take a walk. Would she have touched his wrist if she'd known he was a Jew? "*As Zydu*," he should have said to her and waited for her reaction.

Back in the room he dressed for dinner. He put on his red and blue striped tie inset with tiny gold Danish royal crowns. He also pinned his Danish flag pin into the lapel of his navy blue jacket. He even spritzed himself with some hairspray. His hair was getting long over his ears and curling on his neck. He looked in the mirror and touched his face. No green slime. A ruddy faced Danish yachtsman with the red and white cross Danish flag pin. Did he look like a Dane on holiday in Vilnius?

At the desk when he left his key, the young woman turned to him. He handed her the key. "*Aciu*," she said and smiled. Again, the word for "thank you". Instead of "*tak tak*." She was quite lovely, a touch of the Slav in her slanted eyebrows and eyes. Not as beautiful as the two Danish women, but much more serious. Genghis Khan had left his imprint on the Lithuanians; a hoard of Mongol tribesmen had left them with a touch of the Orient in their features. The imprint of several thousand years of inbreeding. The same as the Poles, a trace of Mongol in their faces, their eyes, their cheekbones. They would deny it, though. He'd once incensed a Polish woman colleague with his suggestion of her Mongol ancestry, so ever since he kept his racial theories to himself.

At dinner he ordered a sparkling wine, a rouge from Alsace, and duck with red cabbage and a clear vegetable soup. He wasn't hungry though. He really needed some fresh air. He would just pick at the food. He was the only single person in the dining room. They were in a glassed-in first floor overlooking the street, all the couples sitting in banquettes covered with imitation velvet, murmuring to each other in the candlelight. It made him think of his own family and his two marriages.

He held his hand up to the candlelight. No green slime on his hand or fingers. Where was Magdalena now, his first wife? Did he really care anymore? Yes he cared; she was still the mother of his daughters. They were in touch with her. After the divorce she'd gone to Santa Fe and with another wealthy Belgian woman had opened a custom jewelry shop on the square. Magdalena was from a family of diamond cutters in Antwerp. When last he'd asked his daughter Alysia about her mother, she said she'd never remarried and was back in Antwerp caring for her elderly mother who had Alzheimer's. Beautiful Magdalena with her cultured French manners, he could never provide her with the refinements she required, season tickets for the opera, a large apartment, designer clothes, they argued over money constantly. He'd borrowed heavily from his father. Poor Maynard, the real Lithuanian Jew, son of immigrants, fighting his way up through the agonies of the auto parts business and the indifference of his professorial son and the son's artistic European wife, sucking away his money. He never complained. Maynard never once complained, but his wife complained. Elaine told her son John that Magdalena was a spoiled European bitch and would soon leave him. His mother was prescient. A year later she did leave him and set up her shop in Santa Fe. He'd been there secretly once, unknown to her, sitting in the sunlight in the square, La Fonda. He watched her in the window of her shop working on a display, her hair in a ponytail and blonde. She looked ten years younger. He never told anyone he'd been there, not even their daughters. It took at least five years to stop loving her.

The duck came. He ordered another glass of wine. He examined his fingers again in the candlelight. He looked up the Lithuanian word for "duck" in his guidebook, *antienos.* In Polish it was *kavka*. In Czech he didn't know, but *kafka* meant "blackbird." Were there blackbirds out there in the square? Of course there were blackbirds in Lithuania, a country full of blackbirds, ugly blackbirds instead of nightingales. He'd looked for nightingales in the sky above Vilnius. Nightingales and Emanuelis' pigeons. And what about Ramona, why did she also leave him, or was that too fresh to talk about? She didn't leave him. They left each other. Ten years together in Evanston and they'd just grown very tired of each other. So she went to California and he came here. Was it that simple? No it wasn't that simple. First the sex gradually dissipated and then disappeared entirely. He began staying nights in his office trying to write a novel that he finally ran through a shredder. Ramona, sweet Ramona, I just grew boring, flaccid, and tired, so you left. She sent him some short note cards from San Francisco and then she moved to Santa Barbara. She found a job as an administrator at a temple scheduling courses, lectures and programs. His daughter Sandra had told him that they lunched together occasionally. Sandra had come up from Los Angeles, but now that Sandra had a live-in boyfriend, she hadn't seen Ramona. He wondered if Ramona had a live-in man. The two of them, living by the sea in Santa Barbara, a nice life. What was he doing in Vilnius? Why would he permit himself to get involved with someone like Leda? What would all the women who had known him as a husband and a father say about him? Did it really matter? Yes it did matter. It mattered to him.

He paid the check and walked outside into the street.

23

HE WALKED OUT OF THE HOTEL to the street and stood in front of the hotel. The name of the street was *Didzioji*. The address of the hotel was *Didzioji* 35. He'd have to remember that if he got lost or just wandered too far. He had the brochure for the hotel folded in his inside breast pocket. It was a lovely spring night. There was no chill in the air. He pulled his sports jacket up snug around his neck, with his Danish crown tie and his Danish flag pin, he wondered if he really looked like a Dane. What were the streets of Vilnius' Old Town section like at night? Were they safe for a man strolling a block or two away from the hotel? He started to walk past the large church across the street and around the corner he saw some lights. It looked like a small carnival, several brown tents, and music from some loudspeakers, folk music. There was a group of young women, girls in peasant costumes dancing on a small stage and people standing watching them. He stood behind the crowd. The girls were very young dancers in flowered peasant skirts and babushkas. They looked like 10-12 year olds dressed in white blouses with embroidered vests and couplets. The same ivory-planed high featured Slavic faces, very serious, a few half smiles. As they danced they took each other's arms and whirled and stamped their boots. To him, the lone Danish observer, the dance was almost like a military march. Should he join them? Step up on the stage, bow to the young girls and their parents and say to them, "*As Zydu*" and take their hands? What would the reaction be of the small crowd watching them? He saw a boy standing behind his muscular, shaven-headed father. The boy was secretly practicing ballet steps behind the father's back. He wasn't going to take the stage and dance with them, though. He just wanted to remain anonymous, invisible. He heard a "pop-pop-pop" sound and turned and saw there was a shooting booth just down the street. He would leave the dancers and try his skill as a marksman.

He walked toward the shooting booth. As he crossed the street he looked up at the street sign, *Subaciaus* Street. He didn't want to just wander around. He wanted to know where he was, if he imprinted each street he'd find his way back to the Astorija without any problems. The shooting booth was much like the one in Copenhagen, only a more tattered-looking tent, almost like Madame Josefina's confessional booth. "You want to be a writer? Every putz wants to be a writer." The old woman's wrinkled face came to him. "What kind of hand is this, silky smooth, not a worker's hand. My Bruno had calluses on his hands from all the rocking horses he made for Polish children in his shop." Suddenly the old woman's wrinkled face and saffron gown drifted away and he was faced by a sullen young Lithuanian teenager with plaits of her blond hair worn around the crown of her head. She was reading a book. She handed him a rifle, a pellet gun, and said something to him in Lithuanian. "Do you speak English?" he asked her. She looked at him blankly. He put the gun down. It was chained to the panel in front of the booth. He took out his phrase book from his jacket and looked up the phrase, "Do you speak English?" *"Ar jus kalbate Angliskai?"* She looked at him without expression. "*Ne.*" Her eyes were the same cerulean blue as the water of the pool. She must be about fifteen or sixteen. One of the young peasant girl dancers who had discarded her flowered dirndl and boots and been graduated to a job as a shooting booth attendant. He wanted the phrase for "how much?" *Kiek?* He had some Euros that he'd changed at the airport ATM. He opened up his wallet and took out the smallest bill, and she took it from him and gave him some smaller bills and coins in change. All this with the same expression. Not a sign of recognition. Nevertheless, in the exchange of money she had touched his wrist and now his count of Lithuanian women who had touched him was up to two.

What were the prizes for marksmanship? There were some cheap little statuettes on a shelf that looked like plaster Chinese pagodas, also a pipe with a bottle of green colored liquid. The liquid was apparently soap that you poured into the pipe to make bubbles. He looked at his fingers on the stock of the gun. They weren't green. Apparently he'd succeeded in washing off the green slime in the pool, but if he placed the requisite number of shots in the bullseye of the paper target clipped to a board at the back of the booth, he could win his own bottle of green slime. There was also a set of wooden nested eggs bearing a reproduction of Vladimir Putin. He shouldered the rifle, took a deep breath and slowly squeezed off his first shot. He just missed the bullseye. A little low. She wasn't watching him. He was still alone in the booth. She had put on a pair of black-framed glasses and was reading her book. Another choice on the shelf in addition to the set of Putin nested eggs was a wooden China blue egg with decals of baby chicks. Also there was a small tri-colored red, yellow, and green Lithuanian flag on a stick. He squeezed off another shot, this one just a little closer and perhaps an eighth of an inch from the bullseye. Now she was watching him. She had put the book down and was staring at him through the black-framed-bottle Russian era eyeglasses. She was wearing tennis shoes and a yellow sweatshirt that had a word scrolled in red on its front, *Taip*. He knew that word. It was the first word in his phrasebook, "yes". He inhaled and said to himself, *Taip* and squeezed off six more shots one after another. Several were right in the bullseye. She came down off her seat when the gun emptied.

So now he had two targets to show his prowess as an American marksman, one from Copenhagen and one from Vilnius. He selected the pipe and bottle of liquid as his prize. He tried to remember his Danish prizes, the photo of the young Queen Margrethe, the wooden royal guardsman, or was it a wooden Viking with a helmet and a fluff of beard? There was something else, but he couldn't remember as he walked further down *Subaciaus* Street into the darkness away from the lights of the carnival. He sat down on a stone bench in a small square. There was a statue there. It looked like a shrouded woman, a religious figure. He looked up at the sky. No nightingales flying, no pigeons. He filled the pipe with some of the green liquid and sent a green bubble floating up into the night sky of Vilnius. It was an easy way to get rid of the slime, just buy a bottle of it and blow it up into the darkness. He couldn't really see the bubbles as they floated out, but the emptying of the contents of the bottle seemed to bring him some kind of relief. When he had finished, instead of taking the pipe and bottle back with him to add to his collection of trophies, he left them on the bench and walked back to the hotel. He traced the street signs he remembered. Perhaps he would sleep tonight. He would dream of the green, viscous bubbles floating in the darkness and hope they wouldn't turn into the faces of the young students standing on the stairs waiting for school to open. That they wouldn't turn into the students' faces or into the tortured face of Bruno Schulz or into the faces of Abba Kovner or Abraham Sutzkever. In this city, even though disguised as a Dane, he was an interloper. Vilnius was a Jewish graveyard and he really had no business being alive here.

Suddenly he decided not to go back to the hotel, but to return to the shooting booth. He wanted to win another prize to bring back some trophy from Vilnius other than the discarded bubble pipe. He would win the nested eggs of Vladimir Putin. Why Putin? Why not Valdas Adamkus, the President of Lithuania, the man from Chicago who looked like a gray-faced, prim, exhausted bureaucrat. Probably the nested eggs of Putin were something Lithuanians liked to shoot at. He approached the shooting booth and took out some of the bills the young attendant had given him. There was no hint of recognition as she made change for him and handed him the same rifle. A man, though, was seated beside her, perhaps her father. Maybe the owner of the concession? He had a wide mouth, light brown thin hair, a sallow complexion. He was holding a rifle that he was cleaning. She hopped back up beside him and began reading her book again. The man though was watching, waiting for him to begin shooting. He felt confident that he could win the nested eggs of Putin. Apparently to win he would have to put all eight shots into the bullseye. He squeezed off the first shot and hit the bullseye, and then again used his new technique of squeezing off all seven remaining shots in succession. He succeeded in shredding the bullseye. Instead of handing him the nested lacquered encased Putin eggs, the man carefully inspected the target and shook his head. He brought it over and pointed to one tiny hole that was partially out of the shredded circle. Instead of Putin, he was given a green plastic bookmark with a reproduction of a human eye inset at the top. The man handed it to him and pointed at his Danish flag pin.

"Dansk?"

He didn't answer. If they were going to cheat him out of his trophy, let them draw their own conclusions.

Back at the hotel he kicked his shoes off, carefully hung his jacket in the closet, and picked up the phone and called Leda in Copenhagen.

While he was waiting for the throaty calling sounds to form their chain and make a connection, he looked at the eye in his new trophy and moved it back and forth in the light so that the eye seemed to be staring back at him.

Suddenly there was a connection.

"*Ciao.*"

"Leda?"

"*Tak.*"

"It's Jonny Levin calling from Vilnius."

"Jonny Levin, my American friend? I have been waiting for your call. I have something here for you, an envelope."

"Do you have your passport?"

"No, not yet. I was promised it today, but it did not come."

"Leda, I'm to meet you in two days in Kaunas."

"So you will meet my friend Dalia instead. I am sad for you. I seem to have paid your money and I think they have cheated me. I paid them five thousand Kroner for a passport. I think you must meet Dalia instead of me. I have a way of contacting her. Just tell me where you shall meet her, what time and place. Did you say Demokratu Square at 4:00? She is my friend; she will be there. Also, her English is better than mine and she is more beautiful and intelligent than I am. She will not waste your money like I do."

"Leda, are you sure you can't get a passport? It would be so much easier if you were there instead of Dalia."

"No, I think I've been cheated out of your five thousand kroner. You'll have to work with Dalia. She will help you. She is a good person."

"Did you get my message where to meet? The day after tomorrow, 4:00 at Demokratu Square in Kaunas?"

"Yes, I have communicated that to Dalia. 4 p.m., Demokratu Square. It is in what we call Vilijampole. The old Jewish section."

"Will she have Braucivius with her?"

"How should I know? If he is alive, perhaps she will bring him with her. Perhaps he is dead or will be too drunk or old to come with her. In any event you have promised to pay her four thousand kroner."

"I said I'd pay her only if she produced Braucivius."

"And if she doesn't, at least pay for her taxi and pay for her dinner. Don't be harsh with her, Jonny Levin. Also if by chance you see my parents, say hello to them for me. Tell them that their daughter is a success as an artist in Copenhagen."

"I will and I'll be kind to Dalia."

"You promise you will do that?"

"Yes."

"Okay. It's a deal. Now I will open the envelope I have for you. Or shall I wait until you return to Copenhagen?"

"No, open it. How did you get it?"

"I went to your hotel to see if you had actually checked out. The old man at the desk thinks I'm your daughter. He said you'd left, but another guest at the hotel left this envelope for you. I'm opening it."

"What does it say?"

"There's a hand-written message, but more important, Jonny Levin, it's stuffed with money. American one-hundred-dollar bills. One, two, four, ten. Actually ten one-hundred-dollar bills and a note. It's written in English, but I can read the handwriting."

"Read it."

"'B.U.R.C.H.I.K.'. Is that a word? 'You checked out and I missed you. You won again. Here's a G.R.A.N.D. I owe you. You are my M.A.Z.E.L.. Call me in N.Y.C. anytime 212-743-2813. Your pal, M.O.O.N.E.Y. P.S. Here's another joke for you.'"

"'A man walks into a tavern dressed as a H.A.S.S.I.D, black hat, ear locks. He's got a parrot on his shoulder. The bartender says, where did you get him? The parrot answers – in Brooklyn, in Williamsburg.'"

"'How do you like that one Jonny, a Y.I.D.D.I.S.H.E.R. parrot.'"

"Leda?"

"What?"

"Just keep the envelope. I'll be back in Copenhagen in three days."

"I will put it in my refrigerator with my eels and my jar of American money. I will have it for you. What did you do, win at the casino? You're a lucky man. When you come back to Copenhagen we'll go to the casino together."

"In three days. When I leave Kaunas I have a flight from Vilnius the next morning, SAS."

"I will be waiting for you, Jonny Levin. I will hold your money for you. Please thank Dalia for me and good luck. I wish you a safe return, my American friend."

24

In the morning he checked out of the hotel to take a train to Mariampole. He'd reserved a room through the concierge downstairs at the Hotel Europejski, Mariampole. The concierge was very helpful and polite and told him he was the only American in the hotel. He knew the train he booked would stop at Paneriai, the Forest at Ponar where seventy thousand Jews were killed mostly by Lithuanian firing squads. The Paneriai Forest was only six miles outside of Vilnius and Paneriai was the first stop on the Mariampole train. He would just get off the train, spend an hour there, and then catch a later train to Mariampole. He'd picked up a brochure in the lobby that offered guided tours through Ponar—a hundred Euros for a guide in a car, a hundred-ten Euros for a guide in a minibus. There was something obscene about taking a guide and a car to Ponar. The Jewish prisoners were forced to walk surrounded by Lithuanian guards, or were forced into trucks or trains. They were then led to sand pits that had originally been dug by the Russians for oil storage tanks. He didn't want some pedantic Lithuanian lecturing him on what happened at Ponar. He knew what happened there. He would take the train by himself and use his guidebook to buy the ticket to Mariampole even though the concierge had offered to send a messenger from the hotel to do it for him.

He didn't have the trouble at the station that he'd anticipated. There was a helpful young man who spoke excellent English that the ticket agent called over to the window. The transaction was easy. He'd even had time to buy two bottles of water and an apple. The ride to Ponar was only ten minutes. He was left standing alone at a small station platform with the gates of Ponar directly across from him. The entrance was marked by a gate that spelled out in horizontal block concrete letters:

PANERIU MEMORIALAS

He walked toward the gate. It had begun to rain lightly, an appropriate gray rain. There was a group of people walking ahead of him, the women with small brightly colored umbrellas, like daubs of paint through the grayness of the rain. He let them go ahead. There was a directory sign and he could vaguely translate it. One of the words indicated a museum. He'd read that there was a small museum at Ponar. The other arrows probably led to the killing pits. He had several photos of Ponar and he knew there were sites of several killing pits grown over with grass but still clearly visible as depressions in the forest. These were the areas where the Jews were led, men, women, and children, forced to undress, and then shot in the head usually in groups of ten so the bodies would fall on top of those previously shot. They were then covered with a thin layer of sand and another ten people would be led to the edge of the pit. He'd examined several of the photos in his room at the hotel with a magnifying glass. In one photo the men were led into a holding area and then made to walk over wooden planking to the edge of the killing pit, each man holding the waist of the man ahead and blindfolded by having their undershirts over their heads. They were surrounded by Lithuanian guards both in the holding pit and on the scaffold that led to the killing pit. There were maybe twenty or thirty guards. They were all dressed in the same uniforms that the men wore in the photo where the women in Kaunas were being led running from a truck. One of the men on the killing platform at Ponar looked very much like Braucivius, the same uniform, the brown tunic, black trousers and boots, shorn hair, but the man's back was to the camera. His face wasn't shown. As he thought about the photo he realized it would be unlikely that Simon Braucivius would have come down from Kaunas to Vilnius. It was more likely that Braucivius would have been part of a killing squad at the 9th Fort in Kaunas. Why would they send him to Vilnius? But the resemblance was there. He'd looked over photos on the Internet of a dozen young Lithuanian men alleged to be killers by a kibbutz museum website site in Israel. The Lithuanian men all looked alike to him. They looked like young acolytes for the priesthood, innocent faces, bland and expressionless, all with tunics, some military cadets with high collars, none smiling, all staring at the camera with no trace of emotion. Were these angelic young faces the men who had killed the Jews? He also knew from his research that no Lithuanian had ever served a day in prison as a convicted Jew killer. Only two men had been convicted, both very elderly. One died and the other was excused from prison time due to ill health.

He arrived at the first of the pits and hung back from the group of people. They were being lectured to by a man in Lithuanian. Some couples stood in the light rain with their arms around each other. The man then began speaking in French. A few of the couples were very elderly, some with canes. He wondered whether some were survivors. The man then switched to English, very poor, barely comprehensible. Apparently he was pointing out the sand walls of the pit. Even with the lush green overgrowth you could see that the pit was walled by sand which was later used to cover the bodies. There was a small plaque written in several languages on a stone at the edge of the pit that, in English, read:

HITLERITE FORCES USED THIS SITE
AS A MASS GRAVE FOR CORPSES

He walked away from the group and their lecturer and went by himself to stand at the edge of another pit down the path. It was almost the same size and was also grown over with grass. As he stood alone staring at the pit, the stench of ashes began to fill his nostrils. He noticed there was another small memorial stone at the front of the pit. There was a paragraph written in English.

IN THIS EIGHT-METER DEEP PIT
THE HITLERITE INVADERS
BROUGHT THOSE
WHO WERE ROUNDED UP,
BURNED THEIR CORPSES, AND
DISPOSED OF THEIR BONES

He shook his head and stared at the stone. "Hitlerite invaders?" What about the Lithuanians? Nothing was said about the Lithuanians. Who were the men with the guns at the killing pits? The innocent priest acolytes in the brown tunics wearing the Lithuanian flag armbands, were they "Hitlerite invaders?" No, many of them were probably local high school boys.

He'd read about the eighty Jews who were shackled together and forced to work as slaves to burn the bodies to destroy the evidence as the Russians closed in on Vilnius. These prisoners had tried to tunnel out through the sandpit and escape. Some of them succeeded and others were killed by the Germans, but a few escaped and joined the Jewish partisans in the forest. By that time the Jews in the forest knew that Ponar was not a resettlement site, but an execution site. One young girl named Sara had escaped Ponar and survived. She crawled out of the pit naked and she was hidden in the Jewish hospital in the Vilnius ghetto. Abba Kovner came to interview her and she told him the story of what really was happening at Ponar. He was only twenty three years old, but both he and Vitka Kempner had listened to the young woman, Sara, and Kovner then issued his famous proclamation to the Jews in the ghetto. He urged them to defend themselves. He told them Ponar was not a place for resettlement, but a place for death. "Better to fall in battle than to be led like sheep to the slaughter," he said. He told them the roads to Ponar only lead to certain death. "Defend yourself." They didn't listen to him though. They didn't believe him.

He thought of Kovner as he stared at the pit and then turned to walk back to the station platform. Before he left, he stopped at a large stone memorial. Originally the Russians had erected a memorial that said nothing about the Jews. Now there was a large memorial stone with a menorah at the base and sections in Lithuanian, English, and Russian:

ETERNAL MEMORY OF
SEVENTY THOUSAND JEWS
OF VILNIUS AND ITS ENVIRONS
WHO WERE MURDERED AND BURNT
HERE IN PANERIAI
BY NAZI EXECUTIONERS
AND THEIR ACCOMPLICES

At last the mention of the accomplices. He turned and walked back to the station platform and stood waiting in the rain for the train to Mariampole under his black umbrella. His nostrils were still filled with the acrid stench of ashes. The train arrived exactly on time.

25

MARIAMPOLE. HE'S AT THE BAR OF the Hotel Europejski, Mariampole. He picked out a taxi to the hotel from the small taxi line outside the station. The driver was a bull-necked huge man who in gestures told him he was a local strong man who could even pull a locomotive along the tracks. He showed him a photo of himself at the railroad station in Mariampole pulling a locomotive. It made him think of Leda's walk on his back to the cadences of Tuwim's "Lokomotywa." He's ordered a lemonade with cherry vodka. Some of the women at the bar were drinking it and it looked refreshing. There were several big beefy men at the bar drinking beer. Perhaps he should have ordered a beer and no one would have noticed him. He liked doing contrary things, so why not a lemonade and cherry vodka? The drink came with a red plastic dagger through three maraschino cherries. The people at the bar were the newly rich arrivistes of Mariampole. He saw their shiny new Mercedes in the parking lot. Some of the men carried purses and were using cell phones. It was a loud crowd, boisterous and laughing. There were two blonde waitresses who kept putting their arms around the men at the bar and rubbing up against them. The waitresses were attractive in denim mini-skirts and black aprons filled with change. Again, the slightly slanted eyes, the high cheekbones of the Slav, their images were reflected in the large mirror behind the bar through a haze of cigarette smoke.

What would his father Maynard have made of this scene? Maynard would have never walked into the bar. He would have just gone up to his bedroom. What about his paternal grandfather Meyer Levin? He tried to picture his grandfather as he sipped his drink and watched the people. Had Meyer been born in Mariampole? The family legend was that Meyer was brought to America at age two as a baby, on the ship in the arms of a family friend. Before Meyer, there was his great-grandfather Bernard Levin. The little old white-bearded man the family called "Burchik." Burchik had been a purveyor in Lithuania, supposedly he sold goods to the Russian army garrison. The story was told that the young Russian soldiers loved Burchik so much they often tossed him up into the air on a blanket in a gesture of comradeship. Burchik probably didn't enjoy being the man on the blanket, so as a middle-aged man he came to America. He left Mariampole in the 1870's. He opened a small dry goods store in Chicago on the South Side. His wife ran the store and Burchik spent most of his time in Shul. Maynard almost every night at dinner would be sent to the synagogue to lead his grandfather home. All that Maynard had that belonged to Burchik was a box of tefillin and a silk prayer shawl. There was only one photo of Burchik and Maynard together, the old man in a derby and a vest standing with his arms around his young grandson.

So this was Mariampole. He hadn't really seen the town, just scenes from the window of the taxi on the way to the hotel. He was the first member of the Levin family to ever return. He looked at his fingers. They seemed to be turning green again. The Lithuanians at the bar were now beginning to sing and were toasting each other by clinking their glasses. His fingers were turning green and the Lithuanians were singing. Also the smoke was too much for him and again he had the same acrid odor in his nostrils that he'd experienced at Ponar.

He finished the drink and stood up to pay the bill. His waitress was singing along with her customers. He held a bill out to her and she made change from her apron, but he shrugged it aside. She smiled at him and gave him a "thumbs up" sign. Apparently the "thumbs up" gesture was universal. Strangely, an Italian phrase that always preceded the movie previews at the local theater in Evanston was *la lingua di ciné est universale.* The phrase tumbled through his head as he entered his room on the fourth floor. It wasn't much of a room, not at all comparable to the Astorija in Vilnius. A refrigerator that hummed with nothing in it, a tiny TV, stiff pillows on the bed, the smell of mold permeating the room. He pulled open the window drapes over the bed and forced a window open. He still had Burchik on his mind. Higher and higher on the blanket while the Russians cheered and tossed him again and again. The tiny old Jew flying higher and higher to entertain the drunken peasant soldiers. Burchik got out of Lithuania though. He had the courage to come to America with his wife and children, to get on a ship in Gdansk, bringing only his tefillin box, his silken blue striped prayer shawl and a pair of silver candlesticks. The candlesticks were now in the apartment in Evanston on the dining room buffet. On the bottom of one candlestick was engraved in Polish, "Fraget w Warszawie."

As he pictured Burchik flying higher and higher on the blanket, he also began to think of Anshel Wasserman. He was the Israeli novelist David Grossman's grandfather, in Grossman's novel "See Under: Love", but he had promised himself no more literary allusions. He'd bundled up all the Israeli writers that he knew and compressed their novels into a bundle of hieroglyphic scrap and left it in the courtyard of the Louisiana museum outside of Copenhagen with the faceless Henry Moore torsos.

But one small mention of Anshel Wasserman, Grossman's grandfather, could be tolerated here. Why not? *Nebuch.* That was one of Anshel's favorite words. *Nebuch.* Perhaps it was a reference to Nebuchadnezzar, but no, there was a glossary that Grossman appended to "See Under: Love" and he defined *Nebuch* as "poor thing." What does that mean and in what context "poor thing"? A sympathetic phrase perhaps like, "Anshel Wasserman didn't have a kopeck to his name. *Nebuch.*" But Anshel Wasserman was from Warsaw. Alright, "Anshel didn't have a groschen to his name. *Nebuch.*" And what about *choloria*? Grossman's glossary defined *choloria* as a Polish curse meaning "cholera." So as an example, the commandant of the concentration camp where Anshel Wasserman was imprisoned, the Commandant Neigel, could be described as "a man who should only be blessed with good health. *Choloria.*" Grossman really wrote some brilliant chapters. One is titled "Bruno." He changed Bruno Schulz into a fish who, after having left the manuscript of his novel "The Messiah" on the pier in Gdansk, slipped into the waters of the Baltic Sea as a fish. Page after page follows Bruno as a fish emanating a strange sound that only fish can hear. "Ning." He becomes the leader of a large squadron of fish following his "Ning" sound everywhere. They constantly try to devour him even though he's their leader, but he survives. Quite unlike the real Bruno who wound up painting fables on the walls of a Gestapo officer's children's bedroom in Drohobycz and was shot in the head by another Gestapo officer who was jealous. He wanted Schulz to paint his child's bedroom with fables. So instead, Grossman leaves Schulz battered and torn, but still alive, as a fish. He leaves him in the sea.

Then he inserts a chapter called "Wasserman." Grossman accompanies his grandfather Anshel Wasserman as the invisible grandson "Momik" to an interrogation by the Commandant Neigel; Neigel the Commandant who can't understand why grandfather Anshel is still alive. Anshel has survived all attempts to kill him. He's survived gassing, shooting, and strangulation. He's the one Jew in the camp that the Germans cannot kill. They bring him before the Commandant who, enraged at Anshel's refusal to die, puts a pistol to Anshel's head and pulls the trigger, but Anshel is unaffected. He even makes a bargain with the Commandant. Anshel Wasserman had been a famous children's story teller in Warsaw. His children's books were published throughout the world. Momik never knew this. The Commandant, though, remembers Anshel's stories, how entranced he and his sister were with them as children. He makes an agreement with Anshel witnessed by Momik, the unseen grandson. The boy, Momik, is Grossman's omniscient observer. The agreement is that if Anshel Wasserman will write a story only for the eyes of the Commandant and read it to him every night before he leaves his office, when Anshel finishes the story, the Commandant will shoot Anshel again and this time he's confident he'll be able to kill him. Anshel will no longer be the one Jew who would not die. In the end, though, Anshel Wasserman survives; it is Neigel, the Commandant, who dies. He commits suicide.

So if Grossman can weave this kind of magical tapestry, why leave it as scrap in the courtyard with the faceless torsos of Henry Moore in Denmark? Why not unravel some of it and let it be read again. If Grossman can do this for Anshel Wasserman, why shouldn't Jonny Levin do the same for his paternal grandfather Meyer. Why not? Or better yet, for his paternal great-grandfather Burchik who had the courage to leave Mariampole forever and bring his family to America. As long as he is in Mariampole, the nest of the Levin family, why shouldn't he permit himself to write just one more little section of his novel? It isn't any good, we know that. It's boring, no one cares about his history of the Levin family. No one wants to read it. It's not really a novel, but this is Mariampole. Five thousand Jews were killed here in one day on September 1, 1941. Why shouldn't he tell a little more of

Burchik's story? Anshel Wasserman wore a silken Cantor's gown, a splendid gown and a tasseled rabbinic hat while he told his story to the Commandant Neigel. So he will imagine himself wearing Burchik's silken prayer shawl and playing with the fringes as he tells more of the family Levin story.

KAENE LEIB (LEE)
AND
SCHMUEL (SAM) LEVIN
THE LEVIN TWINS

Twin sons of my father's brother Herschel (Herschie) Levin. Herschie owned a carpet store in St. Paul. From that store his twin sons built a carpet empire across the U.S. hawking cheap printed knockoff rugs which they parlayed into a tax loss knitting mill in St. Cloud, Minnesota. They then dumped the mill on the townsfolk and they retired from the carpet business each with a million dollars. Leib (Lee) to Miami Beach and the tracks at Gulfstream and Hialeah and Schmuel (Sam) to the Racquet Club in Palm Springs. Neither of them ever married. Both of them owned identical Rolls Royces. So from a horse and wagon that their grandfather Burchik drove to his store in Mariampole, the Levin twins parlayed the American dream into two midnight blue Rolls Royces. What would Burchik say about that? *Nebuch*. Burchik had spent his time in America *davening* in the Shul, lost in the ecstasy of his dream of America. What would he say to the ravenous Levin twins, his grandsons? Did he even know them? Had his prayers been with them? Did he shine his countenance on them as they gambled in Nice and Monte Carlo then brought twin blond *nafkehs* (prostitutes) back to the Negresco. So much for Burchik's prayers as he touched the fringes of his tallis. Even I remember the rapacity of the Levin twins. Herschel Levin, my father's brother's twin sons. One winter, my father drove my mother and I to St. Paul to Herschie's carpet store for a sale on remnants to cover the floors of the house in Glencoe. I remember Schmuel telling the story that if a Polak came to the store and didn't buy, as he left, Schmuel would spit on his coat so the next merchant would know that he hadn't bought anything. From spitting on Polak's coats to dying of a heart attack at center court at the Racquet Club in Palm Springs. *Choloria.* Kaene Schmuel Levin, Burchik's grandson. Should that be woven into Burchik's Mariampole tapestry? And the *nafkeh* Schmuel was living with at the Racquet Club in Palm Springs, a twenty-nine year old call girl from Hollywood, should she be written in? The blonde who gave him artificial respiration on center court. Later she sued his estate claiming he'd given her AIDS. Should she be woven into Burchik's American tapestry? Burchik who sold pins, needles, candles, and soap to feed his family. Burchik who sold stockings, gloves, mittens, combs, lotions, mirrors, hairpins, and lumps of coal. Burchik whose wife would make the barrel of soup before he left for his evening prayers at the wooden synagogue on 14th Street.

Enough. Enough already. Why dishonor Burchik with the Levin twins. Enough. Not here in Mariampole. I am not David Grossman. I don't have that kind of talent. Forget the novel. I'm sorry I ever mentioned it. No trellises of flowers. No flowers.

No birdsong for the Levin twins.

What I can and should do though before I try to sleep is take one more look at the Jäger Report. Forget about writing the novel, put it back in the drawer where it belongs, pull the blinds. No walk tonight like my walk in Vilnius. Pull the blinds and take a shower. Wash off the slime on my fingers. Put some cologne in my nostrils to block out the stench of ashes. Beneath the bed lamp, again take another look at the Jäger Report.

So goodbye Leib and Schmuel (the Mule) Levin. The twins from St. Paul. I won't bury you in my little cemetery in Copenhagen. I promise. No tiny birds overlooking your stones. No tak, tak, tak.

No trellises of flowers.

He opened up the Jäger Report after shaving and putting on a fresh pair of pajamas and some cologne and sat on the bed with only the bed lamp lit. The Jäger Report wasn't difficult to follow. He knew the Mariampole entries, September 1, 1941, 5,090 killed in one day. How many men would it take to kill 5,000 Jews in one day? On the first page of the Jäger Report, it said that only "8-10 reliable men" were assigned to the "raiding squad" from Einsantzcommando 3. Could 8-10 Germans kill 5,000 Jews in one day? No, they would have to have the Lithuanians with them. Who would dig the pits? Who would arrest and hold 5,000 people? Certainly not 8-10 Germans. He knew where the Mariampole Jews were buried. He would go there in the morning before catching the train to Kaunas. He would go to the site and say a prayer. He looked at the Jäger Report to see where the killing squad had been the day before September 1, 1941. They were on

August 31, 1941, in Alytus "31-8-41. 233 Jews." As shown on his map, Alytus was maybe thirty miles south of Mariampole. He measured the band of statutory miles with a small ruler he had in his case and converted the meters into miles. Thirty miles seemed correct. Then also on August 29, 1941, they were in Utena and Moletai where they killed 3,782 Jews "582 Jews, 1731 Jewesses, 1469 Jewish children", but that wasn't enough for August 29th, they also drove to Rumsiskis and Ziezmariai, outside of Kaunas, and there they killed 784 Jews "20 Jews, 567 Jewesses, 197 Jewish children." Could "8-10 reliable men" do this by themselves? Of course not.

It was all incomprehensible. He put the Jäger Report and his ruler down and turned out the light. Tomorrow perhaps he would meet Simon Braucivius. What would he possibly say to Braucivius? He could show him the photographs and the Jäger Report and ask him simply, were you there, did you participate in this, were you one of the men who killed the Jews of Lithuania?

26

DEMOKRATU SQUARE, KAUNAS. He is standing in the middle of Demokratu Square which to him looks like a long abandoned park, a huge gray, dusty field of overgrown grass with chunks of bricks and broken concrete. It's almost four p.m. and he's scanning the sky with binoculars for Emanuelis' pigeons. He's also nervously awaiting the arrival of Dalia and perhaps Braucivius if she's bringing Braucivius with her. Will she even show? This whole adventure in Lithuania could be just that, a very foolish adventure. He looks at his watch. Five minutes to four. The huge square is empty and he's alone. It's beginning to rain again, much like the rain at Ponar. The same veil of rain. Will he be able to see the pigeons through the rain? This morning he had the taxi driver take him to the banks of the River Sheshupe in Mariampole. There was a stone monument there with an engraved plate:

HERE THE BLOOD OF ABOUT 8,000 JEWS WAS SPILLED
MEN, WOMEN AND CHILDREN;
AND ABOUT 1,000
PEOPLE OF OTHER NATIONALITIES
THAT
THE NAZI MURDERERS
AND
THEIR LOCAL COLLABORATORS
KILLED IN A GRUESOME FASHION.

Again the mention of "local collaborators." Who were the "local collaborators?" Dozens of men like Braucivius. None of them were ever brought to justice. He thought of dropping in unannounced at the American Embassy in Vilnius to show them his photographs and copies of his letters and the Jaeger Report. What good would it do? He'd just get more non-answers. No Lithuanian had ever served a day in prison for the murder of the Jews. Members of his own family were in the ash of that field by the Sheshupe in Mariampole. He could tell that to some clerk in the State Department at the Embassy at Vilnius, who would take his name and address and tell him that the matter would be looked into. No - this was a better way, to meet one of the perpetrators face to face. Here in Kaunas, Viljiampole, in Slobodka, face to face. Most of the houses here, if you could call them that, were weathered shacks. Occasionally he'd seen a face, a tired woman hanging her wash from a line. Shy blond boys in leather shorts with razor scooters playing in a courtyard.Very few of the houses were occupied. He tried to close his eyes and imagine the ghetto in 1941, the German *aktions.* Thousands of Jews standing in Demokratu Square being selected and directed to the right or to the left. Children screaming as they were torn from their mothers' arms. Mothers fighting to hold on to them, people being savagely beaten by the guards, the screams, the blood, the panic. And now he was standing here alone.

It was almost four. Where was Dalia? And then he saw her, at least he thought he saw her. A figure coming at him hurrying through the rain wearing a yellow raincoat, walking toward him. It looked like a young woman. Was she alone? Yes, she was alone. No Braucivius. She approached him and now the rain seemed to lighten as he called out to her.

"Dalia?"

"No it is not Dalia."

"Leda?"

"Yes, it is me Leda, Jonny Levin. Leda, your friend from Copenhagen. I've kept my word to you. It is now exactly four p.m. and I am here."

He put his hand out to shake her hand and she brushed it aside and put her arms around him and held her cheek against his face.

"You are soaked, my American friend. Come home with me and we will sit by the fire together and I will dry you and introduce you to my parents."

"Home? You're at your parent's home?"

"Yes, can you believe it? I am reconciled with them. I am staying at their house in the bedroom of my childhood."

"And Braucivius, is he alive? Have you word of him?"

"Yes, very much alive and still living with his whore across the street from my parents' house. No one has seen him for at least a year. A sick old man, a tyrant. But my father says still alive. My father despises him and wishes him dead. Only the good die easily."

"I can't believe all this."

"You have to believe it, Jonny Levin. What other choice do you have? Come, I will take you home with me. What are you doing standing here in the rain in this godforsaken place, Demokratu Square? No one ever comes here. It is the dark heart of the old ghetto."

"No, I have to wait Leda. I promised Emanuelis. I will wait here for his pigeons. He is sending them here."

"Emanuelis' pigeons? They do not come here. They do not fly to Lithuania."

"Yes they do, they come here every week."

She pulled her hood aside and looked up at the sky. "They fly to the Danish isle of Bornholm and then back to Copenhagen. They do not ever come to Lithuania."

"Wait. We will see."

"If they come to Lithuania I will call them down for you. I am an expert in calling them. You saw how I called them down in Copenhagen."

"No, don't call them down. If you call them, you'll interrupt their flight and they won't know how to return. Just be patient. Please, Leda, just be quiet and see if they'll come."

He took her hand and she leaned back against him. "The pigeons will not come to you in Lithuania, Jonny Levin. Believe me. You are being very foolish. You and Emanuelis must both be a little crazy. I have come to meet you, but the pigeons will not come to meet you."

"Leda, please, I want to say a prayer while I am here."

"Yes. I will be quiet. What are you praying for? Are you praying for the souls of the Jews of the ghetto?"

"I will respect that."

He closed his eyes and she leaned back against him.

"May I say something to you Jonny Levin, are you finished?"

"Yes."

"There are some birds in the sky. I see perhaps four birds. Hand me your binoculars."

"Where?"

"Over there," she said pointing. "They are coming in our direction, very high. Can't you see them?" She gave him the binoculars. "I don't think even Emanuelis' Pakistani pigeons can fly that high. They must be nightingales or swallows. I could try calling them down now. Let's see if they'll respond."

"No, don't. Just leave them alone. I see them, a squadron of four. Very high, almost invisible."

"They must be nightingales."

"Lithuania has no nightingales."

"Of course we do. Birds of the night that fly along the rim of the clouds. We have many such birds."

"I can barely see them," he said. "Now I think they're gone."

"No, I still see them, but in a minute they will be gone. So even if you are right and they were Emanuelis' Pakistani tipplers, so what? What would that prove? I see no reason for us to stand here in the rain. I have a car, an old Czech auto my father bought, a Skoda. He gave it to me to pick you up. I have it parked over there at the edge of the Square." She pulled his arm and took his hand and began to walk him toward the car. "Let's go."

"Leda, you have something caught in your hair." He reached out to her and took a small iridescent piece of paper from her hair curling down from the edge of her hood and pressed it flat on his fingertip and showed it to her.

"What is that?"

She took it in her fingers and looked at it and then pressed it onto her palm and held it out to him. "It looks like a star, one of those Jewish star symbols that Marguerite would cut for Emanuelis."

"I think that's what it is."

"So where did you get it from? Did you just paste it in my hair?"

"No, it came from up there." He pointed at the sky. "It came from Emanuelis' pigeons."

"They are dropping Marguerite's stars on Lithuania? Dropping the stars on Kaunas?"

"Yes."

She took his hand and as they walked they saw several more of the tiny paper cuts glistening on the walk and in the rubble of the field.

He stooped and picked some of them up and gave them to her. Two small Stars of David, a Lion of Judah, and a Torah scroll.

She examined each of them carefully and then pasted them all to her forehead, smiled at him and made the sign of the cross. "I cannot believe that Marguerite has sent these to me. Come home with me Jonny Levin. I think you are a man capable of magic. A magician."

27

SHE DROVE THE OLD CAR EXPERTLY. She showed him how to turn on the heater and they drove through the rain through the old streets of Kaunas leading to her house.

"You're a good driver, Leda."

"Yes, I'm an expert driver, but I am much out of practice. Oh, did you see that idiot? He drove right in front of me. No signal."

"Are the drivers here in Kaunas bad drivers?"

"Yes, we are notorious for our bad drivers. You cannot trust anyone to obey traffic signals and they pass you with no horn like that idiot. No warning."

"How far is your parents' home?"

"Not too far, maybe five kilometers. Where are you staying, at a hotel? Do you have a room somewhere?"

"At the Hotel Europejski Kaunas. I stayed at the Europejski in Mariampole and they told me they also had a hotel in Kaunas and booked a room for me."

"Oh, the Europejski. It is an old-style hotel, but quite comfortable. I'm sorry we could not invite you to stay at our home as our guest. We only have two bedrooms. My parents would like to meet you. They have never met an American. They are very curious to meet you."

"How did you get out of Copenhagen? I thought you couldn't get a passport."

"Oh, did you see that crazy woman? She almost hit that old man walking in the crosswalk. She just swerved around him and went on down the street. I only got the passport because of your five thousand kroner. Without that I wouldn't have gotten it. I thought it was certain that they had me on their list as a criminal because I left the country with false papers. But apparently I am not on their list so I got a new passport. It was a miracle. Who knows what saint was watching over me but I got through with no problem, except I had no money left for airfare and I had to pay with the dollars I had saved in my eel jar. I expect you to pay me back."

"Yes I will. And your parents, how did you contact them? I thought you weren't speaking."

"We did not speak for almost three years that I have been in Denmark, but after all I am their daughter. Do you know I am an only child? I know my parents' hearts were broken when I suddenly left Lithuania for Copenhagen. They were very angry with me. I was enrolled at the university in Vilnius to study architecture. At first I would write long letters trying to explain myself, that I want to live in freedom, that I wanted to paint and study art. I only had one or two letters in reply, very cold letters. So I became angry. I turned my nose away from them and felt they had abandoned me as a daughter. But yesterday I simply showed up at the door. My father answered. I don't think he recognized me. I said, 'I am your daughter' and looked at him. He looked at me and then he put his arms around me and we both cried. My mother has been ill. I did not know. She has a stomach ailment that won't go away. I will drive both of them to Vilnius where they have better doctors and better hospitals."

"So they've forgiven you?"

"Yes, we have both forgiven each other. They welcomed me back as their daughter. They need me to care for them and I want to help them. I'll stay here long enough to help them and then I'll go back to Copenhagen. I don't want to live in Lithuania. I want to live in Denmark. I love Denmark; I love my flat and my friends."

You will continue your work with Emanuelis and Marguerite?"

"Yes, of course. Why not? Also I will continue my work as an artist, and as a painter, and a commisionaire."

"Were you surprised when you found Marguerite's stars falling on Kaunas?"

"Surprised?" She touched at her forehead and removed the tiny paper figures by licking her fingers and put the figures in a row on top of the dashboard. "We only have a few more blocks now."

"You weren't surprised?"

"I don't know what they are supposed to mean, the pigeons and the stars. Are they supposed to be some punishment for Lithuania, raining Jewish stars down on us from the heavens? Do you really think that my generation does not know about the killing of the Jews here? No matter what Emanuelis tells you, we know of it. But there were families who also saved Jews. Does anyone speak of them? Who took Jews into their homes and hid them or raised the Jewish children as their own children. Do you think all Lithuanians were killers of Jews?"

"No, I don't think that. I know there were some who risked their lives to help the Jews. I know Abba Kovner, the leader of the Resistance in Vilnius, was hidden by a Lithuanian nun in her convent. He even dressed as a nun and worked in the gardens of the convent. Abraham Sutzkever, another Jewish partisan, was hidden by a family until he joined the partisans in the forest."

"Hiding a Jew was under penalty of death. Do you know that? All of us have been told that by our teachers and by our priests. Still some people risked their lives to help."

"I know that, Leda, but most people did nothing. They just

looked away. And then there were the men like Braucivius who were actual accomplices who joined in the killing."

"So at last you will meet him tonight. I still believe he was a partisan. A man who fought for Lithuania. Iphigenia told me her father, even though she hated him, was a hero. My father doesn't speak to him, though my father has made an arrangement with the policeman who is the lover of the whore who lives in Braucivius' house for us to meet there. We just have to bring a bottle of brandy for Braucivius which I have bought. Also fifty dollars American for the policeman is necessary. If I am successful in taking you to Braucivius you will owe me another four thousand kroner, the money you would have paid to Dalia, plus my airfare. Do you agree to that as a deal?"

"Yes."

"I cannot slap your hand Jonny Levin because I am driving," she smiled at him, "but if it is a deal I will tell you that I have also brought with me your ten one-hundred dollar bills and the note your friend left for you in Copenhagen. You see what an honest woman I am?" She suddenly jammed on the brakes and pointed to a house. "We are here. I will park and you will come with me and I'll introduce you to my parents. Neither of them speaks English. We will have some wine with them and you will warm up, Jonny Levin, and then we will cross the street and meet Iphigenia's father, Braucivius."

Her mother was at the door when they came up on the porch stairs. A very pale, short woman who hung her head shyly as she was introduced to him. She had wisps of gray brown hair in an oval surrounding her face. She had a sharp angular face with thin eyebrows and a hint of former beauty. She was anxiously wiping her hands on her apron. Leda spoke in Polish to her mother. The father had been sleeping on the couch in the living room and got up rather startled to see his daughter and the American man she had brought to their home. He also was short and thin-faced, balding with aquiline features, a furniture factory worker, his hands were stained by varnish. He immediately lit a cigarette and offered the package and when it was refused stuffed it into his shirt pocket. His brown eyes were slanted and yellowed. A man who looked exhausted and furtive, but smiling as he offered wine to his daughter and her friend. Leda spoke to her father in Lithuanian. The mother had also set out a plate of crackers and cheese and offered them with gestures urging both of them to eat.

"We cannot stay but a few minutes," Leda said. "They do not understand English, but I can translate for them if you would like to say something to them."

"Yes, tell them they have a lovely daughter who has been very kind to me."

She blushed and spoke Lithuanian and he could see their faces brighten.

"Also that she is a fine artist, one of the best in Copenhagen, but I don't see any of her paintings here."

"No, they still think of me as an architectural student, not as a painter. I know my father wants to show you some of my architectural drawings."

He reached under the living room couch where he'd been sleeping and pulled out a roll of blueprints and then carefully spread them on the large table covered with a heavy woven lace tablecloth. He opened Leda's drawings of some modern buildings, holding the drawings at the edges and then slowly turning each page.

"He thinks I would be a great architect, that I should plan buildings for the government here."

"Tell him they are excellent. You are obviously very talented and he's proud of you."

"Yes, so talented that he did not speak to me for three years. He's a good man, but a stubborn man."

"Also tell him thank you for arranging for me to meet Braucivius."

She stepped to the table and rolled the plans up and put them back under the couch. Then she spoke first to her father and then to her mother. She talked to her parents in Lithuanian and her father shook his head, but she kept on talking to him rapidly. The mother sat down obviously upset and very tired and drawn. Finally Leda spoke in English looking at her watch.

"Yes, he has arranged for us to meet Braucivius. We are due there right now across the street. He cannot understand why you want to see him, but he has made the arrangement even though he disagrees with your theory that Braucivius was a killer of Jews. He does think that Braucivius is a tyrant and a drunk, but that he was not ever a killer of the Jews. Either was my teacher, the man in the beret in the photo who was my English teacher and I agree with my father. That would be completely out of character for my teacher. He was a gentle man and always kind. He is dead, but I remember his kindness to me as a student." She broke into Lithuanian again speaking to her father as he nodded in agreement. "They used to drink together as friends at the tavern, my father and my teacher, but now we shall drink one toast to all of us. Then you and I will cross the street and you can see for yourself. Let us drink to Iphigenia in Riga and to her sisters and her dead mother, also to my dead schoolmaster and to all of us who are still alive. May there be friendship between America and Lithuania. Also to Emanuelis and Marguerite, my Jewish friends in Copenhagen, who my parents have never met. May our friendship be blessed and to our guest, Professor Jonny Levin from America, may he be blessed." She held her glass up to an old icon of the Virgin Mary on the wall. Then she put her index finger into her glass of wine and passed her finger through the flame of the small candle burning beneath the portrait and licked her finger. "*Na zdrowie* and *Sto Lat*," she said with her eyes glistening. "May we all live to be 100 years," she said and bent and kissed her mother's cheek.

They left the house and crossed the street and stood for a moment in front of Braucivius' house, while the policeman who was waiting for them came down from the porch. He was a thick necked man with a shaven head, his tunic unbuttoned; he had a large belly and a barrel chest. His white police car was left sitting in front of the house with the radio crackling.

"Give me fifty American, Jonny Levin, for this fat pig of the police or he won't let us into the house. I can see he is drunk."

She took the fifty-dollar bill he gave her and handed it to the man with a handshake. He touched his hand to the visor of his cap and then led them up the porch stairs where a woman was watching them from behind a panel of glass in the door.

"There is the whore of the house. Don't worry, none of them understands English. They can barely speak Lithuanian. I haven't been in this house since Iphigenia left, after she attacked her father with a hot iron from the fireplace."

The woman was in her forties, fat faced, heavily rouged with dyed blond hair. She wore high black boots and heels and a short flowered skirt, a pink frilly blouse and a black vest decorated with golden birds. She had large breasts and looked like any hooker you might see framed in the window of a brothel in Amsterdam. She was smoking and coughing.

Leda spoke to her and pointed at the mantelpiece and the woman nodded. The room smelled of cabbage and was filthy. Newspapers were strewn over the furniture. Layers of dust on everything. Only one bulb shone from a yellowed lampshade. It was dark and difficult to see, but Leda removed two frames from the mantel.

"You see they are still here, I can't believe it. The room hasn't been cleaned in years. Here is the same photo you have and here is Braucivius," she said pointing at the photograph. She blew at the dust on the frame. "And this is the medal he received as a partisan." She rubbed the frame. "Do you see it?"

She held the brandy bottle out and gestured toward the woman who found a glass and handed it to her.

"She will take us now to Braucivius and you will see him for yourself."

They walked down the hall corridor into a small bedroom where the stench was almost unbearable. It was a rancid odor of illness and an unwashed body. The shades were drawn and stained brown. There on the bed was an almost skeletal, white-haired man, his face covered with white stubble. He looked like he was paralyzed. He gave them no sign of recognition. His eyes were vacant. There were newspapers all over the bed, cigarette butts were piled in ashtrays by the side of the bed and in plates on the floor. Old bottles of medicine were stacked on a bedside table. He suddenly began coughing and opened his eyes and stared at them.

The woman shouted in his ear and there was still no expression. She kept shouting and then she poured him a glass of brandy.

"She is telling him who I am, Iphigenia's friend, her schoolmate, and that you are my friend." The woman held the brandy glass to his lips and he seemed to awaken and attempted to hold himself up. He pointed at the photo and the medal Leda was holding and said something to the woman. She pulled his pillows back and lifted him up on the pillows and closed his robe around him. Then she took the medal out of the frame and pinned it to his robe.

He held his hand out for the brandy glass and although his hand shook, he was able to drink. He drank the glass of brandy down and gestured for more. Then he pointed to the photo and Leda handed it to him. He held it up to his chest for his visitors.

"Ask him who these women were that he was guarding," Leda said to the woman.

The woman shouted in his ear and he answered gutturally, his mouth twisted.

Leda listened to the woman and then said in English, "He said they were Jews. They were all Jews from Kaunas."

"Ask him what happened to these women," Leda said to the woman.

She spoke to him and he pointed to the photo and held his finger up and then ran it across his throat.

"Did he kill them? Did he kill these women? Ask him."

She pointed to the photo and asked him.

Then she turned to Leda. "Yes," he said, "I killed them. They were Jews and we killed them all."

He touched his medal.

"He was given the medal for killing them. He was a partisan."

Leda translated all this into English. "Do you want me to say anything to him? Do you want me to say something for you, Professor?"

"No. I will say it to him myself." He bent over the old man's face, so close he could feel the stubble on his face and smell the sour odor of his breath. "*As Zydu*," he said to him. And then again, louder, "*As Zydu.*"

Braucivius looked at him for a moment and then drew himself up and coughed and spit in his face.

When that happened he slapped the left side of Braucivius' face as hard as he could. He ripped the photograph from his hands and tore the medal off his robe. Braucivius began shrieking, then spit at him again mumbling in Lithuanian and writhing in the bed, gasping for breath.

He could feel the imprint of Braucivius' face stinging his hand and he turned away and slowly walked out of the bedroom and out of the house, down the street to Leda's car. Leda remained in the house.

For the first time in Lithuania he felt like he was alive. He hoped that he had hit the old man hard enough to imprint his face with the same green slime that had enveloped his own hands and that it would soon envelope Braucivius and like a cancer spread and quickly kill him.

28

HE SAT IN THE CAR AND WAITED FOR HER. He had a cut on his finger and another across his palm. Apparently he'd broken the glass from the photograph. He looked at the frame. It was broken and smeared with a line of his blood. The medal had also punctured his thumb. His hands were shaking and he felt lightheaded as if blood was draining from his head. Leda came down from the porch and got in the car.

"You're bleeding. You've cut yourself."

"I'm alright."

"I have some tissue in my purse. Here hold your hand out." She wiped the blood away and wound pieces of tissue around his thumb like a bandage and told him to close his hand over another piece of tissue and keep it closed.

"We'll go back to the Europejski. You can wash your hand there and I can make you a proper bandage."

"What an awful man. Now do you believe me that he was a Jew killer and executioner?"

"Yes I believe you. I heard what he said."

"He was not a Lithuanian hero."

"No, you were right. I'd been foolish to think that. A very cruel man. I think you may have hurt him badly. His face was turning blue as I left."

"Do you think I may have killed him?"

"If he dies, that's what they will say of course. She asked me who you were. She demanded to know. She wants to report you to the police. She has a cell phone and was calling as I left."

"So let them arrest me."

"They may come after you, but I doubt it. They actually want him to die so they can take the house. It would be very convenient for them if he should die. Anyway I don't think they would ever come after an American. They are not that clever. They are used to dealing with drunks and thieves, not Americans."

"You were there. You brought me to him. They could come after you."

"No, I doubt it. I would just deny everything."

"So you really think I could have killed him?"

"Perhaps, you could have. He was almost dead before you slapped him. When you slapped him it was, as they say, 'the straw that broke the horse's back.' Did I say that right in English? Do they have that expression in America? Anyway he killed himself long ago with drink. He was an awful man and let us both pray that he will die."

When they arrived at the hotel he told her to wait for him in the bar off the lobby. He went upstairs to his room and washed his hands and face almost obsessively. He felt like the spittle from Braucivius was still clinging to his face and he couldn't wash it off and cleanse himself. He tried to mimic the ablutions that must have been taught to the young executioners of Jews that he'd seen in the photographs from the Ghetto

Fighters' museum. The young Lithuanian men in their black military tunics and round white collars. They all looked like priest acolytes. When he finished washing he put his hands out before him and covered the cuts with Band-Aids that he had in his toilet kit. Then still holding his hands like a young acolyte approaching the sacristy, he opened the toilet chamber door and dropped Braucivius' medal into the toilet and flushed it down. He took the photo out of its frame and carried the photograph to the toilet chamber and tore the photograph into little pieces. He then flushed the pieces down the toilet. He washed the blood off the shattered glass of the frame and put the frame in his bag underneath his clothes. So much for Lithuanian partisan heroes. If he had in fact delivered the blow that killed Braucivius, at least he had performed the correct ablutions in his memory.

He went down to the bar. She didn't see him coming and he stopped for a moment and stared at her. She really was a beautiful young woman. She had the same black pearl earring in her left ear that she was wearing the night they met in Copenhagen and the ring through her right ear, her hair falling over her face, held back by a thin red ribbon, perhaps the same ribbon. She was smoking a cigarette. Leda the Swan. He'd forgotten that she smoked.

"You have bandaged your hand. Where did you find those little bandages?"

"I had them in my kit."

"Let me see your hand. Is that the hand that you slapped him with?"

"No it was my right hand."

"I think he will be dead. He had that strange rattle in his throat and was choking for breath when I left."

"When he spit at me I just went into a rage."

"Yes he was a man who could hiss like a cobra. Is that the right word for the Indian snake in a basket? A little man sitting beside it plays the flute and the cobra comes hissing out of his basket and dances, but this cobra, Braucivius, he struck at you, so he got what he deserved."

"It was not my intention. I could see he was a sick old man. I just reacted without thinking of what I was doing."

"You could not let him defile you like that. I would have done the same thing. Remember he attacked Iphigenia, his own daughter, and she struck back at him with a hot fireplace iron. She would be glad he is dead. She hated him."

She took a long drag on her cigarette.

"My dear Jonny Levin, do you know there is a midnight train from Kaunas to Vilnius? You could catch it and leave here. Just as precaution, should they try to come after you and trace you to this hotel. They would not find you. I can drive you now to the station." She looked at her watch. "You still have time, at least an hour. You should go back upstairs to the room, get your things, pay your bill and check out of the hotel."

"No, I'm not going to run. I'm not afraid of them."

"I know you're not afraid of them. You would not be running. What difference does a few hours make? You can sleep on the train, check back into the Astorija and catch a plane to Copenhagen in the morning. They would never come after you in Vilnius. They have no authority there. They are not that sophisticated. Also there you would have the protection of the American embassy."

She put her hands out to him and held his hands across the table. "If I tell you that I believe you, that there were Lithuanians who were Jew killers, that you were right. Emanuelis and Marguerite are also right in trying to preserve the memory of the Jews. Will you then leave?" She turned her face to him. "You see

I have pasted the tiny Star of David symbol to my cheek. I have become a Jew for you. Perhaps now you will learn to think of me as a woman, and not as your daughter. But I ask you first to do only one thing for me. Please listen to me my dear Jonny Levin. Check out of this hotel now. Leave Kaunas now before they can harm you. Please. Go upstairs, get your things." She looked at him, her eyes glistening.

"Okay," he said to her, "wait for me here."

She tossed her hair back and smiled at him. "I'll not only wait, I'll order a vodka for each of us. I'll have it waiting and I'll count your money and we will make a division. Americans drink vodka over ice, they actually have ice here, so we will have one drink together and we'll leave. One last drink. But we will meet again in Copenhagen. We will meet again, I know it. Go now, do as I say."

He went upstairs. The room looked untouched. He even straightened the bed and ran the water in the bathroom sink again to get rid of any trace of his blood. He was on the third floor and had a view of the street in front of the hotel. He looked out the window. There wasn't a police car there. Only a man and woman, an elderly couple both with canes, the man walking ahead of the woman. He picked up his bag, closed the door and held the key as he took the stairway down. If they were waiting for him in the lobby, he would see them. How would he approach them? He had his passport in his inside jacket pocket. Would they take it from him? Would he be able to call the embassy in Vilnius? Was there an American Consulate in Kaunas? All this was spinning in his head. He didn't know the answers. He knew that the Japanese had a Consulate in Kaunas during the war. Chiune Sugihara, the Japanese Consul in Kaunas issued over one thousand transit visas to Jews to escape to Japan through Russia using the Trans-Siberian Railway. Chiune Sugihara of blessed memory. As he walked down the stairs he thought of Sugihara and also the Ninth Fort.

He'd wanted to go there in the morning. He wanted to read the plaque there and say a prayer. Was there even a plaque there? "We are 500, French" "Nous sommes 500, Francais" had been written by Abraham Wechsler of Limoges, scrawled on a wall at the Ninth Fort. Also the Yiddish word *Nekoma* written in blood on the door of a house in Slobodka by a man who was murdered by Lithuanians. He wrote in his own blood as he was dying, *Nekoma* (Revenge). He also wanted to try to find the house in Slobodka. He'd seen a photograph of the scrawl in blood in a publication of the US Holocaust Museum. He doubted if the house had been preserved. What about the Seventh Fort? He also wanted to go there.

But despite himself, he knew she was right. He had no knowledge of how to survive in Kaunas. Emanuelis had warned him of the Lithuanians. He'd told him that Leda could be of great use to him. She was a practical young woman, not a dreamer, not a Professor with his head stuffed full of literary abstractions. So he did as she said. He went to the front desk, checked out and paid them in cash in Euros. He tore up the credit card slip he'd given them and went into the bar and found her. The two of them drank their vodkas. She divided up the money as he directed, five hundred dollars for each of them. She smoked another cigarette and they left the bar separately. She told him to walk three blocks to the right of the entrance. She would be waiting for him.

As he walked from the hotel, he used the same method of remembering street names as he had in Vilnius. *Aleksoto* Street was the first street. No one was on the sidewalk. There was only light traffic on the streets. If they came for him it would probably be in a white car like the one he'd seen in front of Braucivius' house. He tried to act naturally; a man carrying a bag at night in Kaunas down a city street. He looked like a foreigner though, his walk, his clothes. He didn't look like a Lithuanian. The next street was *Valanciaus*. Only one more. She'd said three streets. How had he remembered the man in Slobodka who had scrawled in his own blood *Nekoma* (revenge). He didn't know. And Abraham Wechsler from Limoges, "Nous sommes, 500 Francais". They had just suddenly come to him. This city was full of Jewish blood. Demokratu Square, the Ninth Fort, the Seventh Fort, Viljiampole, Slobodka, all awash in Jewish blood, but it became more real when the dead were given names. So he had killed one of their executioners. 137,000 Jews and now 1 Lithuanian. Was that revenge? *Nekoma*? Hardly. He crossed one more street and there she was in her father's Skoda waiting under a street sign that read "*SV Gertudos*".

He got in and told her, "I still feel like I'm a coward running away, afraid to face them."

"You are not a coward, it is they who are cowards. All my life I've thought of them as heroes, my teacher and even Braucivius and now I see that they were killers."

"If they arrest me and charge me with a crime, maybe I'd be able to bring out what really happened here."

"Do not even think that they would listen to you for a minute. They would just throw you in a cell with the scum of Kaunas until you gave them dollars to buy your freedom."

"They'll do the same to you? They'll say you were my accomplice."

"Accomplice? I don't understand."

"You brought me to them, you arranged our meeting."

"No. They may come to me for more dollars, but they will not involve me. I can bring Iphigenia and her family down on their heads. And they will lose the house, they know that. Also, the old man died of neglect. You didn't kill him by hitting him. He was already virtually dead. They were letting him slowly die like a rat in his hole. They are the murderers, not the two of us. You are not Raskolnikov. Not in the least. Don't think of yourself that way. Ooh la la la. There is the station. I even see a parking place. I am always lucky finding parking places. We have only maybe twenty minutes. I will run and buy your ticket."

"No, I'll buy my own ticket. I don't want you further involved."

"You think, Jonny Levin, that I am afraid of them? They are pigs. Did you see them, how fat they are? The man could not even button his jacket and the woman looked like the mother of a pig. What is the word?"

"A sow?"

"Yes, she looked like a sow wearing a blonde wig that doesn't fit."

She bought the ticket for him and walked with him to the platform and stood with him as the passengers began to board.

"Now we will say goodbye," she said. "I will return, I know that. I will not stay here. I'll stay only as long as my mother needs me."

"I feel like I'm abandoning you Leda. I got you involved in this, deeply involved. But for me you would have had nothing to do with Braucivius."

"You are too much of a thinker, Jonny Levin. You worry too much. Do Jewish men always worry? I got myself involved. It had nothing to do with you. It was my own wish to be involved."

"Leda, please call me in the morning at the Astorija and let me know you're alright. Do you have a phone at home?"

"My father has a cell phone. Can you believe it? He actually bought one. Are you really worried about me Jonny Levin?" She put her arms around him and buried her face in his chest. He was immediately caught up in the fragrance of her hair and placed his lips on the crown of her head. He put his arms around her and held her. She turned her face up to him and he kissed her goodbye. Her lips were soft and moist and she was crying, "I am a foolish woman. I'm actually happy. For the first time you kissed me and instead I'm crying."

The train bell began to ring and other passengers were rushing aboard. She took a chain with a key to her apartment from around her neck and gave the key to him. "Give this key to Marguerite and wait for me in Copenhagen. We are just discovering each other and I think we have much to learn from each other. You will be safe now. Get on the train. Leave Kaunas. I will call you in the morning. I promise to call you at the Astorija."

She squeezed his hand and walked away from him down the platform without looking back. They were the only two people left now and he watched her walking away from him. She turned just once, waved to him moving her hand toward herself, and then the conductor boarded and leaned around him and blew his whistle. Suddenly she was out of sight.

What had she said to him in the bar? She had pasted the Star of David on her cheek and said she had turned herself into a Jew for him so that he would no longer think of her as his daughter, but as a woman. She was very perceptive, but he had never thought of her as his daughter although she was younger than both of his daughters. He had real feeling for this beautiful young Lithuanian woman. He could see Bellow's wizened face leering at him from his wooden coffin, then Bellow's face turned into the face of the elderly woman with gold rimmed teeth wearing a babushka seated next to him. He closed his eyes to the faces and felt the train moving.

He tried to sleep but flashes of Leda kept intruding. Her scent, the sound of her voice, her graceful walk as she disappeared down the platform, the lithe young body, her touch on his hands, how she lifted her face toward him as he kissed her.

Then the photographs began to intrude again and her face was mixed with the faces of the women in Kaunas being led out of the trucks. Then came the little boy in his black cap with his hands bound standing naked at the edge of the killing pit. What was his name? What was the boy's name? Abraham Wechsler had a name. Leda's face was fading now. The print of her lips was fading. All of the faces were receding, even the nameless little boy standing naked with his father at the edge of the pit. He looked out the window at the black Lithuanian night. The woman next to him held her rosary beads in her hand and was fingering the beads and murmuring. She looked up at him and smiled and made the sign of the cross on her breasts. He nodded at her and closed his eyes.

At the Astorija in the morning he waited for her phone call, but it didn't come. His plane would leave at two p.m. He'd had no trouble checking into the Astorija at midnight. A brisk, efficient young woman greeted him in a blue jacket. She remembered him, "The American gentleman" she said in English. Leda was right. There'd been no difficulty with the police. He saw some police at the station in Vilnius, a group of men drinking coffee and laughing. Heavy large men in blue sweaters, a few with pistols strapped to their thighs. One of them looked up at him, a flash of gold-rimmed teeth.

He stood looking out the window watching the street with a cup of coffee he'd made after he'd showered and shaved. Another gray morning. No white police cars. He wondered if the police in Vilnius drove white cars. It was quiet. He'd go down to the pool and take a swim and then bring a croissant from the dining room back to the room and wait for her call. What if she called while he was in the pool? He remembered seeing a wall phone extension by the pool. He'd leave instructions at the desk to put her through to the pool. Even after a shower he still had the feeling that his face was covered with Braucivius' spittle, that he'd been scarred by it. He would wash it off in the pool like he did with the green slime the last time he was here.

When he came down to the pool he saw the same woman and her two boys he'd seen the other morning. The woman was stretched out on a deck chair, smoking and reading a magazine. She looked up and smiled at him slightly as he passed. The two boys were playing the counting game *vienas, du, trys* and then diving at each other and wrestling in the water. He carefully hung up his white terrycloth robe with the gold Astorija crest. Again he was in his boxer shorts with no swimsuit. He dove into the water, the same cerulean blue, down, down, he kicked his legs and forced himself as far down as he could, brushing the bottom with his chest. And then as he moved up he felt the slime disappearing again, washing away with Braucivius' spittle. He smiled, a grin underwater. *As Zydu. As Zydu*, he'd said into the old man's ear and then he'd hit him. He should have closed his fist instead of slapping him. Then he would know that he had shattered his face and that Braucivius would be dead. He would know that he had killed him. He would have the solace of knowing that he was the one who had killed him.

He popped out of the pool and sat on the edge, his feet dangling into the water and toweled himself dry when the phone rang on the wall extension behind him.

"Hello?"

"Jonny Levin, is that you?"

"Leda?"

"Yes. It is Leda, your friend in Kaunas. They told me you were bathing."

"Swimming. I'm at the swimming pool."

"I didn't know you were a sportsman, a swimmer."

"Are you alright?"

"Perfectly alright."

"Did they bother you? Have they contacted you? The police?"

"Yes, they came to my house first thing this morning. Braucivius is dead. They took him away in a black death wagon. They came with a horse and a black wagon. Can you imagine a horse? This is such a backward country."

"What did they say to you?"

"They came to the door and said that you had killed him, that I had brought you to him. They wanted money. Five hundred dollars and they would be silent about it."

"What did you tell them?"

"I told them that they had killed him. They let him die. They watched him die for weeks and did nothing to help him. I wouldn't tell them who you were. I told them if they ever bothered me again I would call Iphigenia and her sisters. Otherwise I would keep quiet and they could have the house. I care nothing for that house. Why should I care? It means nothing to me. If they bother me again they will lose the house. Iphigenia and her sisters will charge them with neglect of their father. Letting a hero of Lithuania die as if he were an animal, a rat in their trap."

"So what will they do?"

"Nothing, nothing at all. I know how they think. Go back to Copenhagen, Jonny Levin, I will call you at your Hotel Angleterre. I will be back in Copenhagen in a month. You have the key to my flat. Hold it and give it to Marguerite and ask her to water my plants. Tell Emanuelis and Marguerite that I know what they are doing and I honor them. Give them each a kiss for me. When I return I will keep helping them. You're a good man, Jonny Levin. I will remember my American friend. I hope we will meet again. I am too sad to talk more. Take care of yourself."

"Leda. Please be careful."

Then she was gone and the phone went silent.

29

HAIFA. HE'S RENTED A HOTEL ROOM at the Hotel Shulamit in Haifa at 15 Kiryat Sefer Street on the 5th floor with a small roof garden overlooking the sea. He has a dish of black pitted olives and is sitting in the roof garden in the sunlight listening to the sound of pigeons in the rafters and the calls of children playing soccer in the schoolyard across the street. He's reading "The Story of a Life" by Aharon Appelfeld. Appelfeld was a friend of S.Y. Agnon who was a mentor to him. Appelfeld also studied with Martin Buber and knew people like the poet Uri Zvi Greenberg who immigrated to Israel from Poland and whom Isaac Bashevis Singer knew in Swider the summer resort in Poland outside of Warsaw. Why has he come to Haifa? Why has he left Copenhagen to come to Haifa? He doesn't really know yet. Maybe to look for Appelfeld. Appelfeld was from Czernovitz on the Romanian border, now part of the Ukraine. He was a child survivor who as a ten year old orphan in a concentration camp escaped and hid in a forest, burrowing like an animal to escape the Germans. He has come to Haifa perhaps to meet Appelfeld or maybe Yehoshua. He met them both once in the States, Appelfeld at a Temple where he read in a Chicago suburb; Yehoshua in Tucson at the Jewish Center. He would like to have coffee with them and tell them about Emanuelis and Marguerite and their pigeons and Leda. Has he abandoned Leda? No. He has helped her abandon him. He was not the man for her. Also she was not the woman for him. That he knew. Despite Bellow's entreaties, he knew that.

Leda is still in Lithuania. She called him before he left Copenhagen. She told him she was right. No one came after her. Their threats were false. She said she was not in danger and neither is he. There's been no further mention of Braucivius since the death wagon came for him. He is not to worry about her. She thinks of him often, but a great change has come into her life. She said she was paralyzed by indecision. She desperately needed money. She needed $1,000. She has a painting she painted especially for him. She would like to make a gift to him of the painting, but she couldn't afford to. She must sell it to him. She took her mother to the hospital in Vilnius and there she met a young doctor who has fallen in love with her and wants her to marry him. She has delayed her return to Copenhagen. Could he send her money to help her? Her mind was on fire. She felt that she had fallen in love for the first time in her life, but she doesn't want to live in Lithuania. If he bought her painting, she could leave Lithuania. Perhaps her doctor friend could study abroad.

He tried to help her. He felt she had earned his help. He sent her a check for $1,000, an American Express money order, and she sent him in return the painting. It was a painting of Braucivius propped up on his bed in his death throes, a face twisted in agony, in his gray robe wearing the medal with a slight trace of blood ebbing from his mouth. He burned the painting and threw the ashes in the river in Copenhagen. He walked with the ashes in a container down Hans Christian Andersen Boulevard to the Christians Brygge at the edge of the Inderbaunen river and dropped the ashes into the river. He returned and stood before the statue of Andersen, touched his hand again, and said farewell to the old faery tale meister. Then he booked a British Air flight to Tel Aviv and took a bus to Haifa and found a hotel room at the Shulamit on Kiryat Sefer Street (the "Street of the Book").

Before he left he said goodbye to Emanuelis and Marguerite.

It was very difficult. He was able to report to Emanuelis that his pigeons were flying over Lithuania, that he had seen them high in the night sky over Demokratu Square in Kaunas. He'd also seen the cuttings that they had dropped, the tiny Stars of David, the heraldic Judaic cuttings, lions, tigers, even a serpent. He didn't tell him about Braucivius. He didn't tell him he had struck Braucivius a blow on the side of the face that may have killed him. He doesn't think he killed him. Even though Leda, by sending him the painting, a death effigy of Braucivius, had implied that he had killed him. He did not kill him. He exorcised the painting by burning it much like the Germans had burned the corpses of the Jews at Ponar. It was that kind of burning. That evening, after he emptied the ashes of the painting into the river, he went to the Glyptotek Museum to a concert, a return performance, by the pianist Jeremy Menuhin playing Tchaikovsky. He just wanted to be alone. The music calmed him. Menuhin became annoyed because some Danish children were playing games in the corridor behind the stage, and he left the piano and quieted them. He'd never seen a performer do that.

So here he is sitting in Haifa in the sunlight wearing dark glasses. He doesn't feel like an assassin (an Arabic word). Maybe more like a Mafioso just in from Chicago. He could be that. A Mafia man from Chicago playing with a dish of olives in the brittle sunlight. He would like to also meet David Grossman. He was particularly intrigued by Grossman's novel *See Under: Love*, much more complicated than Appelfeld. Appelfeld writes in very clean straightforward prose, very little magic. He would like to talk to Grossman about the grandson Momik seeking to make cabalistic combinations of his grandfather's numbered tattoo on his forearm. He is constantly looking in Haifa for tattooed numbers on the arms of elderly people he sees on the busses and on the park benches. So far he has seen perhaps ten numbers tattooed on arms of elderly people. He's keeping count, just like he'd kept count in Lithuania and Denmark of women who touched his wrist. As far as his novel is concerned (assuming anyone but him has concern), he has disposed of it. He took it to Skagen, the Danish artist colony at the tip of Jutland, and stood out on the pier exactly where the North Sea meets the Baltic. He lowered the novel into the sea, page by page, and watched it float out to where the two seas came together. He watched it join the foam of the seas as they merged. So, unlike Bruno Schulz, he did not leave his manuscript in an art gallery. He did not transmogrify into a fish. Instead he is here in Haifa and it is his intention this afternoon to ride the Carmelit down to the ocean and rent a beach chair and sit at the edge of the sea. He has bought a simple blue-lined composition book. He intends to start again, this time there will be no construction of a cemetery. No doves. No trellises of flowers.

The
Jäger Report

The Jäger Report

Commander of the security police and
the SD Einsatzkommando 3
Secret Reich Business 1 December 1941
Kauen [Kaunas]
5 copies
4th copy

Complete list of executions carried out in the EK 3 area up to 1 December 1941

Security police duties in Lithuania taken over by Einsatz-kommando 3 on 2 July 1941.

(The Wilna [Vilnius] area was taken over by EK 3 on 9 Aug. 1941, the Schaulen area on 2 Oct. 1941. Up until these dates EK 9 operated in Wilna and EK 2 in Schaulen.)

On my instructions and orders the following executions were conducted by Lithuanian partisans:

4.7.41	Kauen-Fort VII	416 Jews, 47 Jewesses	463
6.7.41	Kauen-Fort VII	Jews	2,514

Following the formation of a raiding squad under the command of SS-Obersturmfuhrer Hamman and 8-10 reliable men from the Einsatzkommando. the following actions were conducted in cooperation with Lithuanian partisans:

7.7.41	Mariampole	Jews	32
8.7.41	Mariampole	14 Jews, 5 Comm. officials	19
8.7.41	Girkalinei	Comm. oficcials	6
9.7.41	Wendziogala	32 Jews, 2 Jewesses, 1 Lithuanian (f.), 2 Lithuanian Comm., 1 Russian Comm.38	
9.7.41	Kauen-Fort VII	21 Jews, 3 Jewesses	24
14.7.41	Mariampole	21 Jews, 1 Russ, 9 Lith. Comm.	31

17.7.41	Babtei	8 Comm. officals (inc. 6 Jews)	8
18.7.41	Mariampole	39 Jews, 14 Jewesses	53
19.7.41	Kauen-Fort VII	17 Jews, 2 Jewesses, 4 Lith.Comm, 2 Comm. Lithuanians (f.), 1 German Comm.	26
21.7.41	Panevezys	59 Jews, 11 Jewesses, 1 Lithuanian (f.), 1 Pole, 22 Lith. Comm., 9 Russ. Comm.	103
22.7.41	Panevezys	1 Jew	1
23.7.41	Kedainiai	83 Jews, 12 Jewesses, 14 Russ. Comm., 15 Lith. Comm., 1 Russ. O-Politruk	125
25.7.41	Mariampole	90 Jews, 13 Jewesses	103
28.7.41	Panevezys	234 Jews, 15 Jewesses, 19 Russ. Comm., 20 Lith. Comm.	288
		Total carried forward	3,384

Sheet 2

		Total carried over	3,384
29.7.41	Rasainiai	254 Jews, 3 Lith. Comm.	257
30.7.41	Agriogala	27 Jews, 11 Lith. Comm.	38
31.7.41	Utena	235 Jews, 16 Jewesses, 4 Lith. Comm., 1 robber/murderer	256
31.7.41	Wendziogala	13 Jews, 2 murderers	15
1.8.41	Ukmerge	254 Jews, 42 Jewesses, 1 Pol. Comm., 2 Lith. NKVD agents, 1 mayor of Jonava who gave order to set fire to Jonava	300
2.8.41	Kauen-Fort IV	170 Jews, 1 US Jewess, 33 Jewesses, 4 Lith. Comm.	209

4.8.41	Panevezys	362 Jews, 41 Jewesses, 5 Russ. Comm., 14 Lith. Comm.	422
5.8.41	Rasainiai	213 Jews, 66 Jewesses	279
7.8.41	Uteba	483 Jews, 87 Jewesses, 1 Lithuanian (robber of corpses of German soldiers)	571
8.8.41	Ukmerge	620 Jews, 82 Jewesses	702
9.8.41	Kauen-Fort IV	484 Jews, 50 Jewesses	534
11.8.41	Panevezys	450 Jews, 48 Jewesses, 1 Lith. 1 Russ.	500
13.8.41	Alytus	617 Jews, 100 Jewesses, 1 criminal	719
14.8.41	Jonava	497 Jews, 55 Jewesses	552
15-16.8.41	Rokiskis	3,200 Jews, Jewesses, and J. Children, 5 Lith. Comm., 1 Pole, 1 partisan	3207
9-16.8.41	Rassainiai	294 Jewesses, 4 Jewish children	298
27.6-14.8.41	Rokiskis	493 Jews, 432 Russians, 56 Lithuanians (all active communists)	981
18.8.41	Kauen-Fort IV	689 Jews, 402 Jewesses, 1 Pole (f.), 711 Jewish intellectuals from Ghetto in reprisal for sabotage action	1,812
19.8.41	Ukmerge	298 Jews, 255 Jewesses, 1 Politruk, 88 Jewish children, 1 Russ. Comm.	645
22.8.41	Dunaburg	3 Russ. Comm., 5 Latvian incl. 1 murderer, 1 Russ. Guardsman, 3 Poles, 3 gypsies (m.), 1 gypsy (f.), 1 gypsy child, 1 Jew, 1 Jewess, 1 Armenian (m.), 2 Politruks (prison inspection in Dunanburg	21
		Total carried forward	16,152

Sheet 3

		Total carried forward	16,152
22.8.41	Aglona	Mentally sick: 269 men, 227 women, 48 children	544
23.8.41	Panevezys	1,312 Jews, 4,602 Jewesses, 1,609 Jewish children	7,523
18-22.8.41	Kreis Rasainiai	466 Jews, 440 Jewesses, 1,020 Jewish children	1,926
25.8.41	Obeliai	112 Jews, 627 Jewesses, 421 Jewish children	1,160
25-26.8.41	Seduva	230 Jews, 275 Jewesses, 159 Jewish children	664
26.8.41	Zarasai	767 Jews, 1,113 Jewesses, 1 Lith. Comm., 687 Jewish children, 1 Russ. Comm. (f.)	2,569
28.8.41	Pasvalys	402 Jews, 738 Jewesses, 209 Jewish children	1,349
26.8.41	Kaisiadorys	All Jews, Jewesses, and Jewish children	1,911
27.8.41	Prienai	All Jews, Jewesses, and Jewish Children	1,078
27.8.41	Dagda and Kraslawa	212 Jews, 4 Russ. POW's	216
27.8.41	Joniskia	47 Jews, 165 Jewesses, 143 Jewish children	355
28.8.41	Wilkia	76 Jews, 192 Jewesses, 134 Jewish children	402
28.8.41	Kedainiai	710 Jews, 767 Jewesses, 599 Jewish children	2,076
29.8.41	Rumsiskis and Ziezmariai	20 Jews, 567 Jewesses, 197 Jewish children	784
29.8.41	Utena and Moletai	582 Jews, 1,731 Jewesses, 1,469 Jewish children	3,782
13-31.8.41	Alytus and environs	233 Jews	233
1.9.41	Mariampole	1,763 Jews, 1,812 Jewesses, 1,404 Jewish	

		children, 109 mentally sick, 1 German subject (f.), married to a Jew, 1 Russian (f.)	5090
		Total carried over	47,814

Sheet 4

		Total carried over	47,814
28.8-2.9.41	Darsuniskis	10 Jews, 69 Jewesses, 20 Jewish children	99
	Carliava	73 Jews, 113 Jewesses, 61 Jewish children	247
	Jonava	112 Jews, 1,200 Jewesses, 244 Jewish children	1,556
	Petrasiunai	30 Jews, 72 Jewesses, 23 Jewish children	125
	Jesuas	26 Jews, 72 Jewesses, 46 Jewish children	144
	Ariogala	207 Jews, 260 Jewesses, 195 Jewish children	662
	Jasvainai	86 Jews, 110 Jewesses, 86 Jewish children	282
	Babtei	20 Jews, 41 Jewesses, 22 Jewish children	83
	Wenziogala	42 Jews, 113 Jewesses, 97 Jewish children	252
	Krakes	448 Jews, 476 Jewesses, 97 Jewish children	1,125
4.9.41	Pravenischkis	247 Jews, 6 Jewesses	253
	Cekiske	22 Jews, 64 Jewesses, 60 Jewish children	146
	Seredsius	6 Jews, 61 Jewesses, 126 Jewish children	193
	Velinona	2 Jews, 71 Jewesses, 86 Jewish children	159
	Zapiskis	47 Jews, 118 Jewesses, 13 Jewish children	178

5.9.41	Ukmerge	1,123 Jews, 1,849 Jewesses, 1,737 Jewish children	4,709
25.8-6.9.41	Mopping up in: Rasainiai	16 Jews, 412 Jewesses, 415 Jewish children	843
	Georgenburg	all Jews, all Jewesses, all Jewish children	412
9.9.41	Alytus	287 Jews, 640 Jewesses, 352 Jewish children	1,279
9.9.41	Butrimonys	67 Jews, 370 Jewesses, 303 Jewish children	740
10.9.41	Merkine	223 Jews, 640 Jewesses, 276 Jewish children	854
10.9.41	Varena	541 Jews, 141 Jewesses, 149 Jewish children	831
11.9.41	Leipalingis	60 Jews, 70 Jewesses, 25 Jewish children	155
11.9.41	Seirijai	229 Jews, 384 Jewesses, 340 Jewish children	953
12.9.41	Simnas	68 Jews, 197 Jewesses, 149 Jewish children	414
11-12.9.41	Uzusalis	Reprisal against inhabitants who fed Russ. partisans; some in possesion of weapons	43
26.9.41	Kauen-F.IV	412 Jews, 615 Jewesses, 581 Jewish children (sick and suspected epidemic cases)	1,608
		Total carried over	66,159

Sheet 5

		Total carried over	66,159
2.10.41	Zagare	633 Jews, 1,107 Jewesses, 496 Jewish children (as these Jews were being led away a mutiny rose, which	

		was however immediately put down; 150 Jews were shot immediately; 7 partisans wounded)	2,236
4.10.41	Kauen-F.IX	315 Jews, 712 Jewesses, 818 Jewish children (reprisal after German police officer shot in ghetto)	1,845
29.10.41	Kauen-F.IX	2,007 Jews, 2,920 Jewesses, 4,273 Jewish children (mopping up ghetto of superfluous Jews)	9,200
3.11.41	Lazdijai	485 Jews, 511 Jewesses, 539 Jewish children	1,535
15.11.41	Wilkowiski	36 Jews, 48 Jewesses, 31 Jewish children	115
25.11.41	Kauen-F.IX	1,159 Jews, 1,600 Jewesses, 175 Jewish children (resettlers from Berlin, Munich and Frankfurt am main)	2,934
29.11.41	Kauen-F.IX	693 Jews, 1,155 Jewesses, 152 Jewish children (resettlers from from Vienna and Breslau)	2,000
29.11.41	Kauen-F.IX	17 Jews, 1 Jewess, for contravention of ghetto law, 1 Reichs German who converted to the Jewish faith and attended rabbinical school, then 15 terrorists from the Kalinin group	34
EK 3 detachment in Dunanberg in the period 13.7-21.8.41:		9,012 Jews, Jewesses and Jewish children, 573 active Comm.	9,585

EK 3 detachment in Wilna:

12.8-1.9.41	City of Wilna	425 Jews, 19 Jewesses, 8 Comm. (m.), 9 Comm. (f.)	461
2.9.41	City of Wilna	864 Jews, 2,019 Jewesses, 817 Jewish children (sonderaktion because German soldiers shot at by Jews)	3,700
		Total carried forward	99,084

sheet 6

		Total carried forward	99,804
12.9.41	City of Wilna	993 Jews, 1,670 Jewesses, 771 Jewish children	3,334
17.9.41	City of Wilna	337 Jews, 687 Jewesses, 247 Jewish children and 4 Lith. Comm.	1,271
20.9.41	Nemencing	128 Jews, 176 Jewesses, 99 Jewish children	403
22.9.41	Novo-Wilejka	468 Jews, 495 Jewesses, 196 Jewish children	1,159
24.9.41	Riesa	512 Jews, 744 Jewesses, 511 Jewish children	1,767
25.9.41	Jahiunai	215 Jews, 229 Jewesses, 131 Jewish children	575
27.9.41	Eysisky	989 Jews, 1,636 Jewesses, 821 Jewish children	3,446
30.9.41	Trakai	366 Jews, 483 Jewesses, 597 Jewish children	1,446
4.10.41	City of Wilna	432 Jews, 1,115 Jewesses, 436 Jewish children	1,983
6.10.41	Semiliski	213 Jews, 359 Jewesses, 390 Jewish children	962
9.10.41	Svenciany	1,169 Jews, 1,840 Jewesses, 717 Jewish children	3,726

16.10.41	City of Wilna	382 Jews, 507 Jewesses, 257 Jewish children	1,146
21.10.41	City of Wilna	718 Jews, 1,063 Jewesses, 586 Jewish children	2,367
25.10.41	City of Wilna	1,776 Jewesses, 812 Jewish children	2,578
27.10.41	City of Wilna	946 Jews, 184 Jewesses, 73 Jewish children	1,203
30.10.41	City of Wilna	382 Jews, 789 Jewesses, 362 Jewish children	1,553
6.11.41	City of Wilna	340 Jews, 749 Jewesses, 252 Jewish children	1,341
19.11.41	City of Wilna	76 Jews, 77 Jewesses, 18 Jewish children	171
19.11.41	City of Wilna	6 POW's, 8 Poles	14
20.11.41	City of Wilna	3 POW's	3
25.11.41	City of Wilna	9 Jews, 46 Jewesses, 8 Jewish children, 1 Pole for possesion of arms and other military equipment	64

EK 3 detachment in Minsk from
28.9-17.10.41:

Pleschnitza Bischolin Scak Bober Uzda	620 Jews, 1,285 Jewesses, 1,126 Jewish children and 19 Comm.	3,050
		133,346

Prior to EK 3 taking over security police duties, Jews liquidated by pogroms and executions (including partisans) 4,000

Total 137,346

Today I can confirm that our objective, to solve the Jewish problem for Lithuania, has been achieved by EK 3. In Lithuania there are no more Jews, apart from Jewish workers and their families.

The distance between from the assembly point to the graves was on average 4 to 5 Km.

I consider the Jewish action more or less terminated as far as Einsatzkommando 3 is concerned. Those working Jews and Jewesses still available are needed urgently and I can envisage that after the winter this workforce will be required even more urgently. I am of the view that the sterilization program of the male worker Jews should be started immediately so that reproduction is prevented. If despite sterilization a Jewess becomes pregnant she will be liquidated.

(signed)
Jäger
SS-Standartenfuhrer

1. Further information about the Jäger Report can be found on page 234 (et seq.) *The Holocaust: A History of the Jews of Europe during the Second World War,* by Martin Gilbert, Holt, Rinehart & Winston, New York, 1985.

2. Karl Jäger committed suicide before facing trial. He died in his cell at Hohenasberg Detention Center on June 22, 1959. See *Masters of Death: The SS Einsatzgruppen,* by Richard Rhodes, page 276, Vintage Books, a Division of Random House, 2003.

Lowell B. Komie has written four collections of short stories, *The Judge's Chambers, The Lawyer's Chambers and Other Stories*, which won the Carl Sandburg Award for Fiction, *The Night Swimmer: A Man in London and Other Stories*, and his most recent, *The Legal Fiction of Lowell B. Komie.* He is the author of four novels, *The Last Jewish Shortstop in America,* winner of the Small Press Award for Fiction, *Conversations with a Golden Ballerina,* and *The Humpback of Lodz.* In 2006, he published *The Silhouette Maker of Copenhagen,* a novella which has been expanded into the novel, *Hotel Europejski.*

CPSIA information can be obtained at www.ICGtesting.com
Printed in the USA
LVOW09s2231020914

402148LV00002B/212/A

9 780964 195776